HOME FOR CHRISTMAS

Don't run, he thought. He obeyed that thought only because he didn't want to frighten her off. She looked like an animal ready to bolt in the next second.

"Dinner is ready," somebody announced from the back, and more people became obstacles as they passed in front of him on their way to the food.

He felt like a fish swimming against the tide. He forced himself to let a group pass before he continued on his quest. What he needed wasn't on the food table. He felt like he was in a slow-motion commercial, trying to reach his destiny. He hoped he ended where the people in the commercials did: achieving their goals. Elation and apprehension swelled in him at the same time. He felt just as he had the first time he saw her after he realized that he loved her. He wished he could go back to that time. He had been young, but not yet foolish. He wished he could find an eraser to rub out his mistake that came later.

Finally, after too long, he stood in front of her. He fought to slow down his breathing and heartbeat which made it seem as if he had just run all the way from Houston. He lost the fight.

HOME FOR CHRISTMAS

Alice Wootson

BET Publications, LLC
www.bet.com

ARABESQUE BOOKS are published by

BET Publications, LLC
c/o BET BOOKS
One BET Plaza
1900 W Place NE
Washington, DC 20018-1211

All Kensington Titles, Imprints, and Distributed Lines are available at special quantity discounts for bulk purchases for sales promotions, premiums, fund-raising, and educational or institutional use. Special book exerpts or customized printings can also be created to fit specific needs. For details, write or phone the office of the Kensington special sales manager: Kensington Publishing Corp., 850 Third Avenue, New York, NY 10022, attn: Special Sales Department, Phone: 1-800-221-2647.

First Printing: October 2001
10 9 8 7 6 5 4 3 2 1

Printed in the United States of America

ACKNOWLEDGMENTS

To Ike, the love of my life, for his patience, for giving me the quiet I needed to write this novel, for giving me feedback about the male point of view, for suggesting a road trip, and for driving Miss Alice all over the country.

One

Jeff unfolded the letter again and reread it as if afraid the words had changed in the last two minutes. And maybe hoping that they had. He swallowed hard. Hope and fear about the same thing fought inside him, each trying to be the bigger. Ridiculous. He had a choice in this. He could say no. He sighed. But he wouldn't. He had wanted this since his mom had given him his first book of science experiments for his third birthday. He had tried to be enthusiastic when she gave him the book instead of the video game that he had begged for. He smiled. After the messes he had made in the kitchen she had probably been sorry she hadn't bought the game instead. He ran a finger across the letterhead. Had she dreamed this for him when she bought him a chemistry set the next Christmas? He shook his head. He doubted that she allowed herself to hope that much for him. He looked at the letter again, straightened a corner, then slipped the letter back into the envelope.

"Are you almost ready?" His mom came to his bedroom door. She brushed a hand down the front of her blue skirt. "You're going to be late."

"I'm ready."

"You don't think you should have told her before today?" She frowned. "You didn't change your mind about going, did you?"

"I can't change my mind about that. It seems like I've been hoping for this chance my whole life." He pushed the letter into his back pocket. "I can't change my mind."

"Maybe you should have talked it over with Sheila when you decided to apply for the job."

"I wasn't sure I'd get it. Competition for jobs in that area of the space agency is tough. I didn't see any reason to tell Sheila. I knew she'd be upset, so why upset her when it might be for nothing?"

"Jeff, you were number one in your class."

"Every college graduating class has a number one, Mom."

"Not with a double major in math and chemistry." She sighed. "No use discussing it now. It's done."

"Yes, it's done." He adjusted his tie as if it weren't already in the correct position, and walked toward the door. "I'm ready."

"Not quite." His mom walked past him and picked up the cap and gown from the bed. "Who's going to look after my handsome son when I'm not around?" She placed the gown across his arm, but carried the cap herself. "Maybe we can find a foster mother for you."

"I think twenty-two is too old for the foster-care system."

She brushed her hands along his shoulders, smoothing the already smooth suit jacket. "Then maybe we can find you a keeper. You can place a want ad in the paper after you get your first paycheck. 'Help Wanted: guardian for genius who would forget his head and feet if the good Lord hadn't seen fit to attach them to his body.' " She stood on tiptoe, tugged at his shoulder until he bent down, and kissed his cheek.

"I love you, too, Mom." Jeff kissed her forehead as he did every evening. He grinned at her.

His mother, a wide smile on her face, gently wiped away the lipstick she had left on his face. "I don't want

Sheila to think some other girl is giving her competition." She stepped back and stared at him. "I'm not sure waiting to tell her was the smartest thing you ever did." She shrugged. "It's your business." She glanced at her watch. "We'd better go. Mrs. Baker and her daughters will be here any minute, and we can't keep them waiting."

Jeff followed his mom from the room. He watched her stand there looking out the screen door.

It was right to wait to tell Sheila. Tonight they would slip away from his party and go to the bench in the pocket garden at the end of the block. He'd sit her down and hand her the letter. He'd explain why he hadn't told her before. He'd make her understand what an honor it was to be offered the job. She'd see how important it was to him. She knew that to turn the job down would be giving up his life's dream.

He shook his head. *One of my dreams. Marrying Sheila is the other.*

"They're here."

Jeff followed her out the door. *I'm not giving up one for the other. I can have both.*

He got into the car. *Sheila has to understand.*

"You did it." Sheila pulled him around in a circle. "You're number one." She wrapped her hands around his shoulders. "Come here." The quadrangle was crammed with people, but her husky voice made everyone else disappear. She reached up and brushed her hand along the side of his face. "You shaved just for me. Did you know I was going to do this?" She eased his face closer.

"I hoped so." He moved closer still.

"I'm so proud of you, sugar." She brushed her lips across his. "So proud." She kissed him again.

"If you keep on showing me how proud you are, the dean will come take back my degree and I'll be the first graduate to have his graduation revoked for conduct unbecoming."

She kissed him again. "It would be worth it."

"Congratulations, Jeff. You deserve it, man." Weston, who graduated in the second spot, held out his hand. "I probably won't see you again, so good luck with the job in Houston. Don't forget us when you become director of the space program."

Jeff took in a quick breath as if he could suck up the words before they reached Sheila.

"Houston? What's he talking about? What job in Houston?" Sheila frowned and took a step away from him.

"I'll tell you later."

"Tell me what later?" She stepped even farther away from him. "Why can't you tell me now? What are you keeping from me?"

"Congratulations, Jeff," Sheila's father said as he came close to the others. "A college graduate. We knew you could do it. From the time I first met you, I said, 'Here's a young man who's going places.'" Sheila's father held out his hand, unaware of the tension between Jeff and Sheila.

"Thank you, Dr. Miller."

Jeff shook his hand, grateful for his timing. He refused to look at Sheila. If he thought it would help, he'd go find Wes and strangle him.

"Didn't I say that, Marie? Didn't I say that Jeff Hamilton will really go places?"

"Yes, you did, after you got over the fact that your daughter was old enough to date and that you couldn't keep her locked up until she turns thirty, as you used to threaten."

"That was when I thought she was interested in that

Barry fellow. He's probably in jail somewhere now." He frowned at Sheila. "I never did see why you wasted your time with him."

"Now, Bob. That was a long time ago." Mrs. Miller patted her husband's arm before she turned to Jeff. "You have made your mother proud." She kissed his cheek.

"He certainly has." Jeff's mother joined their little group. She exchanged greetings with Sheila's parents. The three talked about Jeff's accomplishments. Sheila didn't say a word. Jeff didn't know if that was good or bad. He sighed. *Yes ,I do.*

"We . . ." Dr. Miller pulled a pager from his pocket and frowned at it. "I'm sorry. It's one of my patients. We have to leave. I thought we'd be able to stay for the reception with President Menchan. Give him our best. We'll see you this evening at your party." He shook his head and turned to Sheila. "I'm sorry you have to leave Jeff right now, but it's only for a few hours. You'll see him tonight."

"Jeff and I have to talk. I'll catch a ride with him."

"I'm sorry, baby," Mrs. Hamilton said. "Mrs. Baker's car is already full."

Dr. Miller walked away, but Sheila stood staring at Jeff.

"What's wrong, Sheila? We have to go." Mrs. Miller touched her daughter's arm. She looked from Sheila to Jeff, then back to Sheila, and frowned. "What is it?"

Sheila looked around. Out of all the people here, she should see somebody she knew, but she didn't. "I guess it can wait until later on today. It has to." Her stare settled back on Jeff.

"I-I'll see you tonight." It was hard, but he met her stare. He owed her that.

She let out a harsh breath and tilted her head. Then she nodded slowly. "You'd better believe it."

Jeff watched her walk away from him. He hoped that

by tonight he would find the words to keep her from doing it again.

He went to the reception for the graduates and their families and friends because his mother deserved it. His whole life she had sacrificed for him: cleaning house for the Wilsons and then working part-time at the Stenson Nursing Home. His mother needed to celebrate the results of her efforts.

Later, if anybody had asked him what he ate at the reception or how something tasted, he couldn't have told them. He introduced his mom to each person who congratulated him and was thankful that his brain was alert enough to remember names as he introduced his mom and the Bakers.

The crowd thinned out and it was time to leave. He had been ready to go when Sheila left. If he hadn't been the graduate, he would have gone with her and her parents. He sighed. *Graduate or no, if Mom and the Bakers hadn't been with me, I would have left anyway.*

He patted his back pocket. The letter was still there.

During the hour-and-a-half ride home, he tried to find the right thing to say. He wished it were a chemistry problem or a math problem that he had to figure out; something with a lot of numbers would be easy. He was used to that kind of problem. Trying to find the words that would make Sheila understand that he had to do this . . . that was impossible. Still, he tried.

Jeff straightened the collar of his deep blue shirt. Sheila gave it to him last Christmas along with the tie. Maybe they would bring good luck to him tonight. She had kissed him when she had given it to him. As he had opened the package, she had stood close enough for a whiff of the perfume he had given her to tickle his nose and settle against memories of her in his arms.

Later they had found a spot to be alone, and he'd gotten closer still. He smiled. Together they had discovered more ways than they knew existed to find pleasure without breaking their vows to wait to consummate their love.

He patted his hair as if it needed it. Sheila had to let him get that close again. He swallowed hard. Where could he get luck if the shirt didn't work? He dabbed on a bit of the cologne that she had given him, too. If he had a lucky hat, that would have gone on his head. He was sure his mom would let him break her 'no hats on men's heads in my house' rule this one time.

He shook his head and went to the kitchen. Maybe his mom had some last-minute things for him to do that would take his mind off the mess he had made.

"Mom." He stopped in the doorway and looked into the kitchen. Every surface was brimming with food. "I sure hope you didn't spend yourself into a hole." The smell of chicken and ham and greens twisted with that of the sweet potato pies that covered the windowsill. He knew that potato salad and macaroni salad were in the refrigerator; he had helped cut up the vegetables last night. Jeff looked around and shook his head. His mom had done more this time than she had when he had graduated from high school, and he had thought *that* was too much.

The table held a platter piled with fried chicken. Sliced ham covered another platter and four different kinds of cheeses filled a third. Cut-up vegetables surrounded containers of dip in two large bowls. Chips and pretzels and cheese curls filled baskets on the counter. More varieties of crackers than he knew they made were in different baskets. "There's enough food here to feed Hannibal's army. You spent too much. Maybe we should have just served cake and punch."

"Cake and punch? For my son's college graduation? Do you really think I would invite all of our friends and neighbors for cake and punch when my only child just graduated from the university? Nothing is too good for my son, the graduate." She smiled. "Besides, I don't want anybody accusing me of stinting on the refreshments." Her smile widened and she patted his arm. "My son, the graduate. I do like the sound of that much better than when I said it after your high school graduation." She laughed and carried the baskets into the dining room. "Grab something and come on."

"We've got twenty minutes, Mom." Jeff took the meat platters and followed her.

"We don't want to wait until the last minute." She walked over to the table.

The extra leaf had been put into the oak table that had belonged to Jeff's grandparents. The table had been pushed against the wall to make more space for guests in the small room. A table cloth with "Congratulations" and "Best Wishes" and streamers scattered over it was spread over the table.

"Come on, university graduate. Let's go grab the rest. Folks will be here soon and they'll be hungry." She went back to the kitchen with Jeff trailing behind. "Besides, somebody always shows up early."

Soon the table was crammed with containers of food.

A large sheet cake sat in the middle of the sideboard that matched the table. Tablecloths with pictures of caps and gowns covered both.

His mother moved the stack of dessert plates closer to the cake and removed the top from the cake box. A picture of Jeff in his cap and gown filled the center portion. She touched the edge of the box.

"It's amazing how they can duplicate a photograph with icing." She moved the box a quarter of an inch to the left and stood back. "There. That looks about right." Jeff watched as him mother shifted two containers to the side. Then she fussed with the napkins and matching plates. "That's as good as I can get it." She grabbed his hand. "Come on. I got something for you. I want you to open it before the others get here."

"Mom. I told you not to get me anything." He let her pull him into her room.

"Since when did you become the parent?" She rummaged in the back of her closet, pulled out a large box, and handed it to him.

"What is it?"

"Open it and find out."

Jeff touched the package. Then he turned it over a few times before he carefully loosened the tape on one end. He tried to slide the box out, but the paper was too tight.

"I know we like to recycle the paper, baby, but just this once, can we rip it?" His mother pulled at the loose end. Jeff hesitated before he finished.

"Mom." Wonder rode his whisper as it eased out. He held up a dark brown briefcase. "Wow." He opened the catch, closed it, and turned the briefcase over and over. He even brought it close to his nose and sniffed the new leather.

"Do you like it?"

"It's beautiful." He opened it again, then closed it and ran his hand over the side.

"Nothing is too good for my executive son. That space center had better watch out. You're going to turn that place on its ear." She took the briefcase from him gently and placed it on the bed. "Have you decided how you're going to tell Sheila?"

"No." He sighed. "Mom, I have to take this job. I have wanted to work in the space industry since I saw that special on television back when I was in grade school. I have to take advantage of this opportunity."

"I know, baby." She nodded. "A lot of kids outgrow their childhood dreams. You didn't."

"I-I just don't know how to explain it to Sheila so

she'll understand what this means to me. We'll only be apart for a year. And I'll be home for the holidays: Thanksgiving and Christmas. And I won't be leaving until August." He sighed. "I guess I should have told her I was applying." A crease folded his forehead, seemed to age him more than ten years. "I thought I was doing what was best."

"I'm not the one you have to convince, baby."

"Anybody home?" Mrs. Duncan called from the porch.

"Coming." Mrs. Hamilton patted Jeff's shoulder. "It will be all right. When the time comes, you'll think of the right thing to say. Just speak the truth to her from your heart."

Jeff followed. *I wish it were that simple.*

More taps and calls through the screen door reached him. Voices mingled. "Where's the graduate?" somebody asked. Jeff forced a smile onto his face and left the bedroom.

The living and dining rooms were filled with guests holding plates of food. Comments of "This is delicious" and "Betsy, you've outdone yourself this time" were met with words of agreement. Friendly conversations buzzed in the air, interrupted now and then by a laugh. A green card table, set up in a corner of the living room to receive gifts, was now overflowing. Jeff was grateful for all of them, but he knew none of the packages held what he needed: Sheila's understanding. He looked at his friends and neighbors and tried to look happy. Everybody was here except the one whom he had to see. What was keeping her? She had to come. She wouldn't refuse to give him a chance to talk to her. Would she?

"Congratulations, man. You made it." His friend Kaleef shifted the paper plate to his other hand and held out his right. Jeff forced a smile as he slapped it with his own. "We all talked about doing this," Kaleef said, "but you're the one who did it." He nodded. "College graduate. My buddy is a college graduate."

"I made it first. Next year it will be your turn."

"Yeah, that's right." His friend from first grade nodded. "It took a year after high school for me to start college, but the end is in sight." Kaleef moved on and Jeff walked over to the door and looked out.

"Looking won't make her come any sooner, son." Jeff glanced at his mom standing behind him. Then the door pulled his attention back to it like a bunch of scrap metal to a giant magnet.

"I know." He sighed. "I thought she'd be here by now."

"Maybe Dr. Miller's emergency took a long time."

"Sheila has her own car."

Wasn't she going to give him a chance to explain? Didn't what they had deserve a chance for an explanation? If she was this angry already, how would she feel after she heard what he had to say?

His mother squeezed his shoulder. "I'll go see if I need to put some more food out."

"Okay," he answered, but he never tore his gaze from the door.

This is as bad as it will get, he thought. *Once she hears my plan, she'll see that it will work. She'll like Houston. She just has to get used to the idea.* He released a harsh breath. First she had to get here.

More neighbors congratulated him, shook his hand, patted his back, and moved on, but no one new came into the house. His mother called him several times to get something from a tall shelf, but he always went back to his job as door watcher.

Finally, when he had just about given up, Sheila stood in front of him; she was still on the porch, too far away.

"What's this about Houston?" Her eyes didn't crinkle with the smile she usually had for him.

He missed the kiss she always greeted him with. He shook his head. The kiss she *usually* greeted him with. He missed the way she held her body against his for a few seconds before she stepped away after the kiss. The deep apricot of her silk dress looked warm and friendly. A delicate lace collar framed the neckline that showed her graceful neck. He wanted to press his lips to her neck; he wanted to feel her pulse jump when he touched his tongue to the spot just below her ear. He wanted to erase the problem between them. Instead he stared at her and hoped he would have a chance for that later. Softness wasn't in her smooth chocolate face. A smile didn't turn her mouth up in the grin she usually wore. Her mouth didn't invite him closer to sample her lips. Friendliness wasn't in her usually twinkling bright eyes.

The calendar showed the beginning of June, but Sheila's eyes reminded him more of January.

"Let's go to the park and talk." He placed his hand on her arm. She shook her arm once, but not again, and not hard enough to knock his away. Wasn't that a good sign?

She strode as if in a race-walking contest. Jeff stayed a step behind. The full skirt of her dress danced around her legs as she walked, but Sheila didn't look ready to dance. Her straight back said "keep away" as surely as if she wore a sign.

Jeff widened the distance between them. Maybe leaving space would give her anger someplace to go. Maybe.

"Okay."

She whirled around as soon as she got inside the wire fence of the neighborhood flower garden. Jeff sighed. Her anger hadn't gone anywhere. Instead it had taken the time to expand and dig in tighter. Jeff closed the gap between them. She was wearing the perfume he gave her every Christmas. That was a good sign, wasn't it? *If she was through with me, she would have worn a different scent, wouldn't she?*

He tried to control the shake in his hands as he pulled the letter from his pocket.

"Read this. Please?" He brushed at the wrinkled paper as if he could make the words more acceptable to her before he handed her the letter. "You know how much I've always wanted this."

Sheila's gaze stayed fastened to the letter. She didn't say anything. Jeff went on, hoping to find something to soften her.

"Ever since I was a kid. I told you about it."

She shuffled the second page to the top without even looking at him.

"We . . . We won't be apart for long." *She must be finished reading the letter by now. Why is she still looking at it? Is that a good sign?* "I'll come home for the holidays. I could even come home some weekends."

He watched Sheila's hands as she slowly put the first page on top, folded the papers carefully along the old lines, and slid the letter back into the envelope as if it was important to her.

"Here." She held it out to him.

Jeff looked into her eyes.

He had seen her eyes wet with tears from laughing at some dumb joke he made. His jokes never were funny, but she laughed at his attempts to be funny. He had seen them wet with tears while she watched a movie that she had to see, even though she knew it would make her cry. "It's a woman thing," she had explained when he questioned her.

He had seen her eyes warm with passion when he held her and touched her in places only he was allowed to touch. He had seen the regret in her eyes match that in his own when one of them remembered that they had promised to wait until after they were married.

He had seen a lot of things in her eyes over the years, but he had never seen the coldness that filled them now. It entered him and wrapped around his heart. Fear sprouted inside him.

"Say something."

"What?" She held her hands out. "What do you want me to say? It's already done." She shrugged. "You made your decision. You made your choice." She handed the letter back to him. He hesitated, but finally took it and put it back into his pocket.

"Baby, we'll only be apart for a year." He reached out to her, but pulled back when she moved away. "I'll be home for the holidays." He used the best words he could find. "Houston's not that far. I can fly home on weekends, even. It's only until you graduate."

"And then what?" She crossed her arms across her chest. Her lips trembled.

Jeff watched her take a deep breath, let it out, then take another. Maybe it would calm her.

"What plans did you make for me for after that, huh, Jeff? What did you plan for my future without telling me?"

"We'll still get married just like we planned. Nothing else has changed." He stepped toward her and put a hand on her arm, but she shook it off and stepped back.

"Everything has changed."

"No, baby." He closed the space again. "We can still get married after you graduate, just like you want."

"I guess then you plan for me to move to Houston?"

"That's where the job is."

"What happened to working for one of the refineries here? You said two of them offered you jobs without your even applying."

"That's true. But—"

"When did Houston come into the equation?"

Jeff took a deep breath. "Professor Burke kept bugging me about the space program. I didn't know that he sent for the application until he gave it to me."

"And you had to fill it out. You couldn't tell him 'Thanks, but no, thanks.' You never told me about that, either."

"I didn't expect to get the job, so I didn't want to upset you, but I couldn't pass up this opportunity. Don't you see?"

"If you didn't expect to get the job, why bother with the application?"

"I-I . . ."

"Never mind." She turned her back on him, but not before he saw tears sparkle on her eyelashes. "I'm going." She didn't face him again, so he didn't know if the tears fell or still dangled there. "We don't have anything else to say to each other."

Her stride as she left him would have made a military officer proud. The soft, gentle woman he loved had been replaced, and it was all his doing. Would he ever hold her again? Would she ever let him close enough to feel her softness next to his hard body? The answers couldn't be no. She had to give him more time to make it clear—time to fix things.

"Wait. Please." She turned. He reached out to her, but he didn't touch her. He didn't want to risk her rejection before he was finished explaining. The more time she stayed with him the longer he had to persuade her that things could still be okay between them.

"I'm not moving to Houston. You knew I wanted to stay here. I told you that. That's why we discussed getting jobs here. We talked about getting a house in my neighborhood. How could you do this? How could you do this to us?" She turned away, and this time she didn't turn back.

"Sheila, wait. . . ."

"You want Houston and I want Philadelphia. Nothing will change that."

Jeff watched her go, but he didn't try to stop her again. He heard her drive off, but he didn't leave the park. He sat on the bench and thought of how big Houston was and how much bigger it would be without Sheila with him.

The next day he called Sheila. The first two times her mother said that Sheila wasn't available. Would she ever be "available" to him again? The third time Mrs. Miller asked him to wait. He waited. He would hold the phone for however long it took for Sheila to decide to talk to him.

"Hello." The hours since he had seen her hadn't melted the frost in her voice.

"Sheila, please. Can we talk about this some more?"

"It won't do any good." Her soft words could have been a hammer shattering his heart. The sorrow that had replaced the frost wasn't any better. Just different. "You're going to Houston and I won't go. My roots are here. Your dream is there. There's nothing to talk about. Good luck. I wish you the best."

He wasn't sure she was gone until the hum came through the phone line. He tried to call back, but there was no answer. The next two times he tried he got a busy signal.

The next morning he was up before dawn, but he made himself wait until after nine—a decent hour, his mom always said—before he called Sheila's house. He was too late. Mrs. Miller said that Sheila had left early. She had decided to drive to Virginia Beach to spend some time with her aunt and uncle.

"I'm sorry, Jeff," Mrs. Miller said when he asked, "but

she told me not to give you the number there. She didn't say how long she'll stay. Probably until it's time for her to go back to school."

Her sigh came over the phone and dropped between them. "I'm sorry things fell apart between you and Sheila." She waited as if trying to find the right words. "I know you'll be successful in Houston. You can do anything you set your mind to." Again she hesitated. "Maybe we'll see you sometime when you come home to visit."

"Maybe."

Jeff let the phone drop back into place. Mrs. Miller was wrong. He couldn't do everything he set his mind to. He couldn't find a way to bring Sheila back to him.

Jeff worked his temporary job until two weeks before it was time for him to go. His mother suggested that he take the time off, but he didn't. He was glad to have something to do. He worked overtime at the department store every chance he got. It didn't take his mind off Sheila, but it filled the hours.

His last two weeks at home were spent buying what he needed to take with him, saying his final goodbyes to his friends, and hoping Sheila would call. He learned that no matter how much you hope, sometimes it doesn't matter. Finally it was time for him to leave.

"You have your tickets?" Jeff's mom smoothed his sleeve.

"Yes, Mom. They're still in my pocket where they were two minutes ago when you asked."

"I want to make sure you don't forget them." She straightened a wrinkle in his other sleeve. "Are you sure you shouldn't wear a suit?"

"Mom, I won't be meeting anyone from the department until tomorrow morning. They won't know what I'm wearing on the plane."

"Well, if you're sure."

"I'm sure."

"Do you have directions to the apartment they got for you?"

"Yes, Mom, but I don't need them, since you made me memorize them." He smiled at her.

"You never know. You could lose that paper. Then what would you do?"

"Call the department."

"That wouldn't make a very good first impression, would it? A top scientist who couldn't keep track of a piece of paper. How could they trust you with expensive equipment and the important experiments you'll be conducting?"

Jeff laughed and kissed her cheek. "Mom, you are something else."

"I'm just making sure you have everything you need. We don't want you to leave anything behind."

"I know."

She left the bedroom, and Jeff didn't have to hold the smile on his face any longer. He didn't have everything he needed. And he was leaving something more important than a piece of paper behind.

He walked over to the window and looked out. Sheila hadn't come home. Her mother had been patient with his two calls a day. She said that she understood. That was nice of her, but it wasn't *her* understanding that he needed.

"Mrs. Baker is here, Jeff."

His mother's voice pulled him from the window. He got his suitcases and left his bedroom.

"Mom. You're sure you don't mind my leaving? After all you did for me, I'm leaving you."

"I told you before, you have to follow your dream.

That's what kids are supposed to do. Most times it takes children away from their parents. That's the way of the world. I left my parents to make a life for myself, you leave to find your future, and someday your kids will do the same. That's how it is." She kissed his cheek. "Some people can't accept that, but that's how it's supposed to be." She patted his arm.

She didn't mention Sheila's name, but Jeff knew that was who she was talking about.

"Besides, I have such a full life that I won't even miss you."

"Right."

"Well, not much, once I get used to your not being here." She smiled at him. "Who knows? I might decide to throw a couple of wild parties while you're gone." She laughed.

"My mom, the party animal." Jeff laughed too.

"Come on," she said. "We don't want to keep Mrs. Baker waiting." She took a small box from the table. "Just a few cookies I baked for you. And a few rolls."

"Mom." Jeff shook his head and followed her out the door. He looked down the street in both directions before he put his luggage into the open trunk. He looked around one last time before he slid into the passenger side.

It was an hour's ride to the airport, but he didn't turn around to look out the back window. Mrs. Baker and his mom kept up the conversation. He answered when he had to, but only then.

Too soon they got to the airport and he got out. If it had taken longer, maybe Sheila would have . . . He shook his head. Sheila was out of his life forever. She didn't want anything else to do with him. She had made that clear.

"I'm coming in to wait with you until your flight is called," his mom said when Jeff suggested that she could leave.

"That's not necessary. I promise I won't get lost on the way to the gate."

"I didn't think you would, but I only have one time to send my son off to his first real job, and I intend to be here for as long as I can. Mrs. Baker and I worked it out. We even found a spot last week where she can wait for me." She took his arm. "Come on; you don't want to miss your flight."

"I have an hour. I never heard of a flight leaving early."

"Don't get smart with your mother. Over here." She pointed to the right and led the way to the check-in line. "Do you have your tickets?"

"Yes, Mom." Jeff laughed. He pulled on the lightweight jacket he carried over his arm. He chuckled as he took the pouch from the pocket.

"Well, it could have fallen out. Move up a bit."

Jeff slid his suitcases along the floor and closed the space left when the man in front of him moved up.

He checked in, then followed his mom up the escalator. In spite of being a foot taller than she was, he had to lengthen his stride to keep up.

"Mom. Slow down."

She looked back at him and waited for him. "I don't want you to miss your plane."

He stood beside her. "If I didn't know better, I'd think you were anxious to get rid of me."

"You know that's not true." She frowned. "Don't you?"

"Absolutely. That's one thing I know for sure." He kissed her cheek and wrapped his arm around her shoulders.

They went the rest of the way to the gate faster than he wanted but slower than she wanted.

"Do you want to sit?" He pointed to the rows of gray seats fastened together.

"Not really. How about you?"

"I've got hours ahead of me sitting in the plane. I want to stretch my legs as long as I can."

He walked to the large window and looked out, even though they were facing the back and he couldn't see who got out of the cars that came to the front of the airport. Sheila wouldn't be coming on a plane. She drove to Virginia Beach. Besides, arriving passengers were already gone from the plane by the time it reached these gates. His mother moved beside him.

"At least they sent you first-class tickets. You'll have a little extra leg room."

He was still staring out the window when his mother touched his arm. "They called your row."

Jeff walked to the end of the line. He looked at the people passing by in the hallway to make sure.

"Good-bye, Jeffrey." She wrapped her arms around him. He bent down and let her kiss his cheek. She tightened her hug as he kissed her. "Take care of yourself, son."

"I will, Mom." He watched her blink hard. "I'll see you for Thanksgiving."

"You call me before then."

"Yes, ma'am." He waved and stepped through the doorway. He looked at the people passing by once more before he walked down the narrow hallway taking him to his future without Sheila.

He came home for Thanksgiving, but Sheila was never home when he called. He went over to her house on Saturday and again on Sunday before he left. Her mother had been polite. She seemed sorry both times when she told him that Sheila wasn't home.

He tried writing to Sheila, but stopped when he realized that she would continue to send all of his letters back.

By Christmas he had allowed himself to hope she would see him. Christmas was the time of miracles, wasn't it? Why shouldn't there be a miracle for him?

He went to her house as soon as he got home. There was no miracle waiting for him.

"She went out." Mrs. Miller stared at him. Sadness filled her eyes. "She went out with Bill Clayton." She continued to stare, but it softened. "She's dating him now." She touched his arm. "I'm sorry, Jeff."

Somehow the right goodbye words found their way through the hurt building inside him. The walkway was smooth, but he stumbled anyway. It didn't take her long to get over him. *I'm still hurting and she's already moved on to somebody else.*

He was glad when it was time for him to go back to Houston. If his mother weren't still living here, he'd never come back.

Two

Snowflakes drifted down as if not sure where they wanted to go. A slight breeze swirled, and the flakes whirled before slowing back to a lazy pace. Jeff Hamilton fastened the last two buttons of his overcoat, put his free hand into his pocket and, in spite of the cold, smiled. His first purchase tomorrow would have to be gloves.

His smile widened as he walked over to the cab at the front of the line outside of the Philadelphia International Airport terminal. He held the bottom of his coat together as the wind tugged at it. He had forgotten how cold Philadelphia could be in December, but he wasn't sorry that he came back.

Eric had thought he was crazy when Jeff had told him that he was leaving Houston. He had calmed down a little when he realized that Jeff would still be involved with the operations of the company, only from Philadelphia. Jeff breathed in the cold air and nodded. This was where he belonged.

"Where to, mister?" The cabdriver's accent belonged in a place where sunshine blanketed beaches and people looked for shade, not where they sought shelter from the cold and the next ground cover would be white. Jeff looked at the sky. Maybe tonight. If this snow quit fooling around and got serious, they might have a good coating by morning. He felt like a kid with a new sled. His smile eased away. Not that he had ever had a new sled. He shrugged. His secondhand sled had skimmed over the snow as well as any new sled could.

"Yo, mister. You want to go somewhere or not?"

A jet flew over almost low enough for Jeff to see the numbers. He forced his attention to the driver.

"Sorry. Yes."

The driver popped the trunk and Jeff placed his suitcase inside. When he closed it, the air was crowded with snowflakes the size of popcorn kernels. Another gust fanned the bottom of his coat open. He added warmer pants to his mental shopping list.

He climbed into the back of the cab and gave his address, but had to repeat it when another jet shrieked overhead, erasing every other sound. A lot of people were leaving Philadelphia.

He leaned back as the driver eased into traffic. How many were leaving home? How many would take eleven years, as he had, to discover that they belonged here?

The driver left the airport, and Jeff looked out the window at the mountain of chewed-up metal bits inside the fence they were passing. Smashed-up hulls of cars waited nearby for their turn. A pile of crushed washers and dryers formed their own rusting pile. The scrap-metal business looked the same as it always did. When he was younger he had passed this company on his way to church. He had wondered then if anyone ever used the metal or if they shredded it just to save landfill space. His smile returned. Scrap metal like this had helped him get to the point that he could buy a dozen sled factories if he wanted to.

They sped over the Platt Bridge and past the refineries that wore lights like year-round Christmas trees. The driver stopped for a light and a kid approached asking to wash windshields. Jeff shook his head. Even in this weather. How many took their quarters home to the projects on the other side of the overpass? How many helped put food on their tables? The light changed and the driver turned onto the Schuylkill Expressway before Jeff could say anything. As they zipped along he was glad that he had enough sense to arrive between rush-hour traffic. That was one thing he hadn't missed.

He stared out the window at center city passing by, but he wasn't seeing the buildings. Large brown eyes in a milk-chocolate face loomed up from his memories. Soft lips that he had kissed more times than he could count, but not enough times, trembled as they had that last time he saw her. He remembered how tears had danced on the edges of Sheila's eyelashes that day. How he had made them appear. How stupid he had been to think that he would find something better in Houston than he had here. He doubted if he was the only one who had ever thrown away something perfect to search for something better. He sighed. Even if he were correct, it wouldn't make him feel any better. In this case company wouldn't ease the misery filling him.

What was Sheila doing? She was probably married by now. He swallowed hard. When he had seen her at his mother's funeral ten years ago, she had been engaged. He had even talked to her, for all the good it did. Nothing had changed. He insisted on going back to Houston when he was finished taking care of business, and she was staying here where she wanted to be. He shook his head. No, nothing had changed back then. His life was in Houston and her life was here. She was content with Philadelphia while he wanted more. Sheila wanted to marry her new fiancé and Jeff still wanted her. But on his own terms.

He sighed. He had wanted her, but not enough to give up his fledgling business in Houston and move back here. He was known as a business genius, a man who knew how to take nothing and turn it into something.

He should have been known as a man who was an idiot when it came to his personal life. One who knew how to take something and destroy it.

He swallowed hard. Maybe she had a couple of kids. Enough time had passed. Would they look like her? Would they have that dimple in their left cheeks that deepened when they smiled? They should be his kids. That was the way they had planned it. They would graduate, get married, have a family. Then he spoiled it.

"You coming home or just visiting?"

"Coming home." He was grateful to the driver for grabbing his attention. No matter how many times he went over it, the ending was the same: he had accepted a job in Houston with the space industry and Sheila had stayed in Philadelphia and made a life for herself here without him.

"You coulda picked a better time to come back. We're supposed to get an accumulation." The driver leaned forward and turned up the heater. "Times like this I ask myself why I was crazy enough to leave Jamaica." His voice softened. "I could be walking through the market complaining about the heat instead of trying to get warm." He laughed. "Of course, I wouldn't have any money to buy anything in the market had I stayed home." He laughed again, but it quickly drifted away. "If I coulda found me a job, I'd still be there where I belong." He let the silence in. Jeff knew about being where you belonged. His thoughts flew back to Sheila.

Was she still teaching? He nodded. Probably so. She had planned to be a teacher back when they were at Central High School together. He had had more scholarship offers than the rest of the class combined, but he had decided to go to Cheyney University. His mother had dreamed of going there, but she couldn't afford college. He went for her. Sheila's SAT scores won her a full scholarship good for any college, but she followed him to Cheyney.

She hadn't hesitated about choosing her major. Her course load was heavy in math, but she hadn't planned to work for a corporation: she wanted to be a middle school math teacher. And that was what she did.

At the church after his mother's burial, Sheila had come over to him. She told him that she was teaching. They had talked about her job, her family, people they had gone to school with, and what everybody was doing. They had talked about everything except what had happened between them, and that maybe one of them had had a change of mind.

Then a man had come over and taken Sheila's hand as if he had a right to.

"Hi. I'm Bill Clayton, Sheila's fiancé," he said. He held out his other hand to Jeff.

Jeff spoke to him. He remembered the manners his mom had taught him and even took the hand that Bill had offered when what he had wanted to do was get as far away from that truth as he could. How could a word like *fiancé* cause so much pain?

Jeff had worked to finish putting his mother's affairs in order as if he had two days to complete the task instead of as long as he needed. He had disposed of his mother's belongings, shipped the things he wanted to Houston, and left the house where he grew up as empty as it was when his mother had bought it.

He had finished sooner than he expected to, put the house in the hands of Carolyn, an old high school classmate who had become a realtor, and left earlier than he had planned. He had no reason to stay any longer. And no reason to come back. Until now.

He hadn't tried to see Sheila again before he left that time. What for? He was a math person, but he couldn't count the times he wondered if he did the right thing in not calling her. Or in going back to Houston. Or in leaving Philadelphia in the first place.

The cabdriver drove through the swirling snow as flakes began to gather on the road. When they turned onto Lincoln Drive Jeff couldn't help the anticipation that grew within him. At least he had one thing to look forward to: his new house. He hoped the house was as grand as he remembered, but that wasn't important. He would have bought it anyway. When he told Carolyn to get the house for him regardless of the cost, she had questioned him to make sure he meant it. When he also told her that he didn't intend to see it first and that he would pay whatever price the owners asked, she insisted he send her a letter stating that. "We go way back to high school, Jeff, but my boss will want something in writing."

Carolyn hadn't said it, but Jeff knew that her boss wanted to make sure they weren't wasting time with him. He understood. He'd do the same if he were in her place, especially if the buyer made an open offer on such an expensive property as he had.

Faxes had flown between them, papers were signed and mailed, and the sale was completed within two weeks of his offer. Carolyn had said it was because he had paid way too much. She was probably right. She knew about his background, but she couldn't understand why he had to have this particular house so badly that he didn't care about the price. He was only sorry that his mother wasn't alive to move in with him.

The driver stopped at the red light at Wissahickon Avenue and Jeff smiled. The city had finally fixed the dip around the grate at this spot. He and his buddies had called it the unplanned speed bump. Where were his old friends now? How many had been dumb enough to leave and stay away? In spite of his being "the Brain," the nickname they had given him, they all were probably smarter than he had been about making important life decisions.

The car started again. Jeff glanced at a man running along the path in the park on the other side of the creek. Another rode a bike from the other direction. Joggers and bikers never did care about the weather. The cab followed the curves in the drive that followed the curves carved by the Wissahickon Creek centuries ago. Jeff watched the passing scenery, thinking about how some things stayed the same and some things didn't, and wishing he could change one thing so it was the way it should be.

"Is this the right house, mister, or did I make a wrong turn somewhere? You got a key or something to get us in?"

Jeff looked at the wrought-iron gate attached to the ten-foot-high stone wall on both sides of it. The gold trim covering the curlicues of gate hinted at what lay on the other side, but it didn't begin to give the true picture, if things were as Jeff remembered.

"This is the right house. Give me a minute."

He got out, walked to the left side of the wall, and pushed aside a neatly trimmed bush. He entered the code that Carolyn had sent him. The gate parted and slid silently into place at the sides.

He got back in and rode up the slightly sloping driveway that wound to the right. Sycamore trees, their branches bare of leaves, stood along the way. Limbs swayed with the gusts that arranged the snowflakes as they fell. A coating like vanilla frosting lay where the branches met the trees. Another coating clung to the Belgian blocks making up the driveway. Late-afternoon snow painted the slopes of each stone, and shadows filled in the sides so that the driveway looked like a patchwork quilt of blue and white squares.

"Here we are." This time the driver got out and lifted the suitcase. "Don't look like nobody is home."

Tall, narrow leaded windows flanked the wide door, and a leaded Palladian window spread across the top of the doorway, but no light escaped from the large stone house.

"There is now." Jeff paid the driver. "Keep the change."

The driver looked at the money. "You want me to take that suitcase inside the house for you, mister?"

"I can handle it."

"I hope you don't have to go food shopping today. You know how people around here are when the weatherman says that four-letter word. They act like they won't be able to get out to the stores for weeks." He smiled. "To tell you the truth, my wife went shopping this morning." He shrugged. "Better to have and not need than the other way around, you know." He got back into the cab. "What will you do about the gate? You gonna leave it open or you want me to shut it after I go out?"

"It will close automatically behind you."

"Okay." The man smiled. "Welcome home. I hope you have a merry Christmas. I know it's early, but if the city can put up street decorations and the stores can decorate their windows and put out Christmas merchandise before Halloween, I guess I can say 'Merry Christmas' at the beginning of December."

"I don't see why not," Jeff said. Maybe the man's wish for him would come true. Miracles happened at Christmastime. The one that first Christmas night wasn't the last. Why shouldn't he expect one of his own this year? He shook his head. It would take a miracle for his Christmas to be merry. "I wish you the same."

Jeff carried his suitcase up the snow-covered porch steps. The gray porch floor shone through small drifts as if a fresh coat of paint had been recently applied. He had to remember to thank Carolyn for that. The legs of white wicker furniture peeked out from the bottom of the green plastic covers protecting the furniture from the weather. Small piles of snow nestled in the folds of the covers on what must be a sofa and two chairs. The wind blew, and swirls of snow flew in from one side of the porch, skipped across the floor, and jumped off the other side.

The snow was coming down as if the last forty-five minutes had been practice for the real thing. He was glad it had waited until his flight had arrived.

He opened the lockbox on the door, again using a combination provided by Carolyn, and removed the key. As he opened the door, snow swirled as if looking for a new place to play. Jeff placed the suitcase down on the gray marble tiles covering the hallway floor and quickly pushed the door shut.

He looked up at the high-ceilinged hall made larger by its emptiness. How had he had forgotten the wide plaster molding circling the square of ceiling, penning in the crystal chandelier that he remembered from long ago? How many times had his mother cleaned the prisms? He flipped the switch and rainbows sparkled on the walls while shadows hid in the corners. When he was young, he used to watch the rainbows dance whenever a breeze stirred the crystals. Who had cleaned them last?

He walked a few steps farther into the hall and touched one of the fancy twin columns standing guard at the wide doorway leading to the living room on the left. These he remembered, too. His mouth set in a hard line. He had dusted these columns more times than he wanted to remember. Each summer and school holiday he had come to work with his mother until he was able to convince her that he was old enough to stay at home on his own. At first he couldn't reach past the middle of the column even on tiptoe. His mother had to use a stepladder to reach the top. The summer he turned fourteen was his last to help her. He had managed to dust almost all the way to the top without the ladder. Before then he had also graduated to dusting the knickknacks and pieces of African art scattered throughout the house that Dr. and Mrs. Wilson collected during their travels. Jeff ran his hand around a column.

They were narrower than he remembered. He looked up to the tops flaring out and curling under. But not as tall. He smiled. He had grown another six inches since he had last dusted them.

He opened the small box inside the closet beside the door, looked at the monitor screen and watched as the cab cleared the grounds, and the gates slid back into place. Then he walked into the living room. The walls were bare except for a new coat of paint, but he remembered the paintings of African and African-American scenes that had covered these walls when his mother worked here. No traces remained now, and it was no wonder: Dr. Wilson had retired several years ago, and he and Mrs. Wilson had moved back to North Carolina, no doubt taking their art with them.

Another family had moved in a few months later, but had moved out within the year when the husband's job transferred him to Minnesota. The house had lain empty until now.

"Six bedrooms and three floors are more house than most folks want nowadays," Carolyn had said. "Those who might want this much space are afraid to commit to this kind of expense. Look what happened to the last family. They barely got settled when they had to move." She paused. "I have to warn you: it's still going to cost you plenty. The house is in move-in condition. Are you sure about this?" He had assured her that he wanted the house regardless.

Jeff walked across the newly refinished oak floors. His footsteps echoed because there was nothing to catch the sound and slow it down. Area rugs would help take care of that. He touched the brass sconces inside the doorway. Carolyn had been right about it costing him, but it was worth it. She didn't understand his need to own this house. She couldn't. He wasn't sure he did himself. Being able to call it his made him feel as if his mother would be pleased.

He moved to the wide window in the middle of the three in the bay. Flakes fell as close together as raindrops. He shivered. Rain never created this much coldness. He closed the heavy brocade drapes he bought from the last owners as part of the purchase agreement. Then he left the window. The dark green drapes weren't what he wanted, but they would help keep out the cold until he bought new ones. He'd ask Carolyn to recommend someone to make the new drapes. He turned up the thermostat on the wall beside the doorway.

His footsteps made the silence seem stronger, reminding him that he was alone in the house. He wrapped his arms around himself, then went over and turned the thermostat up another five degrees. Area rugs would help fight the chill, too. He had forgotten the cold. Eleven years was too long to stay away and not forget something. His memories of other things were as fresh as if they had happened this morning. The hurt was as sharp, too. Was she happy?

He went to the dining room. His furniture would fit nicely when it arrived the next day. He looked out of the large window in the bay that was a twin to the one in the living room and smiled. The ground was covered with snow, but the bird feeder was still there. His smile widened. He had spent many hours sitting on the wide windowsill watching the birds come to the feeder.

Once, when he was about seven, Mrs. Wilson saw him

and he had jumped down, afraid he had caused trouble for his mother, but Mrs. Wilson told him it was okay. She got a book of birds from the library to show him. Then she sat with him and helped him identify and read about the birds that came to feed. Before she left the house that day, Mrs. Wilson took him into the library and showed him where the book was kept.

"Anytime you want to check on birds, you come get this book. If you promise to be careful, you can read the books over here, too." She took him over to the last bookcase. "These books belonged to our kids. Books aren't any good if they aren't read." She squeezed his shoulder. "I'll tell your mom that it's okay for you to read any book in this bookcase." He took another book from the shelf. She had left him there, but he hadn't noticed. He hadn't noticed anything until his mom came and got him for lunch.

The floor-to-ceiling shelves were empty now, but by next week his own books would claim their places. He didn't have any kid's books, though. If he hadn't thrown away what he had with Sheila, maybe this bookcase would hold books for his own kids. Maybe by now he'd have at least one child as interested as he was in identifying birds that came to the feeder.

He picked up the phone from the floor in the hall. A dial tone hummed in his ear. So far things were going according to his plans. He called Carolyn.

"Fine," he said when she asked how he was. "I am standing in my hallway using my house phone, and I thank you. My flight was on time and uneventful, and I thank the airline for that. Even the weather is providing me with a welcome-home snowfall." He nodded. "Okay, snowstorm, if you insist." He laughed and leaned against the wall. "Great. Thanks even more for that. I was afraid to ask. Did you at least get to the supermarket before the weathermen caused a panic?" He laughed again. "I'll understand if you tack on an aggravation/snow hysteria fee to what I owe you for the groceries." He nodded. "Since my car arrived safe and sound yesterday, I guess I'll have to come to you. It probably won't be until Monday. My furniture will be arriving tomorrow so I'll be busy getting things where they belong. Since I'm too old to enjoy sleeping on the floor, I'm on my way to the Holiday Inn in Valley Forge." He shook his head. "I'll be all right. Driving in snow is like riding a bike: once you learn how you never forget." He shook his head. "No, I haven't. I'll check out the rest of the house tomorrow. I'd better get to the hotel before my body uses up the rest of my adrenaline supply and I collapse right here." He laughed again before he hung up.

He went to the back door and set the alarm before he stepped out onto the wide porch. Drifts of snow lay along the sides. A thin coating covered the rest of the porch floor. As he watched, more snow joined what was already on the ground. *I have to get a snow shovel,* he thought. *And salt, too.*

Carefully he made his way down the back porch steps and across the paved area to the building made of the same stone as the house. Originally it had been a carriage house, but some owner had converted it to a five car garage. Who needed five cars? He shrugged. A family with five drivers. The house was large enough. He smiled. He planned to get a new car next week. One driver, two cars.

Using the key Carolyn had left beside the phone, he released the garage door. It slid into place overhead, but he didn't go inside. He breathed in deeply and let it out slowly. His car was in his garage in his house in Chestnut Hill. He laughed. If garages could choose, he doubted if this one would have accepted his car. The ten-year-old Geo Metro had been his first car. He had bought it used from a rental agency, and it had had a year's worth of miles on it when he got it, but it was his. He brushed his hand across the newly waxed hood. He hated to take it out in this weather, but it was all he had for now. Car shopping had been at the top of his list before warmer clothes had moved it down.

He got in and followed the cab's tracks down the driveway. He was on his way. He was about to test his theory about never forgetting how to drive in snow.

He got to Stenton Avenue and should have turned right and gotten onto Route 309, but he didn't. There were a lot of things he should have done in his life that he didn't do.

He turned left and followed the route the bus used to take when he lived in Philly. Did the SH still go this way? Was the stop the same as it had been when he rode up here from his neighborhood of tiny row houses?

He drove down the street that was not on the way to the hotel and stopped across from the house that shouldn't concern him anymore. He turned off the motor, but he didn't get out. He had no right to be here. He had thrown away that right like so much trash.

He stared at the redbrick twin. Sheila's mother's rose garden was still in its place. A few stubborn leaves still clung to the stems. They weren't as stubborn as he was. It wouldn't take the leaves eleven years to realize they were wrong.

He looked at the rosebush closest to the step leading to the front door. He managed a slight smile, but his eyes didn't participate.

One time he caught the devil from Mrs. Miller because he had picked off two roses and given them to Sheila.

"We never break roses from a bush," he remembered Mrs. Miller saying. "We clip them, and we do that very carefully." She had gotten her special pruning shears and made him fix the damage he had done to the bush. Then she made him listen to the reasons why care was needed and how to properly cut a bloom.

He swallowed hard. No pruning shears nor tool of any kind existed to fix the damage he had caused. Mrs. Miller should have explained that relationships were even more valuable than any rosebushes. He shook his head. Would he have paid attention if she had?

The snow stopped, but coldness covered the car and seeped in, filling the spaces and nudging him. He shifted, but still he hadn't gotten the courage to go knock on the door. *What can I say? Maybe I'll just leave.* He didn't follow the *maybe.* He sat and stared at the door as if he expected it to come to him.

The front door opened and he blinked. Two little girls, pigtails bobbing up and down, raced down the sidewalk and stopped at the royal blue Pontiac parked at the curb. His breath caught in his throat.

"Don't be in such a hurry." Sheila laughed as she opened the back car door. The girls giggled as they scrambled in. They sounded like Sheila had when she found something to laugh about with him. He wished he had a right to laugh with them.

Jeff felt as if his heart had shriveled into a ball and lay naked and exposed. He had no protection from the pain that found its way inside him and gripped his heart. The cold he felt was worse than any the weather could bring. *What did I expect? That she put her life on hold and waited for me to realize the truth?*

Even through eleven years and rolled-up windows, her voice was the same as he remembered. So was her laughter as it dragged a memory a lot older than eleven years to the surface of his mind.

Her father had surprised her with a puppy on her sixteenth birthday, after he had told her that it didn't make sense to get a pet, since she'd be going to college in two years. That day, Sheila had tumbled and rolled around on the floor with the puppy, laughing as he licked her and jumped all over her. Happy. She had named the cocoa-colored cocker spaniel Happy.

Jeff had more memories than he could count of her laughing and smiling. His strongest memory, though, was of her with tears in her eyes as misery, mixed with goodbye, filled her face. He had put both the tears and the misery there.

He let out a hard breath. She didn't know it, but she had just paid him back.

He watched her drive away and wondered how she could not feel his pain from across the street. How could she not know he was there? How could she not feel the intensity of his regret?

She never even looked his way. He shook his head. Maybe it was better that she not see him. What would he say? *I'm sorry? I changed my mind and you should do the same? Leave your husband and bring your kids? Give me one more chance to prove my love for you?* He sighed. As despicable as it was, if he thought it would work, he would beg her to do just that.

Flakes appeared and covered his windshield, but they were too late. He had already seen too much.

The window was completely covered before he accepted that he couldn't change what had happened. Not what had happened eleven years ago; not what had happened a few minutes ago.

He started the car and tried to get away from this latest proof of his stupidity. Getting Sheila back into his arms again seemed as impossible as changing the past.

Three

"I hope you had a good night's rest, sir." The clerk handed Jeff the receipt. "Thank you for staying with us."

Jeff picked up his suitcase. It wasn't the hotel's fault that he hadn't slept any better than if he had used the floor at his house. He got on the road that led to Chestnut Hill. Maybe coming back hadn't been such a good idea. It wouldn't be the first time he had made the wrong decision. Was it worse to see her and not have her or not to see her at all?

He was still wrestling with his own "half a loaf or none" dilemma when he parked across the street from the post office. He had to make sure that his change of address had gone through and to pick up any mail that he had forwarded to make sure that part of his move was in place. He glanced at his watch. Nine-fifteen. Maybe the usual Saturday crowd was still home.

Luck was with him. A few minutes later he was finished. He glanced through the few pieces of mail as he left the building.

"Sorry," he said as he bumped into someone. He reached out automatically to keep the person from falling.

He looked up from the letters and into a pair of eyes that he never expected to see up close again. Black specks that he had called her eye freckles held his stare.

Time stopped moving forward even though his heart raced on and threatened to burst through his chest. He forced his lungs to take in air and let it out. Then he tore his attention away from her eyes and caressed the rest of her face with his gaze. Smooth milk-chocolate skin beckoned to him as it had long ago, as it had in his dreams too many times. She was more beautiful than he remembered.

He pulled his hand from her arm when what he wanted was to pull her closer. He tightened his hand around the letters he was holding to keep from touching the dimple in her left cheek, to resist the desire to brush his thumb across her full lips, to prevent himself from pushing back her hood and burying his fingers in her curls to feel if they were as soft as ever, as soft as they were in his memories and dreams, to stop himself from leaning forward and sampling her mouth to see if it could possibly taste as sweet as he remembered. He forced himself not to wrap his hands around her shoulders, not to ease her close and fit her body to his once more. He didn't let himself try to make his dream of a second chance come true.

"Jeff." His name whispered from her and floated to him, and he remembered how it tickled his ear when she said his name as he held her close and touched a sensitive spot. He remembered the place behind her ear. He remembered how her body had tightened as she called his name when he caressed her and touched where only he was allowed to touch. He remembered too much from that one word.

"Sheila." *To say that I've missed you would be the biggest understatement of all time.*

"I-I heard that you were back."

She didn't offer him her hand, and it was a good thing. Gloves or not, if he touched her hand, he wouldn't be able to let her go.

Did her hands still get cold even inside her gloves? Had she finally found a pair to keep them warm?

Each winter when they were going together, she bought a new pair, trying to find some that would live up to the manufacturer's promise. Several years he went with her and listened as she questioned the salesperson and was assured that this pair would keep out the cold. They never did find a pair warm enough. Instead they began a ritual: each time they met he had pulled off her gloves and rubbed her hands gently, until their entire bodies were heated close to the boiling point. He'd pretended his purpose was to warm her hands, but he'd really needed the feel of her skin next to his own; they weren't fooling themselves. He had always kissed her palms before she eased her hands from his and pulled her gloves back on so they could both cool off.

He didn't follow the old ritual this time, though. This time he kept his hands to himself. This time it was too late to warm each other. Years too late. Even if she hadn't found the perfect gloves, it wasn't his concern any longer—and it was his fault. She had a husband to warm her hands now. Jeff swallowed hard. Did her kids get cold hands the way she used to?

"I got into Philly yesterday. How have you been?" *Have you missed me as much as I missed you?* He blinked. *You couldn't have. You have a husband and kids for company.*

"Excuse me."

A woman coming out of the post office broke the connection. Jeff automatically took Sheila's arm and eased her toward him. His breath had trouble finding its way out. Even through her coatsleeve he felt her warmth. She used to share her warmth with him back when he deserved it. They used to warm each other when they were in college. Late nights of studying together in the winter were ideal. Sometimes they actually did study something other than each other.

"I-I've been fine." She eased her gaze from his and her body away from him and he let her go. He had no ties to her anymore. He had cut them.

"How are your parents?" *I won't ask about your husband and children.*

"They're both fine. Dad cut his medical practice to part-time. He's teaching two classes at Temple Medical School. They still live in the same house." She smiled, and Jeff knew the meaning of bittersweet. "You know Mom will never leave her prize roses."

"Yes, I remember her roses." Did Sheila remember the time he had picked two white roses from her mom's bush? Was the memory of the kiss she gave him after her mom left them alone still as fresh in her mind as it was in his?

"I'd better go." She took another step away from him, eager to continue her life without him, but he wasn't ready to let her go yet. Not so soon. He had just found her again.

"And your brother. How is Robert?"

"Robert is fine, too. He's married."

"I hope he's happy. He's a nice guy."

"He's happy. He's been married for years. He and Cynthia have a couple of kids."

"That's nice." He watched as she broke free of his stare as if she had just realized that it was him she was talking to.

"Bye. It was . . . Bye." Sheila turned to leave.

"I saw you outside your mom's house with your two daughters yesterday. Are they twins?"

He hadn't meant to mention that. If he wanted her to stay a while longer, why didn't he comment on the Eagles or the Sixers? Why not ask about the weather prediction for today? This week? This winter? Why not mention anything else except something so painful? Why was he asking something that would just push the knife deeper into his heart? Was that possible?

"Daughters?" She frowned, but was still as beautiful as ever. Then her eyes widened the way he remembered when an idea struck her. "Oh, Tammy and Tonya. Yes, they're twins." Her frown returned as if it weren't finished. "What were you doing outside the house?"

He shrugged. "I was thinking of coming in to say hello to your mom."

"Did you go in?" Her frown deepened, as if she was afraid he had disturbed her mom again.

"No, I left. I figured that your mom probably didn't want to see me anyway." *I could barely handle the pain that seeing you with your kids caused. I didn't need to stand in her hallway where we had kissed under the mistletoe our last Christmas, as if we needed an excuse. Do you remember? Did she hang mistletoe again this year? Do you and your husband kiss there?*

"Mom would have welcomed you. She always did like you. She didn't hold anything against you." Sheila slid her gaze from him. "Sometimes things happen and it's nobody's fault." If any noise had been in the air, he wouldn't have been able to hear her words. "Some things are meant to be and some things aren't." Sheila stared at the sidewalk. "Mom said things don't always work out the way we plan." She looked back at him and smiled. Her smile was gentler, softer, than the one he remembered from years ago. Still, it was strong enough to cause the ache in him to grow like a fertilized weed. Until now he hadn't known that he had space inside for his hurt to expand.

"Your mom's a nice lady. I don't know if I could be that gracious if someone had hurt my daughter the way that I hurt you. Sheila, I—"

"That was a long time ago." She took a deep breath.

"Excuse me." Her smile disappeared, as if she suddenly realized that he didn't deserve it. "I-I have to go inside. I-I have to pick up a package before they close." She held up a crumpled yellow slip. "Then I have errands to run. A lot of them." She backed away another step.

A man excused himself and passed between them, widening the space. Why didn't he pass behind Sheila?

"I understand." He felt himself nod. *I just don't know how to make you understand and . . . And what?*

If she did understand and forgave him, then what? Her life had moved past their time together. There was no place for him in it anymore. Nothing stayed the same. Even the strongest weed can be destroyed if you treat it the right way. A relationship didn't stand a chance when somebody assaults it the way he had damaged theirs.

Sheila had learned how to put her time with him aside and go on with her life. He thought he had, too. Until yesterday.

A woman jostled past them on the sidewalk, and Sheila moved even farther away from him. She was still close enough for him to touch if he reached out to her. He would have, too, if it weren't too late.

"Maybe I'll see you again sometime. If I don't, have a merry Christmas. Good-bye, Jeff." Her voice was softer than he had ever heard it before. They had never actually said good-bye that last time. They had just showed it.

Jeff let her go because he couldn't think of any way to keep her with him. And because he didn't have the right to, anyway.

He stared at the post office door long enough for three people to go in and come out before he admitted that it would do no good to wait for her. She wasn't coming to him when she did come out. She would go home to somebody else. To the life she had built without him.

There had been tears in her eyes. Was it the cold? Regret over what had happened between them? Or was it her old hurts that seeing him made her remember? He didn't want to know. There was only a one-in-three chance, but he was afraid of the answer.

He got into his car and didn't let himself look back, as much as he ached to do so. If he did, he might go back to her even though there wasn't anything he could do to change things between them. She had another life now, and another man was part of it. She was married with two kids. Married to somebody else, mother to somebody else's kids.

He drove to his empty, lonely house. This evening, after his furniture was in place, it would still be empty and lonely. No matter how many things he put in it, his house would always be filled with loneliness. Maybe he should have stayed in Houston.

Sheila leaned against the wall just inside the post office door. She had to make her aunt learn to put the correct zip code on the mail she sent so it would go to the correct post office; so she wouldn't have to take a chance on seeing somebody she didn't want to again. She clutched her hands to her middle, as if that would shrink the ache inside her. She didn't want to see him again, did she?

"Are you all right, miss?" An elderly man was talking to her. He touched her arm. Sheila focused on him. His touch wasn't like the other one. She could still feel Jeff's hand on her.

"Yes, thank you." She took a deep breath and forced a smile onto her face even though tears would have come easier. She should have been prepared. She knew he was coming back. How could she not know?

Last October, the *Philadelphia Inquirer* had devoted a full page in its City and Region section of the Sunday paper to Jeff Hamilton's return home. She hadn't read the paper before she got to her parents' house for dinner as she did every Sunday. Her mom had met her at the door with the section of the paper in her hand.

"Have you seen the paper?" she had asked. She remembered hoping that her mom didn't have bad news to share with her.

"I'll tell you over a cup of tea. Dinner is just about finished," her mom had said. The memory was as clear as if it were happening now.

Sheila had followed. Her mom usually insisted she take off her coat and hang it in the hall closet before doing anything else, but she didn't that day, and Sheila had worried that something terrible had happened to someone she knew. She never thought that somebody's return could be terrible and that she was the one affected.

"It won't take long for the water to boil." Her mom had gotten the tea and mugs with one hand, as if she hadn't realized it would have been much easier if she had put the newspaper down.

"What's with the paper, Mom?"

Sheila shook her head as she remembered how her mother had wiped a drop of water from the counter and hung the cloth on the rack above the sink. She smoothed it out, shifted it so it hung evenly, then smoothed it again. Slowly she turned and stared at Sheila. Except for the stirrings of the water in the kettle, the kitchen was quiet.

Why do I remember such unimportant little things? She blinked. Because they weren't so unimportant. She remembered that she had touched her mom's arm and questioned her again. Her mom had finally faced her and stared at her long enough for Sheila to question her again. Before she could, though, her mom spoke.

"There's something in this morning's paper that you should know about." Her mom opened the paper, but she didn't hand it to Sheila. "He's coming back."

Sheila remembered gripping the cup in front of her as

if afraid it would try to escape, the way she wanted to. She didn't need to ask who.

Her mom continued. "He bought a house in Chestnut Hill—the one his mother used to clean."

Then she had held out the paper as if she hadn't already told Sheila the most important news that it contained.

Later, after she ate a meal that she didn't taste, after she tried to convince her parents that she was fine, after she made it the few blocks home without remembering how, then Sheila curled up on the sofa in her apartment and opened the paper.

Sheila had read it enough times to erase the words, if that were how it was done. But it didn't work like that. Even if it did, it was too late. The news had already happened. When she had finally folded the paper to set it aside, the words looked just as fresh as when she first looked at them, and the news was still something that had already happened.

That night she went to bed without watching the eleven o'clock news for the first time she could remember. She didn't need any more news. She had already heard more than she could handle.

She crawled into bed wishing she would wake up the next morning and learn that it had been a nightmare; that Jeff had changed his mind.

The next week's edition of both the *Mt. Airy Times Express* and the *Chestnut Hill Local* had reported Jeff's expected return. As if that weren't enough, she had lost count of the number of phone calls she had gotten from friends who remembered that she used to date Jeff and wanted to make sure that she knew that he was coming back. "Used to date" didn't begin to explain how things had been between them.

The two months since the article about Jeff first appeared had scurried past as if anxious to get out of the way. This year Sheila couldn't blame the swift passage of time on the coming Christmas holiday and the flurry of activities necessary to get ready for it. When would she see him? Would he look the same after more than ten years? Would he remember her? How could she keep from seeing him? What would she do when she did?

Her best friend, Aisha, had called the day before, after Sheila got home from school.

"I know you heard that he's back."

"Yes, every day for the past two weeks somebody has called to remind me that he's coming back." *Too many somebodies.* "As if I could forget. It's like there's a relay telephone system set up to give me a count down."

"No, no. I don't mean that he's *coming* back; I mean that he's back. He spent last night at the Holiday Inn in Valley Forge. I have a friend who works there. She went on and on about this fine man who checked in who looked like he stepped out of *GQ* and how she racked her brain trying to think of a way to get him to really notice her. She said she considered offering to come back in the morning instead of working her regular shift. What are you going to do about it?"

"About what? He can spend the night wherever he wants. It's none of my business. Tell your friend good luck and to watch her heart."

"You know I'm not talking about last night, and you know you don't wish anybody good luck with Jeff. Girl, opportunity usually only knocks once. This must really be important for it to make a return visit. Maybe it's the season. You know, Christmas miracles and all that. I know you intend to take advantage of it."

"Things ended between us eleven years ago when he made his choice. What he felt for me wasn't strong enough to make him choose me when it was newer. Anything that we had is dead, buried, and disintegrated."

"What you had is dormant and long overdue for revival. You never got over him. You two were meant for each other. You knew it from the first time you saw him. You didn't give up then, why do it now? Don't you remember how you went after him?"

"I remember." She shook her head, trying to keep the memory from coming and knowing her efforts were useless. "It's too late for us. I have to go. See you tomorrow for lunch." She hung up.

Of course she remembered. How could she not remember? She had noticed Jeff the first week after she got to Central High.

She had turned from her locker one day and there he was fifteen lockers down. Even this long after, she smiled. She knew it was fifteen because she had counted after he left. He was frowning. His generous mouth was set in a hard line. Noises from the other kids filled the hallway, but Jeff was quietly reading a book that looked like the dictionary on the stand in the library, and trying to open his locker at the same time. He looked as if he were older than sixteen. The cleft in his chin was the only thing softening his face. She had wanted to make him smile, to find out what caused the frown that creased his forehead. She, who wasn't interested in boys, suddenly found one who grabbed her attention.

In spite of her pain now, her smile widened. As she had walked closer to him, she had to keep tipping her head back to keep her gaze on his face. He was a basketball jock. With his height, he had to be. She walked past without speaking to him. She didn't have the kind of looks that attracted jocks. She shook her head. She still remembered the pang of regret that had gone through her.

"You must be talking about the Brain," Aisha's brother said when Sheila had described Jeff. "He's number one in his class and so far ahead of the others that they decided to battle for the number two spot and leave number one to him. Math and science are his life. Most of the time he isn't even aware of the rest of us humans. Forget him. Unless you have equations or theories written all over your face, he won't even see you."

But she had made him aware of her. Her persistence surprised even herself. She had managed to be at her locker whenever he was at his. At lunchtime she had always found a seat near him. Not that he noticed. He spoke back, but he never looked at her. A book was always propped up in front of him. Most of the time he ate as if paper would have tasted as good as his lunch. She glanced over his shoulder once. His book had more numbers than words.

Finally, after months of this, and agonizing during a whole weekend over how to approach him, one Monday she took a deep breath and went to the table determined to get more than a "Hi" from him.

"What are you reading?" She took a deep breath and slid close to him.

He had looked up, the frown in place like every other day. "A book about chemical theories and their implications." He had shrugged. "You probably wouldn't be interested."

"Do you think I'm too stupid to understand?"

"No." His frown had deepened. "I said you probably wouldn't be interested, not that you wouldn't understand." He shrugged. "Most people aren't interested. They find it boring."

"Why are you interested?"

"The landfills are full. There's only so much space on this planet. We need to find a way to reuse things."

"We recycle. I see those black containers at the curb in front of everybody's house every week."

"But we don't do enough." He had leaned toward her

and his frown was gone. His eyes, the color of her daddy's coffee, sparkled like those of a kid with the latest video game. "I know there's a way to use what we throw away to manufacture new products cheaper than to make them from scratch. I just have to figure out the process. Plastics and metals. Do you know how much space we can save in the landfills if we recycle all plastics and metals? Especially plastics. Do you know how many years it takes for them to break down?"

Jeff didn't wait for her to try to answer, and it was a good thing. She had no idea, but she was interested because he was.

He had explained what he had in mind. He drew diagrams and charts in his notebook as he talked to her. She had looked at the paper, but all she had seen was his hands and how strong they looked. She could almost feel his hands holding hers. She pictured his hands around her, holding her close to him as the two of them danced to a slow song. Any slow song.

"Do you dance?" She blurted it out, but she didn't try to take it back.

"What?"

The bell had signaled the end of lunch, and she was spared having to explain what dancing had to do with whatever he had been explaining to her. She had really been saved by the bell.

Sheila sighed. Jeff had done more than read about chemistry and talk about recycling. He had developed a process to fuse plastics and metal into an inexpensive hybrid material. He started working in a government lab and ended up with his own corporation. He had chased and caught his dream. But first he had left her with her own dream destroyed. It was her own fault. She knew he was more interested in proving his theory than in anything that had to do with her. That had been obvious from the beginning.

She should have sat with her friends through high school. She should have gone to another college. It would have been safer. And less painful. She sighed. But would she have spent the rest of her life regretting it?

Four

Sheila stood against the wall, imprisoned by her memories, so mixed up that she didn't know if her regrets would be stronger if she hadn't gotten her wish for Jeff's attention and his love or if things had gone as she had wanted.

What would her life be like if she had never persisted with him? What if she had eaten every lunch with Aisha, as she always did before she went after Jeff? What if all she knew about him was what she read or what others told her? Why hadn't she been contented to look at "the Brain" from afar and admire him? What if she had never fallen in love with him? Had never had her heart ripped apart when he left her? Even Jeff hadn't developed a process to repair hearts broken by love. If her love for Jeff hadn't ruined her for every other man, would she be married to Bill? Would Tonya and Tammy be her daughters, as Jeff thought?

"May I help you, miss? Do you have something to pick up?"

The clerk dragged her back from her wondering. Sheila looked around the post office. She was the only customer left. She frowned. How did he know that she had come to pick up something?

"If you give that to me, I'll get it for you." He pointed to her hand.

She glanced at it. The yellow slip of paper looked as if it had been in her hand for weeks instead of . . . Her frown deepened. How long had she been here? She handed him the slip and he went to the back. She shook her head. This was bad. If the post office hadn't been empty she'd still be lost in her freshman year of high school trying to figure how to change what had happened into something with a happier ending.

"Maybe you want to make sure people have your correct zip code," he said when he came back. "You'd get your mail quicker. Actually, this must have been processed by someone who knows your correct address and zip. Normally we would have sent this back, or at least over to the right branch." The clerk handed her the package.

"Thank you. I know it should have gone back, and I appreciate whoever fixed things. I'll try again to make sure my aunt gets my zip code right the next time. This used to be her zip code and I don't live that far from this branch, so I guess that's why she has such trouble remembering."

Sheila left the building. *I definitely will tell Aunt Sadie again and hope she gets it right.*

She took the Christmas package that her aunt Sadie sent from Savannah as she did every year. Sheila walked to her car in a daze. A car coming toward her blew the horn and she quickly opened her door, got in, and closed the door. She shut her eyes and sighed.

Jeff looked the same, but different. Snowflakes had nestled in his hair, giving a preview of what he would look like years from now. She had expected to watch his hair turn gray as their love for each other grew. She blinked, trying to keep away tears that threatened to fall. Somebody else would be in his life now. Some other woman would grow old with him. Someone from his new world so different from hers. She swallowed hard.

The crease in his forehead was there to stay. She used to rub her fingers across it to make it go away. Evidently nobody did that for him now. After the crease smoothed over, she would trace a finger down his warrior's nose and brush across his full lips before she kissed him.

She opened and closed her fingers and shook her head. Just now she had had to look closely to see his laugh lines. He had learned to laugh with her. Not much, but a little. Today his face looked as if he hadn't laughed since he left her. It looked as if *serious* was the only thing it knew how to show now that they were apart. She shook her head again. *Don't flatter yourself. If he thought you were so important, you would have heard from him during those long years.*

She chewed her lower lip. She always did indulge in wishful thinking. She sighed. Jeff had finally filled out his tall frame, but it looked like all muscle. His chest was wider, stronger-looking, but still inviting. Would it feel the same beneath her head? Did he have more hair on his chest now? Would his heartbeat synchronize itself to hers if she were close enough for long enough? If she were touching the whole length of his body with hers?

In high school and college he had run every morning before school or every evening after school and lifted weights in the gym three times a week. He had claimed that he could zone out and think when he was exercising. He looked as if he still followed his same regimen.

She stared out the window. He looked just as solid as before, as if his arms still promised her safety. As if she could lose herself in his embrace and he would protect her from all harm. She swallowed hard. The only harm had been from him. She closed her eyes again. Would his lips, his mouth, taste the same: sweet and addictive? Would his body tighten against hers if she touched her tongue to the dimple in his chin? She smiled. He had told her to call it a cleft chin, not a dimple. After that her nickname in private for him had been Dimple.

She started up her car. If a teardrop hadn't landed on the front of her coat, she wouldn't have realized that she was crying. Another fell, and she wiped at it. She ordered her tears to stop, but it didn't work. She hadn't expected it to.

What did his women friends call him? Women in his crowd would have something more sophisticated than Dimple. Was there a special woman? She knew he had women friends. Men in power always attracted women—usually beautiful women. She shook her head. As good-looking as he was, Jeff would attract women even if he were as poor as dirt. Look at the way she went after him in high school. If he had been a jock, she wouldn't have tried to get his attention. She wouldn't have wished he would see her as she wanted him to. She wouldn't be fighting old hurts. She sighed. Why hadn't he been a jock?

Someone had once said, "Be careful what you wish for." She wished she had followed that advice.

She drove home colder than the outside temperature could be blamed for. She rubbed her hands along the steering wheel. Her hands were colder still because he hadn't kissed them as he used to when they were 'going together.' What would she have done if he had? Going together. A silly phrase that told nothing.

He wasn't married. The papers would have said so if he were. But would a special woman join him later? Would they live the "happily ever after" life that she and Jeff had dreamed of when their dreams were the same?

She pulled into a spot in her apartment building parking lot and let the little heat that had collected in the car turn cold. Still, she made no move to get out.

Her thoughts drifted back to high school as if something back there pulled at them. How she had persisted with Jeff; trying to make him really notice her.

It had taken a few weeks of listening to him explain his theory and how he planned to put it into practice— and a coming school dance—to make her ask him about dancing again.

"I work."

He told her that he worked after school on Fridays and from nine to nine on Saturdays. On Sundays he went to church. "We need the money, but my mom won't let me work during the rest of the week. She said I need to spend my time on my schoolwork. She didn't want me to work at all, but I made a deal with her: as long as I ace all of my subjects I can keep on working."

"You work every weekend? Every single weekend?" Sheila tried to keep the disappointment from her voice. How would she ever know how it felt to be in his arms?

"Yeah. Every weekend." Then he had looked at her as if seeing her for the first time. "If I didn't, I'd go with you to the dance." He laughed. "Even though I don't know how to dance." Then his laugh disappeared. "You could teach me."

Something flared in his eyes. Something Sheila had been waiting to see since she had first noticed him. She knew the same emotion showed in her own.

If the bell hadn't rung they might still be sitting at the lunch table staring at each other. The lunchroom monitor came to their table. They grabbed their books and rushed from the lunchroom.

"Is ten o'clock too late for me to call you?" he had asked as they went down the hall. Sheila felt her heart lift just remembering that day. "On Saturday, I mean? I can call earlier on Sunday, if you want me to," he had said, "but I don't get home until ten on Saturday. Are you allowed to get calls during the week?" They were outside her classroom.

"No. Yes. I mean, ten o'clock isn't too late on Saturday, and yes, I'm allowed to get phone calls during the week, and yes, I want you to call me." She had scribbled some numbers on a scrap of paper, frowned at them, scratched them out, then written the correct phone number.

She smiled as she remembered. Jeff had finally noticed her. She wasn't just somebody for him to explain his ideas to anymore.

Sheila never did remember what her next class had been about. If the teacher had given a test, she would have failed it unless every answer had been Jeffrey Hamilton.

All the way home she planned what she could say to convince her parents that it was important for them to bend the rule about late calls. It took a while, but she succeeded.

Jeff called the next day and they talked for hours. She made sure she was at home in time for his call, even on weekends. He gave her another reason to look forward to vacations from school: he didn't work every minute they were off.

It was Christmas vacation before Jeff met her parents. He came to dinner and he and her father had discussed Jeff's theory. Her father seemed to understand what Jeff wanted to do. When her father learned that Jeff loved chess, that was it. He was in, even though it was rare for her father to win a game. Sheila had called it Christmas magic.

She and Jeff had talked about their dreams and what they wanted out of life. She finally got to be in his arms, and it was more wonderful than she had imagined. Standing with her body against his made her want things that she didn't even understand.

All through high school and their college years they had discussed making a life together, but neither Houston nor leaving Philly had ever been mentioned. She had talked about her plan to be a junior high teacher in Philly. Jeff hadn't questioned it. He had planned to get a job in the area after he graduated.

Sheila opened the door to her apartment, stopped, then went back for the package that she had left on the front seat. It had cost her too much emotionally to forget it.

She slipped it under the large tree that stood in the corner of her apartment and shifted the gifts around to make room. She plugged in the tree. She needed her spirits lifted. Usually Christmas lights did the trick, but not this time. She looked at the lights and wasn't sure which twinkling was caused by them and which was because of the tears in her eyes.

The weekend after Thanksgiving she had put her tree up as usual. Lights and tinsel sparkled and bounced off the ornaments. The angel at the top glimmered in the light, her gossamer skirt catching any air movement. Other angels hung among the ornaments. Still more from her collection stood on the mantel, the tabletops, and the windowsills. Angels, messengers of miracles. Why didn't one have a miracle for her?

Holly swags hung over the doorways and shared the mantel and windowsills with the angels. But no mistletoe hung anywhere.

Aisha didn't understand why Sheila went to so much trouble decorating, since she lived alone. She didn't understand the magic that Sheila felt with her Christmas decorations in place. Her home would be decorated even if she were the only one who saw it, but her annual open-house party on the twenty-eighth just gave her an opportunity to share with others, as one of the Kwanza precepts suggested.

She brushed the black hair of the large angel doll with the beautiful chocolate face who took up the entire end table. Sheila's mother had given it to her when Sheila moved into this apartment.

Sheila turned the knob under the angel snow globe and watched as she turned to the music of "Silent Night." As she looked around, Sheila was tempted to believe in Christmas miracles again.

Jeff still wore the same cologne. As much money as he had, he still wore the inexpensive scent that she had given him every year for his birthday when they were going together. Who bought it for him now?

She shook her head. It wasn't any of her business. She sighed. Probably one of the women he was with in one of the pictures in *Newsweek* or *Time* magazine. Maybe the one in the featured article about him in *Ebony* magazine three years ago.

She went into the kitchen to make a cup of tea. Miracles didn't happen anymore. Why hadn't he stayed away? She could manage her feelings if he weren't here. Why didn't he leave her with the illusion that she was over him?

She rubbed her hands up and down her cup and wished it were bronze-colored skin covering strong, warm hands belonging to the only man she had ever loved. She swallowed the lump that formed in her throat. The man who didn't love her enough to stay with her. She forced her tea down, one sip at a time.

She wasn't going to think about him anymore. What was gone was gone, and nothing was going to change that.

The phone rang and she looked at her watch. *Darn it.*

"I'm leaving right now. I'll be there in ten minutes."

She turned off the Christmas-tree lights, grabbed her

coat, blamed Jeff for making her late, and rushed to meet Aisha at the restaurant.

If she had remembered as soon as she got home, she would have tried to back out of lunch with Aisha. If she thought she could. No. Aisha would never let her get away with that. Ever since she could remember, they had been having lunch together on Saturdays when they didn't have other plans.

At the restaurant she took a deep breath and walked over to the table where Aisha sat.

"The only way I'll stay for lunch is if you promise not to talk about Jeff." She stood as Aisha stared at her.

"Okay, if you're sure you don't want to talk about him."

"I'm sure." She took off her coat. "I never did like discussing something after it was over."

"That's true."

"In school I never talked about a game the next day no matter how badly we beat the other team or how badly we were beaten. Maybe I discussed a movie if it was a really good one, but never something that already happened, no matter what." She slid into the booth. "Or rather, seldom something that already happened. Remember?"

"I remember."

"I never discussed a test after it was over, not even when we got the papers back. Remember?"

"Yes, I remember that, too."

"It's over between Jeff and me and I'm not going to talk about it."

"Okay."

"The usual, ladies?" The waitress stood with the pad in her hand.

"Yes. A cheesesteak with fried onions and peppers. And unsweetened iced tea, please. How about you, Sheila?"

"I'll have the same." She put her napkin on her lap. "I won't talk about Jeffrey Hamilton."

"I can understand."

"He's part of my past—my distant past even."

"Yes, he is."

"He only came back to Philly because he's ego-tripping. He bought the house because he could afford it. Once the novelty wears off, he'll sell it and move on to some other city to find a new way to save the world."

"Probably so."

"Don't get me wrong. I'm not criticizing the work he's done. We all benefit from it. The whole world does. I'll admit that. He's just not dependable in personal relationships."

"That's right."

The waitress brought their orders and left.

"He looks the same." Sheila picked up half of the sandwich but put it back down.

"Yeah?"

"I ran into him at the post office this morning; or rather, he ran into me. Literally. He was preoccupied. You remember how he would get."

"I remember."

"That hasn't changed, either." Sheila stared at the sandwich, pulled a piece of meat from the end, and popped it into her mouth. "I should have let Daddy pick up the package from Aunt Sadie. That's why I was in the wrong post office. I don't know why she can't get my zip code right. I've had the same zip code forever." She took deep breath. "Daddy offered to go, but no, I had to do it myself. Miss 'I don't need anybody to do anything for me.' That's me." She sighed. "He looked the same. The very same." She stared at her plate. "He felt the same when his body touched mine, too. Even through all of our clothes, he felt the same."

"What did he say? What did you say?"

"I don't want to talk about it. Okay?" Sheila took a bite and chewed slowly.

"Fine with me." Aisha took a bite of her sandwich. "I know this is bad for me. I can feel the grease oozing into my arteries and fastening to the walls. We have to switch to healthier food. Next time we'll have a salad with grilled chicken breast." She took another bite. "It won't taste as good as this, though." She blotted the sides of the sandwich with her napkin and looked at the grease soaking into the paper. "I'll do what I always do: hoard my fat grams during the week and splurge again next Saturday." She laughed.

"I can't make it next week. I promised the girls we would go ice-skating. It's supposed to be a regular thing as long as the rink is open. Why don't you come with us?"

"If people were supposed to be on the ice so much, they wouldn't need so many clothes to keep them from freezing and their feet would have built-in skates. I only go out in the winter when I have to." She took a bite. "The bears have the right idea: hibernation until the weather gets warm again." She chewed. "Give me a call when you get tired of the weekly freezes."

"Okay." Sheila frowned and looked at her sandwich as if she wasn't sure she was supposed to eat it. "It's okay to keep with old tastes in food. Why hasn't my taste in men changed? It's been over between us for eleven years. Why am I still stuck in the same rut? He's not. He moved on when he moved away. He left me behind and never looked back. Why can't I?"

"Beats me."

"You saw the pictures of him in those magazines. I showed them to you. Remember?"

"I remember." She took another bite.

"All of those fancy-dressed women he dated. Dates.

In every picture he was with a different woman, all of them beautiful. He forgot about me, didn't he?"

"It looked like it."

"Today was a fluke. He lives in Chestnut Hill and I live in Mt Airy. I work during the day and he's living off his fortune. He'll do his running around while I'm at work. I won't run into him again. There's no need to." She took another bite.

"Probably not."

"There are people who live in Chestnut Hill whom I have never seen, will never see."

"That's true."

"He'll probably be one of them."

"No reason why not."

"That's what I say. No reason why not. Not a one." She picked up her sandwich. "I'm going to enjoy my lunch. I'm not going to discuss him. He's not worth my time."

"That's right." Aisha picked up the piece of onion that fell from her sandwich. She smiled.

They finished eating in silence, although Sheila's thoughts should have been loud enough for everybody in the restaurant to hear.

She spent the first part of the silence trying to convince herself that she had seen Jeff for the last time, and the last part trying to be happy about it. She was glad when they were finished. She had to assume that the sandwich was as delicious as it usually was.

She went back home and turned on the tree lights. Then she lit the fat candles scattered along the mantel. Cinnamon, pine, bayberry, and spices drifted into the air, filling the room with Christmas smells.

She sat on the couch and stared at the flickering flames, smelling the scents and wishing that one of them was the aroma of a familiar men's cologne. She sat as the flames and twinkling lights became the only lights in the room. She sat as if waiting for her wishes to come true.

Five

The moving van was pulling up outside the gate to his house when Jeff got back from the post office. He was glad to have his furniture, but he was more grateful to have something take his mind off his meeting Sheila. He should have been prepared. He knew it would happen—prayed it would happen. Was it ever possible to prepare for something so painful?

He led the van to the house and they unloaded. Jeff had to make a few changes, but most of the furniture went where he had planned to put it. It was nice to know that he could still get some things right, even if it they weren't the important things.

The men left and Jeff started unpacking boxes. The kitchen was first. He had to have a way to make meals. He always did prefer home-cooked meals. He wasn't going to think about the meals that Sheila's mother had cooked and that he had been invited to share. Nor would he remember the times Sheila had fixed dinner for him when they were in college.

When he had moved to Houston he had complained about having to eat out every day. His mother had sent him a basic cookbook. When he complained about how complicated cooking was, she had told him to look on it as a kind of chemistry. He smiled. The book was in one of the boxes, but he didn't need it anymore. He had moved beyond basic years ago.

He concentrated on where to put everything. He almost didn't have time to think about Sheila. Almost. He would have enjoyed cooking a meal for her to show her how far he had come since he had burned a can of soup. He blinked. He had come too far from some things.

He unpacked the cast-iron skillet that his mother had given him during his visit home that first Christmas after he'd left. He hadn't wanted to take it, but she insisted that he did since she had two. "Every home needs a decent frying pan, and those are the best." He had carried it back to Houston in the bottom of his suitcase. The next time he had come home it was to bury her.

He hung the pan on the rack hanging over the granite-topped island. Mrs. Wilson's set of copper-bottom pots and pans once hung there. He had his own set of similar cookware, but his mom's skillet had the front spot.

At two o'clock his stomach reminded him that lunch-time was long gone. He got a hoagie from a store nearby. After tasting it, he promised himself a hoagie from a real hoagie shop as soon as he got the house in order. Was Delassandro's still on Henry Avenue? He put the half-eaten sandwich in the trash and went into the dining room.

He opened the box labeled *China* that the men had put on the table. They had insisted that he check for breakage. He had insisted that it didn't matter; even if something was broken it couldn't be replaced.

He emptied the box, setting the wrapped pieces on the table. He removed the tissue paper and set each piece in its old spot in the huge mahogany-and-fruitwood china closet. He had given this set to his mom the first Thanks-giving he came back. He had shopped every store within a ten-mile radius looking for the perfect set. She told him he should have saved it for Christmas. He told her he didn't want her to wait.

He ran his finger around the gold-trimmed edge of the white bone china. She had opened it that morning and they had used it for Thanksgiving dinner and again for Christmas. Two times. She got to use it only two times. He stood the platters in the grooves at the back of a shelf. It wasn't fair.

She was working only one job. He had looked forward to the time when he could tell her that she didn't have to work anymore. After all the years of working two jobs and taking care of him, just when she could cut back, a massive heart attack got her.

He had tried to talk her into moving to Houston during their Christmas together, but she had refused. Just as somebody else had refused to move with him.

He concentrated on finding the perfect spot for each piece of china. That way he couldn't concentrate on anything else. Several times his thoughts drifted from china dishes to a perfect face with a perfect kissable mouth, but he yanked his mind back.

Dishes were harmless to think about. He finished with the dishes and moved to the living room. There was plenty to keep him busy there.

It was early evening when Jeff pulled the painting of a family at dinner from the packing box. He placed it on the wall across from the sofa. The Wilsons had hung a landscape in that spot. Jeff had bought the painting from an artist in Houston because it reminded him of how Sheila described Sunday dinners with her family.

Every Monday when they were in school he had looked forward to her story about dinner the day before. He used to wonder if it was as happy a time as it seemed when she told it. She never came right out and said that they had a good time; she had just told him what somebody had said or did, or a funny story somebody had heard and passed on to the rest of the family.

The first Sunday during their Christmas school vacation her parents had invited him to come to dinner with Sheila. It wasn't like the painting—it was better—but the painting was as close as anyone could come to capturing it.

He stood back and checked to make sure it was straight. Did they still have dinner together every Sunday? Did Mrs. Miller still make her sweet-potato pie for dessert? Sheila had always brought him a slice for lunch on Monday. He swallowed past the lump that had formed in his throat. Did her husband like the pie as much as Jeff did? He sighed. Maybe so, but her husband couldn't love Sheila as much as Jeff did. He shook his head. As if that made any difference.

He went upstairs to the smallest back bedroom and stared at the boxes covering the floor. It was a good thing he didn't have any furniture to put in here right away. How had he accumulated so much stuff that was important enough to him for him to bring with him?

He took the boxes labeled *Linen closet* into the hall. He had just arranged the towels and washcloths on the shelves and was starting on the sheets when the phone rang. He didn't feel guilty about having an excuse to take a break.

"Just checking," Carolyn said. "How's it going? Did the movers get there as promised or is it the floor tonight?"

"They were here when I got back from the post office. My furniture is in place, so I have a bed to sleep in. I finished unpacking the kitchen stuff, and you bought food, so I have no excuse for going out to eat—except that I'm tired from unpacking so much stuff. I think I'll just open a can of soup for dinner tonight." He nodded.

"Yes, Mother, I know it's past dinnertime." He paused. "And yes, I know it's important to have balanced meals. I promise that tomorrow I'll prepare a meal a nutritionist would be proud of. Hey, you want to come over and see for yourself?" He nodded again. "Six o'clock will be fine. Sure, you can bring dessert." He smiled. "Anything you bring will be greatly enjoyed, whether you bake it or somebody else does."

He hung up. Somebody would be here to take his mind off another Sunday dinner.

He decided to set up his computer next. He used the library because of the view of the backyard. Everything was covered with snow, but he remembered how he felt as if he were in a forest when he used to sit on the window seat. He had to get cushions. And maybe a couple of bird feeders for this section of the yard, too.

He checked his E-mail and reassured Eric that he would keep his promise to be available whenever he was needed. In order to keep Eric from panicking, he had promised to go back to Houston from time to time, but that shouldn't be necessary. The company was operating successfully. It could continue to do that without him. He could keep in touch by computer and fool around in the lab that he planned to build in the apartment over the garage. That was what he enjoyed anyway: the experiments and discoveries. Eric liked the business end.

Jeff opened other boxes and put his books on the shelf. He hesitated when he came across the books from his childhood. One was the book on birds that Mrs. Wilson had given him for Christmas after she learned that he was interested in them. He didn't know who would ever read them, but he put them on the low shelf where Mrs. Wilson had kept her children's books.

Jeff worked until midnight and was so tired that he almost didn't think about Sheila. He almost didn't imagine what it would be like to share his bed in his house with his love.

He crawled into the massive mahogany four-poster and tried not to imagine Sheila wrapped in his arms, her softness nestled against his hardness, making love with her, drifting off to sleep and waking with her in the morning to make love all over again.

He tried not to imagine all that. He turned off the lamp, stared at the ceiling, and tried harder.

He got up at dawn as if he had somewhere to go. After his usual breakfast of pancakes and one sausage, he went back to unpacking, still trying not to imagine sharing his house with Sheila.

By the time he looked at the clock, he had finished with the dining room and it was too late for lunch. He smiled as he took the empty boxes to the back porch.

Snowflakes floated down to join those already making his backyard an advertisement for a winter wonderland. The wooden bench, tucked off to the side facing what he knew was a redbrick walkway, wore a white coat that matched those of everything else in the yard. The path led to a play set that the Wilson kids had used when they were young. He had played on it after he convinced his mother that he was old enough not to break his neck falling off the wooden fort at the top. Every ten minutes she had checked on him and nagged him to be careful. At the time he had complained that she took all of the fun out of playing. She had told him to watch his tone of voice.

He sighed. No one would use it now, even if it was still there. Did Sheila's girls have a set in their yard? Did they like to climb and swing and slide? Sheila liked the swings. Once they had stopped at a playground and had a contest to see who could go the highest the quickest. The winner got to name the prize. He asked her for her best kiss—as if any kiss from her would be otherwise. She had said her prize would have been the same thing.

The wind rustled the bare branches against one another and Jeff went back inside.

By late afternoon Jeff stopped working to fix dinner. He had finished putting away his clothes and he had almost finished in his bedroom. All that was left was to put out the personal touches that made his room his. Bit by bit he was getting there.

He was setting the dining room table when Carolyn rang the bell.

"For you." She handed him a Christmas cactus in bloom and kissed his cheek. "The blossoms will probably be gone by the time Christmas gets here, but you can enjoy it until then. I guess it decided early was all right." She held up a cake box. "Dessert. The first visit to a new home should be sweet to ensure much happiness. I hope you like chocolate."

"Absolutely. Thanks. How was the driving?"

"I managed. I'm glad I only had to travel main streets. The traffic melted most of the stuff. I'm also glad I don't have to be out late tonight. The temperature is supposed to drop and freeze what hasn't evaporated. They issued the usual 'don't drive unless you really have to' warning for the early-morning hours."

"We'll be through well before then. I prepared a simple meal, not a banquet." He smiled as he set the plant and cake box on the marble-topped table in the hall. Then he helped her off with her coat. He had barely hung it up when she brought up the subject he had hoped to avoid until the pain of earlier today had dulled.

"Have you seen Sheila yet? I know you two used to have a thing for each other."

Jeff stood facing the inside of the closet as if he still

had something to do in there. His smile disappeared, chased away by the question. He thought about forcing it back, but that demanded too much effort. He took a deep breath, then turned to face her.

"Yeah. I bumped into her at the post office this morning." He didn't mention parking outside Sheila's parents' house. He wasn't ready to face that memory again. He was glad he hadn't decided to smile. He didn't feel like it anymore. Neither did he feel like talking about Sheila. "Come on out to the kitchen."

For a while, deciding how to cook the chicken hadn't left space for thoughts of her. Not much, anyway. Now Carolyn dragged them out again, and they were as powerful as if they had used the time to gather strength.

Carolyn followed him and brought more questions with her. "Well? Has she forgiven you for dumping her?"

"Don't you think you're being too subtle, Carolyn? Why don't you come right out and be direct?" He picked up the bowl of mixed vegetables.

"You and I go too far back to tiptoe around any subject. Besides, tact was never one of my strong points." Carolyn took the bowl from him.

Jeff picked up the platter of chicken and led her into the dining room, but wished there were a way to ask her to not follow him.

"Beautiful dining room set." She ran a finger across the tabletop. "I love dark wood." She rubbed her hand along the creamy brocade covering the back of the end chair. Lovely." She set the bowl next to the platter and looked at him. "How did it go with Sheila?" She put her hands on her hips and faced him. "Jeff?"

Jeff went back to the kitchen. Carolyn followed as it he were pulling a string attached to her. He picked up the rice pilaf and left the kitchen, and she grabbed the bread basket and followed. He went back for the iced tea and she went back and got the gravy boat. He turned to face her. He had run out of things to get.

"Have a seat." He pointed to the chair facing the window. "Evidently she got over me."

"Why do you say that?" Carolyn eased into the armed chair. "Seats made wide enough for the modern figure. Beautiful." She shifted position. "How do you know she got over you? What happened to make you say that?"

"Do you want to say grace or should I?"

She stared at him. "You do the honors. It's your home."

Carolyn's echo of Jeff's "Amen" had barely faded when she repeated her question.

Jeff made her wait until they had served themselves. When they had finished, the pain of what he had to say was still as strong as when he had seen Sheila for the first time in too long. "I saw her on Friday outside her parents' house. She was with her twins."

"Her twins? What twins?"

"Her daughters." He had to push to get the words out. "Tammy and Tonya." He was usually terrible with names. Why did that have to change now?

"Tonya and Tammy?" Carolyn laughed and shook her head.

"What's so funny?" New shards of hurt poked at him, and Carolyn was laughing. "Those are beautiful names. The girls are beautiful." Any names Sheila chose would be beautiful, and any daughters of hers had to be beautiful, too.

"There's nothing wrong with those names. They're perfectly lovely. But those aren't Sheila's kids."

"What do you mean, they aren't her kids? I saw them with her. From what little I could tell by what I saw, they look like her."

"I guess that's understandable, since they're family. They're her nieces."

"Nieces?"

"Yes. As in her brother's children. Did she tell you they were her kids?"

"No. But she didn't tell me they weren't when I mentioned that I saw her with them. Are you sure they aren't hers?"

"Not unless Robert and Cynthia gave them to her."

"Robert and Cynthia?"

"Sheila's brother and his wife. Remember Robert? Three years ahead of you at Central? Tammy and Tonya belong to them." Jeff continued to stare as Carolyn went on. "You must know him. You dated Sheila for years. He must have been at home some of the time."

"Yeah, I remember good old Robert." Jeff's smile came out of hiding. "His kids, huh?" Jeff's heart soared but crashed immediately like a kite that had suddenly lost its wind. "You mean she doesn't have any kids yet."

"I've known Sheila since we were in third grade at Mt. Airy Elementary. I don't think she's the kind of woman to have a child unless she's married. As far as I know she's not even seeing anyone right now."

"She should be married to that guy Bill by now. I met him at Mom's funeral." He swallowed a lump. *If only Mom had lived long enough to enjoy the life I've made. And maybe she could have kept me from being stupid for so long.* He blinked. "Nobody stays engaged for ten years." If he were Bill, he wouldn't have waited to marry Sheila any longer than the law required. He would have . . . He frowned. He did worse than wait. He left her.

"She *was* engaged. They never got married. Sheila broke it off after a few months. She wasn't engaged long enough to even make wedding plans. Bill is married to somebody else now. They have a couple of kids, too. I see him from time to time." Carolyn stared at Jeff. "Sheila's not seeing anybody special now."

Jeff's heart raced as if he were at the end of a marathon. He dropped his fork to his plate. The clatter was nothing compared with the clamor inside him. "Are you sure about that?"

"Unless Sheila eloped since I saw her a week ago, she is not married. She is not even dating anyone special. I feel as if we need an interpreter here." She leaned closer to him. "Jeffrey Hamilton. Mr. Brainy. Am I getting through to you? Sheila Miller is not married. Not to Bill Clayton. Not to anybody."

Why hadn't Sheila corrected him? Why had she let him assume that the girls were hers?

"Jeff? Are you still with me?" She tapped the table between them.

"I'm here." *At least my body is. My mind is somewhere else—about a twenty minute ride from here. Fifteen if I hurry and make all the traffic lights.*

"I don't need to ask how you feel about her."

"Why did she let me think that?"

"You'll have to find that out for yourself."

"Maybe I should go over there. I mean now. What do you think?"

"You really do have it bad. You're asking me for advice." She shrugged. "Here it goes: you need to be as methodical with this situation as you are with your formulas. She must have a reason for letting you believe that she's married. Don't you think you should think about that before you go charging over there? What will you say to her?"

"I don't know." He shrugged.

"Look. Why not take time to think this through? Sheila's not going anywhere."

"I know." That had been the problem. Sheila wasn't going anywhere.

"Neither are you. You just bought this mansion. What's the rush?" She patted his hand.

He shrugged again. "I want to talk to her." He frowned. This was harder than creating the process that he had developed. Some had called it a miracle breakthrough. Right now he needed a real miracle. "I need to talk to her—to explain. . . ."

"What will you say that you didn't say years ago? We're back to that. Think about it. And finish your dinner. You didn't slave over a hot stove to cook a meal that's not appreciated. Besides, you can't have dessert until you eat your dinner, and trust me—you don't want to miss dessert."

Jeff smiled. Carolyn was right. He didn't have to hurry. Sheila wasn't going anywhere.

He picked up his fork and took a bite. Then he took another. If he didn't know what he had cooked he wouldn't have been able to tell anyone what he was eating. He had to think of the best way to approach Sheila. Not everyone got a second chance. Maybe it was the season. Maybe it was a fluke. Maybe it was meant to be. Whatever the reason, he had to proceed carefully. He couldn't afford to mess up a second time. He'd never get a third chance.

"Delicious." Carolyn placed her napkin on the table. "I didn't know you had it in you. Maybe your chemistry genius carried over into the kitchen."

"Thanks." Jeff looked at his plate. For somebody who had finished the whole meal without tasting a thing, he had done an excellent job of eating.

"I'll help clear." Carolyn stood. "The sooner we clean up the sooner we can have dessert."

Jeff laughed. He would have laughed even if nothing was funny. Sheila wasn't married.

After they'd cleared the table, Carolyn carried in their cake slices and Jeff carried the coffee mugs. Sheila wasn't married. He went back for the sugar and cream, brought the sugar bowl, and went back a second time for the cream.

"What do you think?"

"About what?"

"The cake." Carolyn put a forkful into her mouth.

Jeff tasted it. "It's good."

"Good? Good? A kid the week before Christmas is good. This cake is sinfully delicious."

"Do you think she's home now?"

She put her fork down. "I think you should take time to think this through. I have an idea. Are you going to the annual community Christmas party? It's next Saturday. Sheila will be there. She's always there. And she always makes butterscotch brownies." Carolyn laughed. "They are delicious, but I doubt if you would come just for brownies."

"Party? What party?"

"Jeff, concentrate. Pretend there's going to be a test later. I guess you didn't have a chance to read through the "Welcome Homeowner" packet that I left on the counter under the fruit basket, so you are forgiven. However, I just explained it to you. You must remember the neighborhood holiday party. You came with Sheila so many years that some folks asked me what street you lived on. A couple of years ago we moved it from the last Saturday before Christmas to the first Saturday in December. Everybody complained about being busy with last-minute things like shopping and putting up their decorations. Just like I will be again this year." She laughed again. "Christmas comes on December twenty-fifth every year and every year, I can never get ready early." She sighed. "This year is no different. So. Will I see you there? Your name comes up every year. You can talk to Sheila then."

Sheila wasn't married. She had never been married. He felt better about that than he had a right to.

"Are you coming?"

"Where?"

"To the party." Carolyn dragged her words out as if he needed longer than normal to understand them.

"When is it?"

"Honestly, Jeff. You haven't changed a bit. You're still preoccupied. What is it this time? A way to turn carbon dioxide into pure oxygen? Or maybe a process to make the ozone layer seal the hole in itself?"

"Nothing like that." *I have something more important on my mind.*

"Listen carefully. As Mr. Saunders used to say in history class, 'Feel free to take notes.' The party is at the community center next Saturday at six o'clock. It's still a covered-dish affair. You can pick up something from a supermarket. I like the buffalo wings from Superfresh—hint, hint—but you decide. This will give you a chance to see the folks who knew you when you spent more time here in Mt. Airy than you did in your own neighborhood." Her voice softened. "People have been wondering if you'd ever come back. We figured that you'd outgrown Mt. Airy."

"Not so. I've missed this neighborhood. I never found another like it." He laughed. "If it's not too cold tomorrow, I plan to walk along Germantown Avenue from the shops in Chestnut Hill down to Mt. Airy." *It's not on the avenue, but I might even end up at Sheila's house, if I can decide what to say. Why wait for a whole week?* He frowned. *Because I don't know the words to make everything right between us.*

"You *have* been away too long." Carolyn chuckled. "This is Philadelphia in December. Of course it will be cold. It's called winter. See you on Saturday. Close to six o'clock. None of that 'fashionably late' stuff. We start eating right away."

"I'll be there."

They finished dessert and split what was left of the cake. Carolyn wished him luck and left.

Jeff stood at the door long after Carolyn's car had disappeared down the driveway. One week until he'd see Sheila. He gave the kitchen a final once-over. By then he would have figured out the best approach.

A wide grin spread across his face. He'd see Sheila, and it wouldn't be for only a few seconds. His grin slipped into a straight line.

Would she be with somebody? She wasn't engaged, but maybe she had somebody that Carolyn didn't know about. Anything was possible.

He went into the living room to unpack a box of art pieces from his collection. He set wood carvings from his trips to Africa and pieces from a trip to Mexico on the curio shelf in the corner. *Almost anything,* he corrected himself. He set two carvings of African deities on the mantelpiece.

He had to make sure a relationship with Sheila was included in the possible things.

He opened another box, took out a small bowl, and placed it on the middle shelf of the mahogany-and-glass unit he had brought with him. A week. He had a week to figure out how to get rid of the *almost.*

Six

Sheila stood with the rest of the congregation. She even managed to sift the words for the benediction from the other words swirling in her mind.

"Hug ten people," the pastor said. "But don't count."

She turned to Mrs. Dixon and gently enfolded the older woman in her arms. She smiled as she made her way out of the pew. These hugs were easy. She had known many of the members since before she started back to church after her college graduation. Some had watched her grow up. She returned Mr. Garrett's hug. The only emotion associated with these hugs was care and affection. The person who could pull stronger emotions from her wasn't in church.

"See you in a little while." Mrs. Miller hugged her daughter quickly. "I'll give you a proper hug when you get to the house. Right now I'm in a hurry-up mode, the same as every Sunday during football season." She glanced at her husband, who was making his way to the choir room. "I don't know what he'll do if there's no football in Heaven. He'll probably talk the Lord into letting him organize a league." She squeezed Sheila's shoulder. "I'd better go. His subtle beckoning is becoming more obvious the longer I stand here. I should make good on my promise to drive my own car so I can make sure I get my hug quota." She turned to hug Mrs.

Greenhowe before the woman moved on. "But I'm afraid he'd turn the expressway into a raceway if I wasn't in the car with him." She shook her head. "As it is, I have to be a backseat driver from my place beside him in the front seat." She looked toward the back. "Let me go before he comes to get me." She laughed as she made her way to the back, hugging people as she went.

Sheila hugged her way out as she slipped through a pew at the side. She stopped at the tape ministry room. If she wanted to know what the service had been about, she had to buy the tape. She had tried to follow the sermon, but Jeff kept getting in the way. It wasn't the pastor's fault. His sermons were always clear and powerful. It was Sheila's own fault. She had to find a way to control her thoughts, to block out any disturbing influences. Influence—singular. Jeff's image appeared. She shoved it away, but it came back clearer than before; tall, serious, snow adding salt to the pepper of his hair, the same intense look that he had worn yesterday. The same look he had worn when he chose Houston over her.

If she remembered that she hadn't been his first choice, she shouldn't have to work as hard to concentrate when she played the sermon later.

She tucked the tape into her purse and made her way toward the back of the line of people greeting the pastor at the front door. She got two more hugs as she picked her way to her car in the lot across the street. She stepped over the piles of snow at the curb, grateful for the men who had cleared the way and salted the sidewalk early that morning.

She eased out of the lot and down the street.

Why didn't I tell him the truth about the girls? Why did I let him think that they are mine? She lifted her chin. *It's none of his business. Nothing about me—none of what I do—is any of his business anymore.*

She turned on the radio and tuned to the Eagles game. The score was tied and the Eagles had the ball, but as much as she loved football, she had trouble concentrating on the game, too.

She spent the ride home trying not to feel guilty about deceiving Jeff. *I didn't lie to him.* She just hadn't corrected his misconception. She must have imagined the pain in his voice when he mentioned the twins, the hurt in his eyes when she dared to look at him. It was all wishful thinking on her part. *If he still cared about me he would have contacted me during the last ten years. Ten years. Serves him right.* He should be hurt.

She sighed. He couldn't hurt as much as he had hurt her.

The score was still tied when she turned off the motor. What had happened when the Eagles had the ball?

She went into her apartment, but didn't bother to turn on the television as she usually did when she changed her clothes to go over to her parents' house. This was not her day for mind control.

She had a problem. A big problem. It was Jeff-related, but it wasn't Jeff. She drove over to her parents' house, glad that she had somewhere to go.

"Better late than never," her father said as he hugged her. "Come on in. The Eagles are about to score." He hurried back to the den at the back of the house.

Sheila followed, watched McNabb score a touchdown on a quarterback sneak, then went into the kitchen.

"Why don't you stay and watch with your father?" Her mother hugged her. "I have things covered here. Actually, everything is ready. Your brother and his family aren't coming today; they're going to Cynthia's parents' house for dinner." She took a casserole from the oven and placed it on the gray granite counter. "I'm just waiting until halftime to serve." She shook her head. "I knew your father was a football nut when I married him, but I didn't realize how bad he was. Still is." She laughed. "I should have had a clue when he made sure that we didn't get married during play-off time in case the Eagles made it that far." She shrugged. "Not only is love blind, but it makes you blind, too." She laughed again. "Come on. We may as well watch." Sheila giggled as she followed her mom, who was only a little less fanatical about football than her father was.

At halftime they all carried something from the kitchen to the dining room table and took their usual seats. After they were settled, Sheila took a deep breath and planned how to say what she had been thinking about since she had seen Jeff yesterday morning. Was it just yesterday?

She took each parent's hand. She tried to clear her mind of everything except the prayer of thanks her father was giving. She had barely said her "Amen" when she took a deep breath and blurted out what had been on her mind.

"I think I'll skip the community party this year." Sheila glanced at her mother as she took the bowl of green beans from her.

"What?" Her father turned toward her.

Mrs. Miller stared at Sheila, who slid her gaze to the bowl of vegetables. She stared at it before she passed it to her father.

"The party is the same every year. Nothing changes." Sheila moved her plate a little to the left. How could she tell them that she was afraid that something had changed this year? She blinked. "Besides, I have so much to do." She shifted her plate back into place, picked up the bread basket, and passed it to her mother.

"Um-hmm." Her mother looked at Sheila, took a roll

from the basket, and set it on Sheila's plate. "You forgot to take one."

"Oh. Yeah. I did." Sheila looked at the butter dish, but didn't take any before she passed it to her father.

"Like what?"

"Ma'am?"

"What kind of things will keep you from attending the party the way you have every year since we've held it?"

"You know. Things." Sheila waved her hand in what she hoped was a nonchalant manner. "I have a lot of things to do."

"It's Christmastime. Of course you have things to do." Her mother lifted a piece of roast beef from the platter and placed it onto her plate. She passed it to Sheila, who stared at it before she took a slice of meat and set the platter down. Her mother continued talking."We all have things to do. That's why we moved the date two years ago."

"I know." She let out a deep breath. "I just don't feel like going this year."

"Sheila Miller, I know for a fact that you finished all of your Christmas shopping before Thanksgiving just like you do every year. You probably have less to do to get ready for the holidays than anyone else in the city." She took the bowl of roasted potatoes that her husband handed her. "You have to go to the party. That's that." She passed the bowl to Sheila, who remembered to put a piece on her plate before she set it down.

"Of course she's going to the party." Dr. Miller looked at her as if seeing her for the first time.

Sheila let her gaze slide away from him. She handed him the sugar bowl. "I'm not going this year, Daddy. I can't." She shook her head. "I'll go get the cream for you." She rushed from the table, wishing the kitchen were far enough away for her to think of a good reason. Other than the real one.

"Sheila."

Sheila handed her father the creamer. She tried to avoid eye contact, but she never could with her father.

"Baby . . ."

Sheila felt her body tense. She should have known this wasn't going to be easy.

"We'll talk about this after dinner," her mother said as she cut her meat.

"There's nothing to talk about." Her father buttered his roll. "She knows she's going. She always goes. Every year since we decided to hold it. Next thing you know, she'll be talking about taking her tree down tomorrow. What next? No decorations at all next year?"

"Daddy, I—"

"Let's talk about that later, Bob," her mom said. "Right now let's enjoy our meal so you can get back to the game." She turned toward Sheila. "Is the beef tender enough for you? I wanted to change the herbs and spices that I always use, but I didn't dare. You know how your daddy fusses if I change it."

"No sense tampering with success. It's perfect the way it is." He cut off a piece of beef and put it into his mouth. "Delicious. Like always. Couldn't be any better."

"How would you know? You never want me to fix it any other way."

"Marie, you know you can cook any way you want to. You're doing the cooking. It's your kitchen. When folks are doing the cooking, I don't tell them how to do it."

Her mother laughed. In spite of the turmoil churning through her, Sheila laughed, too.

"Bob, I love you." Marie laughed again.

"Okay. Maybe I make a little suggestion here and

there. Just little ones." He sipped his coffee. "But the final decision is always with the cook." He looked at Sheila. "I hope you don't mess with the recipe for the chicken you're going to fix for us on Wednesday, though." He frowned. "You don't plan to change that, do you?"

They all laughed.

They finished the meal and went back to the den. The party wasn't mentioned during the rest of the game, but often whenever Sheila stole a look at either parent, her glance met theirs.

After the Eagles won the game, they went back to the table for dessert.

"About the party . . ."

Sheila set the plate with her father's slice of pie in front of him. It took all of her energy to keep her hand steady.

"Bob, why don't we let Sheila think about it? We'll see her on Wednesday. Maybe by then she'll change her mind."

"I hope so." He cut a piece of pie and put it into his mouth. "Not go to the party," he muttered. "How ridiculous. Out of the question."

"Let her think about it until Wednesday. Okay?"

"It has to be okay."

"Do you think the Eagles will make the play-offs this year?"

The discussion turned to games left and home-field advantages and never touched the Christmas party again. Sheila left wondering what she could come up with between now and Wednesday, when her parents came over for the meal she fixed every week. She had to admit that the reason she gave was weak. Why had he come back?

* * *

The doorbell rang and she went to let her parents in. Three days didn't help her find a reason for skipping the party. She didn't have to have a reason—she was grown and this was her decision—but she wanted something to tell them. Soon they were seated at the small table in the dining area.

"How was your day at school, baby?"

Sheila smiled at the question that her father asked every Wednesday. "Fine. I'm still trying to find some tutors for the kids who are in danger of failing. Especially math. We haven't been able to find a replacement since Dalton Architecture and Building relocated to Baltimore last October. I knew it would be difficult to find somebody to replace the ones they sent us, but I expected to have someone in place by now. I've been doing what I can, but I can't work with all of those who need it. One more person would help."

"I would offer," her mother said, "but the poor kids would be worse off when I finished than they were when I started. My math professor made me promise never to go near a math book again. I was happy to agree." She shuddered. "Numbers are so final. They don't give you any leeway or choices, like words do."

"I wish I could help out," her father said, "but between my practice and the classes I teach at Temple, I work during the hours that you need someone."

"I know, Dad. Don't worry. I'll find someone." She patted his hand. "How about a small piece of cake? I made your favorite like I do every week."

"A large piece would be better, but your mother won't let me have it. She has a thing against normal-size helpings. I know you have some vanilla ice cream to go on the side."

Sheila chuckled as she went to the kitchen. She was still laughing when she came back with their desserts on a tray.

"I know you heard that Jeff Hamilton is back."

Her father's words stopped Sheila's hand. She tightened her hold on her fork to keep it from trembling the way she was trembling on the inside.

"Yes." The piece of cake fell off the fork and landed on the edge of her plate. She was glad she hadn't been holding a bowl. She moved her fork to a different spot.

"Bob—"

"No fewer than three of my patients today made it a point to let me know."

Sheila felt as if the room itself were waiting to see what would happen next. She moved her hands to her lap and hoped her father had left his doctor part at the office and hadn't noticed the tremor in her hands before she hid them in her lap.

"I know."

"Are you okay, baby?"

He touched her shoulder, and she looked at him. She took a deep breath. The tenderness in his eyes and his voice made tears fight to show themselves in her eyes. She swallowed hard.

"I'm okay."

"Have you seen him yet?"

"Yes." Sheila stared at her plate. After she'd see Jeff in her mind every day for more than a year after he left, it had tapered to about twice a week. When she was very busy and very lucky, a week and a half passed between the times he insinuated himself in her thoughts. Then came last Saturday. Now Jeff had taken up residence at the front of her thoughts again.

"What did—"

"Bob, did you see Mrs. Barton today? I saw her last week and she told me that she had an appointment for today."

"Yes, she came in this afternoon. Sheila—"

"I need you to do something when we get home. I

need you to help me carry the decorations down from the attic. I want to put up the tree tomorrow."

"All right." He turned back to Sheila. "Sheila—"

"I'm thinking that maybe we should try putting the tree in a different spot this year. What do you think?"

He wiped his mouth and stared at her. "I think you'll put it where you've put it every year since we've been in the house: in front of the bay window in the living room."

"I guess you're right. I remember the time I tried to change and put it in the corner of the dining room." She laughed. "I thought you and Sheila would disown me."

"Honey, you don't mess with tradition. I also remember the time you said you were going to have roast beef instead of turkey and ham." Both parents laughed.

Sheila smiled as they continued the story that had become a tradition, interrupting each other at the same spots where they always did.

She shook her head and her smile left as if she'd shaken that away, too. A rich bronze face drifted to her mind, shoving aside tradition and all memories except those of him.

His shoulders had been wider than she remembered. She swallowed hard. He wore a heavy jacket, but she could tell that his chest was still solid and strong. The ache inside her grew. She let out a long sigh to make room for it. How many times had she run her hands over those muscles? A slight smile found its way back. She had teased him that she could identify his chest among a whole bunch of others. She blinked hard as she remembered his words: "I don't want you testing that theory," he had said. "You might find one that you like better." She swallowed the lump filling her throat.

After he left her, she had tried. She thought that if she tried hard enough, she could make Bill the one.

"Sheila." Her father jerked her back to the present. When her mother started to interrupt again, her father held up his hand and continued. "I waited until we finished eating, but you didn't bring the subject up, so I will. You have to go to the party on Saturday. For one thing, you have to make your butterscotch brownies. Between them and your mother's sweet-potato pie, you two put the others to shame. I don't know why they bother bringing desserts."

"It's not a competition, Bob."

"I know that's what they say, but you know that everybody tries to outdo everybody else. Ray Anderson always brings some new concoction that he worked on all year."

"And you always stuff yourself while raving over it."

"I have to encourage him. He puts so much effort into it."

"Between Ray's latest dish and Mrs. Pearson's coconut cake, you'd encourage all of it away and nobody else would get a taste of them."

"You know you only allow me a tiny taste of anything good." He turned to Sheila. "If you want to experiment with a new dessert this year instead of brownies, it will be okay."

"I'll still make the brownies, and you and Mom can take them."

She stood and picked up the bowl of sweet potatoes.

"I know he has something to do with this. What did he say to you? Don't give him the satisfaction."

Her breath caught on the way out. She forced it out with her words. "I'm sorry, Daddy. I can't go to the party." She went into the kitchen.

Her father followed, carrying the platter of chicken. "I think you'll be sorry if you don't go. Why should you care more about what happened than he does? He's over what was between you. If he wasn't, he would have been in touch long ago. He didn't even have the decency to apologize before he left. He didn't deserve you. You're better off without him." The serving fork clattered off the platter when he set it on the counter.

"He called, remember? I wouldn't talk to him." She blinked. "Then I left; I ran away to Virginia Beach." She sighed. "It didn't make any difference. He wasn't going to change his mind and neither was I. When I was so happy for him, I didn't know about Houston."

He frowned. "I don't know how he could make a decision like that without discussing it with you."

She sighed. "It doesn't matter now. It happened so long ago. Too long ago." He last words were so faint that only she was sure what she said.

"If it doesn't matter, then why not go to the party?"

Sheila was searching for a reason when her mother spoke.

"I think your father is right on this one." Mrs. Miller set the broccoli and bread on the counter beside the platter.

"I know I am. Look what you accomplished since he left. You kept it together in spite of him and finished college. You're the math department head at your school. You could go even farther if you want to." He folded his arms across his chest. "It's good that you found out what he's like in time. It's easier to break things off before the marriage than after. Not as complicated." Sheila cringed. "I'm sorry, baby." He patted her shoulder. "I didn't mean to hurt you." He shook his head. "Sometimes I say the wrong thing, trying to be helpful."

"I know, Daddy." She hugged him and took a pile of dirty plates to the kitchen.

"You know, he might not even be there."

Sheila closed her eyes and leaned against the counter. Her father was right. She had survived all of these years without Jeff. Why should she be afraid of a party that he might attend? Why should she miss the gathering of her friends and old neighbors because of Jeff? He had messed up her life once. Why should she let him do it again? Besides, she didn't have to stay even if she went. She could speak to everyone and then leave, if there was a reason to. If he was there. She tightened her mouth. She would go to the party. Jeff probably wouldn't be there. He didn't know anyone from the neighborhood anymore. Why would he be interested? He had outgrown their community years ago.

"Why don't you ask Malik to pick you up for the party?" her mother said. "He always comes anyway. You would think he still lives in the neighborhood."

"You know we're not fussy, Daddy. As long as somebody brings food for us and canned goods for the food bank, they're welcome to attend."

"You know he has a crush on you," her mother continued. "He has liked you since you were both in the fourth grade." Mrs. Miller scraped a plate and put it into the sink. "Even in high school he hung around you, but you didn't notice him. Back then you only had eyes for—"

"Malik and I are just friends, Mom. I heard that he's got somebody." Sheila cut off her mother's words before she finished. Maybe it wouldn't be as painful that way. She took a deep breath. "But maybe I'll call him later this evening and see if he's going. I haven't talked to him in a while. I kind of miss his company."

"Suggest that he bring a dessert. Tell him about the cakes from that bakery on the avenue. You know the one I mean. Their chocolate cake is unbelievable."

"Robert Miller. One day I'm going to tell your patients what a hypocrite you are. Pushing them to eat fresh fruit for dessert and all the while trying to overdose on pies and cakes yourself."

"Don't forget cookies. Especially homemade chocolate-chip."

They laughed as together they cleaned the kitchen.

After the discussion that her parents had every week, they left with two slices of cake for her father as they always did: one for later tonight with a glass of milk and the other for lunch tomorrow.

Sheila smiled and went to the phone. It would have been nice to talk with Malik again even if Jeff hadn't moved back home. She swallowed. How long would it be home for him? How long before he left to chase a dream that could only be found somewhere else? How long before he decided again that there was nothing in Philadelphia worth staying for?

She didn't know the answers to any of those questions. She waited for Malik to answer the phone and tried to convince herself that she didn't care.

"How have you been?" Sheila asked when Malik answered the phone. "I know I haven't called lately, but the telephone works both ways, you know." She laughed, but stopped suddenly. "I have a favor to ask. Are you going to the community party on Saturday? . . . Good. If you don't have a date, do you want to go with me? Strictly as friends, of course." She sighed. "Yeah, I know he's back. I'm hoping he won't be at the party, but I don't want to be bothered by him. I need somebody to run interference just in case, and I couldn't reach an Eagle fullback." Her smile came back. "Thanks. I owe you a whole bunch of ones." She laughed. "Okay. Fair enough. I'll make an extra batch of brownies just for you." She laughed again. "Yeah, it still starts at six o'clock. You know how they look at folks who bring their food late. See you then."

She hung up feeling more at ease. Even if Jeff did

come it wouldn't matter now. Malik had promised not to leave her alone with him. After Saturday she wouldn't have to see Jeff again. If he even came. If he did, all she had to do was make it through that night.

She left for school early on Monday. No new snow had fallen, but the temperatures had. What snow was on the ground had frozen and made driving rough.

When she was looking for an apartment she had wondered whether or not it was a good idea to live within a few miles of school. Today she was glad she did. She was also glad the custodian had cleared the parking lot.

"Mrs. Watkins said for you to stop by her office," Helen, the secretary, said. "It won't take long."

Sheila got her keys from the hook and went into the small office off the main one.

"I read your article in the *Times Express* about how much we need tutors," Mrs. Watkins began. "A realtor called and said that he's trying to line somebody up from his office. Two retired English teachers from the neighborhood volunteered to tutor in English. Hang in there. Somebody will fill in the gap in math. The groups are too large for you to keep doing it by yourself. We won't even think about next semester when you take your graduate class."

"I know. I hope somebody volunteers soon," Sheila told her wearily.

"At least they have somebody to work in English. Maybe some of the kids could avoid having to repeat a grade because of it. We'll take this one subject at a time. Just having somebody for English should decrease our number of failures."

"That's true. Still, some of the kids need just a little help in math. Somewhere they didn't grasp a key concept and it's giving them trouble now."

"We'll do what we can and hope for a miracle," Mrs. Watkins said.

"That might be what it takes."

Sheila went to her classroom trying to think of who else she could approach for math. She did her best, but the kids in the large tutoring groups had different weaknesses. She needed help.

Seven

The rod maple in the Jeff's backyard looked as if somebody had been hard at work decorating for Christmas. Snow lay along the branches and nestled in the hollows formed where they met the tree. More snow clung to the windward side of the bark. Sunlight, inching over the treetops outside the wall to the back of the yard, sparkled off the winter blanket as if flakes of gold had been hidden among the snowflakes. Jeff leaned against the windowsill. The scene looked like the Christmas tree display at the farmers' market where Sheila's father always bought their tree. Sheila had talked him into going with them one year. He had always avoided going with his mother when she bought theirs. The year with Sheila he had loved it. He shook his head. She did love Christmas, and went all out with the decorations. When she was in college, she decorated her room and volunteered for the decorating committee for the buildings. In spite of that, she still made sure she came home on the weekend that the family decorations went up.

He had thought about getting a tree this year for his new house. He could start a few Christmas traditions. They had to start somewhere. He had teetered between yes and no for the last few days. *No* won the battle. He turned from the window.

Traditions were made by at least two people. No one

would see a tree here except him and he wasn't in a festive mood. Right now the Grinch was jollier than he was. He sighed. What did he expect? He was home, but he hadn't been here for so long that it may as well have been any city. Any city where it snowed. He smiled slightly. Did the kids in her neighborhood still go sledding down the street they had nicknamed Rat Road?

In spite of the trouble that it caused, Jeff loved to see snow. It transformed everything—even cans of trash—into works of art. He even loved going out in it. He'd go for a walk along Germantown Avenue, as he'd told Carolyn he was going to do. He shook his head slowly. *It was a good thing it was a school day. That helped him decide not to go to Sheila's house.* He frowned. Did she still live there? If she didn't, how often did she visit her parents? What did she do with her free time? He shook his head. There was a lot he didn't know about her anymore. Did she still like to decorate for Christmas? If she had her own place, who did she decorate for now? A woman as beautiful as she had to have somebody special in her life. Carolyn couldn't know everything.

Sheila was beautiful inside and out, but Jeff thought now of the outside: her soft body that had always welcomed his touch; her sensuous mouth sweeter than anything else he had even tasted; the look of regret in her eyes that mirrored what he felt whenever they separated and reminded each other of their promise.

He went to the kitchen and made a pot of coffee, even though something cold would be better at cooling him off. Every time he thought of her it was the same thing: his body temperature rose like a sudden fever. What time did the stores open on Germantown Avenue? He needed something to take his mind off Sheila and put him in the Christmas spirit.

At ten o'clock, Jeff was backing out of the garage. The chemical he had spread over the driveway had worked. Tomorrow he'd call the man with the snowplow and make arrangements with him. Later today he'd buy a snow shovel and boots, but now he was taking a trip to the past.

He pulled into the parking lot near Borders bookstore. The building was probably close to a century newer than any of the other shops. He walked around the corner to Germantown Avenue. Cars took every metered space along the street. Water from melting snow trickled over the Belgian blocks covering the avenue. Small streams ran along the curbs. Maybe by tonight the streets would be dry and the only ice would be along the curb.

He looked down the tree-lined street. Tiny lights winked among the tree branches of the sycamores marching down toward Mt. Airy. Heavy ropes of evergreens hung over every store doorway and outlined every window. Inside the windows, more thick greenery framed whatever goods were for sale: antiques, shirts, sweaters, toys, paintings, baked goods. Holly berries battled with the lights to catch the eyes of the shoppers darting in and out of the stores. Jeff took his time. He had no reason to hurry. He, who usually went directly to the store he wanted, made his purchase and left, now strolled along, looked at each window display for a long while before moving on. The last time he had walked along here, Sheila had been with him and it had been May. Most of the shops were the same. He was the one who had changed.

The clanging of the bell across the street caught Jeff's attention. A man dressed in a Santa suit stood on the corner beside a red kettle. Jeff smiled as he made his way across the street. He took out a few bills and dropped them in the kettle. He mother always dropped money in the kettle. She told him that, when he was young, several years when money was tighter than usual, the Salvation Army had provided the toys under the tree for him. Maybe now he was helping a kid under the same circumstances.

He moved past a window with a display of red, black, and green tartan sweaters and slacks. He had stood in front of a window like this with Sheila, planning to buy her the sweater that she admired for the next Christmas. She had known what he was thinking.

"Don't you dare spend that much money," she had said. "Wait until you get your first paycheck from your first real job. There's no rush."

When he did get that paycheck, he was in Houston and Sheila was here and he no longer had a right to buy her anything.

He crossed the street again and went into the hardware store that had probably been here since there was a Chestnut Hill. Sheila had said that her father found things for his house here that he couldn't find anywhere else.

Jeff bought a snow shovel, one of the last two on display, and left. He walked along wishing merry Christmas back to smiling people who didn't know him, but wished him happy holidays anyway. This he also remembered: the smiles and greetings from strangers in this area.

He stopped at the bakery and looked at butterscotch brownies in the display case. Then he bought a cinnamon bun and headed back to his car. Maybe he'd come back to look at the rest of the shops when he could look in a shop window and not imagine Sheila's reflection beside his.

He drove to the mall, where he and Sheila had never gone together. It didn't take long to buy winter clothes. Even if he didn't stay in Philadelphia long, he needed warm clothes to get him through this winter. He frowned. Where had that thought come from? Of course he was staying. If she could manage without him all these years, he could survive, too.

He put his bags into the trunk. It wasn't all his fault. Not telling her about Houston ahead of time—that was on him. Not loving him enough to leave Philly and go with him—that was on her. She hadn't loved him enough. She couldn't have. He shrugged. Maybe he hadn't loved her as much as he thought, either. If he had, wouldn't he have given up his dream and taken a job here?

If she had loved him, wouldn't she have been willing to go with him? If she had loved him, she would have gone with him even if it was halfway around the world. Houston had schools. Schools always needed good teachers. He shook his head. How do you resolve clashing dreams? He sighed. You can't. You let them die and you move on. He headed for a car dealership wondering how long dead dreams could haunt you.

Jeff made a deal for a four-wheel-drive Lexus. The dealer offered to have somebody follow him home in the Metro so Jeff could drive his new vehicle. Jeff told him they could drive the new car. Within an hour he had taken the man back to the dealership and his second car was in the garage.

He took his packages into the house, put the things away, and went to the kitchen. He put on the coffeepot and opened the cinnamon-bun box. One of the perks of being grown was having dessert and calling it lunch.

He checked his E-mail, then reached for the phone. Sometimes not even E-mail was fast enough for some things.

"Eric, settle down. At what stage did you run into the problem?" He nodded. "What have you tried so far?" He frowned. "Try one other thing before you dismantle all of the machinery." He talked his old partner through the process. "Let me know if it works. If not, we'll try something else." He shook his head. "I really don't want to come back there right now. I know I promised, but I think we can fix it without my being there." He nodded. "Yeah, I'll come, but only if nothing else works." He hung up. *I just got here.* He wasn't ready to go back; not even for a short while. He needed to see if he could fix something more important than a piece of machinery.

He went back to the kitchen and looked at the packet Carolyn had left. The announcement about the party was on top. The green sheet with bold black letters stood out. He stared at it as if he were having trouble reading it.

He wouldn't know anyone, no one but Sheila and her parents, and her parents wouldn't want to have anything to do with him. Neither would Sheila. She made that clear when she let him think that she was married and had a couple of kids. Outside the post office, she couldn't wait to get away from him. He swallowed hard. Just like he couldn't wait to get away from Philly eleven years ago? And again ten years ago? He frowned. Why hadn't he tried to see her after his mother's funeral? It didn't matter that she was engaged. She wasn't married. If he loved her so much, why had he turned tail and run? He had never been a quitter. If he had been, a lot of the problems he had solved would still be in existence. Why, with the most important thing in his life, had he quit without a fight?

What good would it do to see her again? What would it do but rub raw his old wounds that had reopened when he saw her? Maybe he should skip the party. He still had a lot to do to the house. That was what he should do. Stay home. Find something to do here. Even as he thought that, he reached for the phone and called the supermarket. They might need this much notice for the platter he was ordering. Besides, once he placed the order, he wouldn't cancel. He shook his head. He wouldn't back out anyway. He wasn't a quitter. Not this time. He had gotten a little smarter over the years.

He went upstairs to unpack some more things. He

hoped that deciding where to place things and whether or not to wait until after the holidays to finish furnishing the bedrooms would occupy his mind. But he didn't expect it to.

By late Saturday afternoon he and Eric had spent enough time on the phone to make him glad that he owned stock in the company. A new problem cropped up each time they solved an old one. How much of it was just jitters on Eric's part because Jeff wasn't in an office down the hall? How much was because Jeff had always come up with a solution instead of making Eric think the problem through for himself? It was true that the business end of the company had been Eric's strongest asset, but Eric knew everything about the manufacturing process they had developed. He and Jeff had discussed everything at each stage of development. He had been there with Jeff when the machinery was first assembled. He was in on every decision at every stage of development. He had to learn to trust his own judgment. And he'd have to—at least for the rest of the night. Jeff had a party to attend and a Christmas miracle to hope for. But first the star of his miracle had to be there.

He brushed down his pants one last time and pulled at his shirt so it hung just so. Some of the men would wear suits, if tonight was like eleven years ago, but Jeff wouldn't. He wanted his shirt to catch the eye of someone special. He usually didn't wear colors this bright anymore, but the long-sleeved knit was the exact color of the shirt Sheila had given him their last Christmas together.

He smiled. It wasn't the same shirt, of course. Even if eleven years hadn't passed and the shirt wasn't worn out long ago, it wouldn't have fit him. His lanky years were over. Would Sheila notice that the royal blue was the very same shade of that other shirt? Would she care? Would she even be there?

He went downstairs trying not to dwell on questions that he had no answers to. He drove to the supermarket, got the platter and drove to the center. It was too late to change his mind, but he was still having second thoughts when he drove into a spot in the parking lot. It looked as though everybody was here. He scanned the lot for a blue Pontiac, but didn't see it. Disappointment and relief were tied for being the stronger. He went inside. He didn't have to stay long. He'd just speak to people he knew, leave the food, and go home.

Sheila looked at her bed. Every item of clothing that could possibly be considered party clothes was there. This was ridiculous. She pulled the blue dress back over her head and put it on the bed. She'd have to fix her hair again. She grabbed the red dress she had first put on and pulled it on again. The matching sweater came next. A Christmas color. The brightness didn't mean that she had to feel as happy as the dress looked. She smoothed the fitted skirt over her hips and fought the urge to change into something less formfitting. He wasn't going to be there. He didn't know anyone anymore. Why would he come? Even if she flattered herself that he would be tempted because she would be there, she had taken care of that. He thought she was married with two kids. He wouldn't come to try to see her. He wouldn't be interested in seeing her, anyway. She was part of his old life. Ancient history. He had built a new and better life without her. She added a touch of color to her cheeks and lips. *Good for him.*

The doorbell rang just as she put the last jeweled clip in place in the French twist at the back of her head. *Good.* She couldn't change her mind about her dress again.

She went to let Malik in.

"Hi, beautiful." He kissed her cheek.

"I'll bet you tell that to all the girls."

"Only the pretty ones. So what's the plan if we run into you know who? Am I your friend, boyfriend, or significant other? Am I the jealous type who stays glued to your side or am I the understanding type who gives you your space? How do you want to play this?"

"I haven't figured all that out yet." She touched her ears. "I forgot my earrings. Be right back."

"You're not running from the questions, are you?" he called after her.

"You saw that I didn't have my earrings on." She clipped on diamond teardrops, took a deep breath, and went back to Malik. This was not the smartest idea she had ever had.

"With you in that dress, why would you think I looked at your ears?"

"Don't talk like that or I might change again."

"That bad, huh?"

"Yeah." She took a deep breath. "Okay. Here's the scenario: we're more than friends but not quite significant others. Okay? Just stay close. Don't leave me alone with . . ." She swallowed hard. ". . . with anybody, okay?"

"There was a time when that would have been more than okay, but that was back in the day." He smiled. "If Darlene were here you'd be on our own, or she'd be with us, and there's no way she'd let anybody think I was with anybody but her." He grinned. "What can I say? She loves me. As it is, you're lucky she likes you. She doesn't entrust the care of me to just anyone."

"I'll send her a thank-you card and call her, too. When is she coming back?"

"Tomorrow. I hope her grandmother doesn't back out. Last year it was all Darlene could do to talk her into coming up here for the holidays. You would think this was a foreign country instead of three states up I-95. I'll never understand why she wants to stay in the backwoods of Virginia, anyhow." He shrugged. "It's her grandmother's decision where she lives. She's lives in the house where she was born. She's eighty, but still lives alone and does everything for herself, including tending a garden in the summer that gives enough produce to feed a neighborhood. She cans, too. If this year is anything like the last, Darlene will come back loaded with jelly and preserves, canned tomatoes, and who knows what else." He laughed. "Her grandmom volunteers twice a week at the nursing home near town. She said she goes to cheer up the old folks." He laughed again. "Are you ready to go?"

"As ready as I'll ever be. Let me get the brownies. Then we can leave before I change my mind." She went into the kitchen.

"That is not an option. I didn't come over here to leave by myself. Besides, I need to be with somebody from the neighborhood so they'll let me in." He took the pan from her and watched as she locked the door.

"You know they think of you as part of the neighborhood. The one year you had the flu so many people asked about you that I was tempted to make a sign and pin it on my back."

"They're nice people." He followed her down the steps.

"What did you bring?" Sheila shifted the bag of canned goods to her other hand.

"Macaroni and cheese. Real macaroni, not from a box. I hope you father's not disappointed about the cake."

"Don't worry about it. If he wants a cake from that bakery, he can buy it. Watch how he eats your macaroni." She frowned. "I didn't know you knew how to make macaroni from scratch." She got into the car.

"I don't. I don't have to. I have connections. Mrs. Zachary, my next-door neighbor, is famous for her macaroni and cheese." He started the motor. "I talked her into making some for me to bring tonight." He glanced at Sheila. "Don't look at me like that. Mrs. Zachary likes me. She said that I remind her of her grandson."

"You took advantage of a lonely old lady."

"Mrs. Zachary is busier than I am, and she has family all over Philadelphia. It was a business deal. She said that I overpaid her, but I convinced her that it was worth it." He drove into the parking lot at the community center. "It is, too. Wait until you taste it."

"You didn't sample it? They won't find a scoop missing when they uncover the pan?"

"Of course not." He laughed. "She made a small container just for me."

They each got their food containers and bags of canned goods. Sheila grabbed the bag with her dressy shoes and went toward the center.

She glanced around the lot. She had no idea what kind of vehicle she was looking for. If she did know, she wasn't sure if she wanted to see it. She picked her way across the lot looking for ice patches the plow might have missed.

"Merry Christmas," Mrs. Connors, the block captain, greeted them as they walked through the door. The white tassel on the tip of her Santa hat flopped over the side of her head. It looked as if it belonged on her gray hair. "Come on in, Sheila. Good to see you." She hugged her. "You too, Malik. Just about everybody is here. It was a brilliant idea to move the party to this weekend." She laughed. "Too bad I can't claim credit." The door opened again and she turned from them to greet the next person.

Sheila and Malik made their way to the kitchen to the side of the room. Sheila wondered if "everybody" included the person she wasn't sure she wanted to see.

They handed the food containers to three people who called themselves this year's Food and Glee Committee.

"You're just in time, Sheila," Mrs. Johnson said as she made space on the table crammed with the other containers. "As soon as our husbands finish covering the tables at the back of the hall we can start to eat." She put a serving spoon into Malik's macaroni. "Looks delicious. Everybody always saves their appetite for this party." She looked around at the food.

"It's a good thing they come hungry, too," Mrs. Marino added. "Look at all of this. It looks like enough food to feed an army for a week, doesn't it?"

"Yes, but come look at the table after the party is over," Mrs. Taylor said. "I always wonder how everybody can bring a dish to feed eight people and there only be smidgens left." They all laughed. "We decided to put the canned goods for the shelter in here this year." She pointed to the barrels in the corner. Paper with Christmas images covered the containers that had been donated by a moving company. "Last year those containers were in the way out beside the door in the main hall. Also, because we didn't have enough space in the ones we had last year, we added two more barrels." She looked at the pile of canned goods heaped above the sides. "Looks like we have to find one more for next year. I don't think the shelters will complain." She pointed to the hallway. "We also added another coatrack, but we still put them at the back of the large room."

Sheila and Malik hung their coats on the already full rack in the hall. Next year someone was sure to suggest that they add another rack, too. Sheila changed from her boots to the red open-toed shoes she had brought. She pulled the sling-back strap in place.

"Don't forget." she touched Malik's arm. "Don't leave me. I mean with anyone. I don't mean *not* with just anyone. I mean don't leave me with . . ." She chewed on her lower lip.

"I know what you mean. We'll pretend to be a commercial for that extra-strong glue. Okay?"

"Okay." She smiled at him. "Thanks, Malik." She took a deep breath as they went to join the others. She was worried for nothing. He wouldn't be here.

Sheila walked into the large room and stopped just inside the door. Last year she had been on the decorating committee and she thought they had done a good job. This year the committee had really done it up right.

Lights twinkled around the front of the stage where Jack the Joker, the neighborhood DJ, was setting up his equipment as he did every year. Drapes of light icicles hung along the top of the stage, bouncing light off the hardwood dance floor.

Red and green crepe-paper streamers crisscrossed the room, dipping up at each brass-and-frosted-glass globe covering the ceiling lights. Paper snowflakes, caught in the slight breezes caused by movement in the room, danced and twirled along the streamers, bumping into paper bells hanging next to them.

A tree nearly as tall as the room stood to the side of the stage; an angel, with outstretched hands and widespread delicate wings, seemed to hover over the top. Tinsel wound around the tree, circling its way to the bottom. Lights twinkled all over, giving their glow to the glass and satin ornaments sharing their space. Construction-paper chains labored over by the kids at the day-care center on Germantown Avenue wove among the ornaments. More paper snowflakes, made by the children in the after-school programs, were tucked wherever there was space among everything else. Underneath the tree, finding the space taken by gifts already in place, more gifts for the children and their mothers in the shelter near the high school tumbled out and spread beyond the tree. The committee would take them to the shelter the following week, along with the canned goods.

Next Friday afternoon the neighborhood kids would have a party in this room and exchange Pollyanna gifts that they made. Sheila smiled. She was looking forward to helping with it, as she did every year.

The high windowsills and the front of the stage were draped with thick ropes of berry-studded greenery. Huge wreaths with large red bows hung on the wall between the windows. Electric candles glowed from the center of each windowsill, reflecting in the windows. Several more electric candles shone among the thick red and green real ones set along the center of the tables that the committee was piling with food.

Sheila looked at the roomful of people. Many were already seated at the tables scattered around the room, forming a semicircle around the dance floor. Each table held a fat candle in the middle, and the scent of bayberries from the table near her wafted into the air and caught Sheila. She breathed in deeply and captured one of her favorite scents. Other neighbors stood talking in small groups.

Conversations buzzed and mixed in the air with Christmas lights and Christmas smells and holiday anticipation. Often a laugh squeezed in. Sheila smiled. She was glad she had come. Her father was right: why should she miss this because of someone who never missed her?

Red and green and white were the dominant colors of clothing chosen by the neighbors, as if they had checked with one another in order to coordinate. An occasional blue dress or skirt or blouse or shirt was thrown in for contrast, different shades of blue, from the palest to midnight blue. Even royal blue. Royal blue. Her breath caught in her throat.

The back of a shirt the exact shade that she remembered from years ago molded muscles that looked like the ones that she remembered. She squeezed her hands into fists to try to get rid of the tingling in her fingers. Her hands had traced over that back, knew every spot where one muscle met another, where they tightened as her hands glided over them. The black pants below the shirt hugged lean hips and molded to the backs of thighs that looked too familiar, that her hands had caressed. She swallowed hard and was sorry her dress didn't have pockets. Why hadn't he worn a sweater? Or a suit jacket?

"Do you want to go find a seat?" Malik was standing beside her, but he sounded half a block away. "There's an empty table near the dance floor."

She must have said yes, because Malik took her hand and led her away from her memory.

She placed her hand on the back of the chair that Malik held out, but she didn't sit. Instead she tightened her grip, as if the chair were the only thing holding her up; exactly the way she felt.

"Do you?"

"Do I what?"

"Want some punch?"

"Yes." She nodded, jerkily.

"What's wrong? To use an old cliché, you look like you've seen a ghost." He followed her gaze. "Or more likely a blast from the past."

Jeff turned and stared at her as if she had sent a message to him to come to her. She hoped not. She didn't want to talk to him. She wanted him to keep away. She had never wanted him to come back. She shook her head. She hadn't.

He said something to the people he was talking to, but he was still looking at her. He followed his gaze as if it were a path leading straight to her. She knew how an animal felt caught in a trap. Or a deer in headlights. Was it too late to leave? She could use the door in the kitchen leading to the yard. She could walk home if Malik wasn't ready to leave. She could . . .

She watched him come closer. Her heart raced, but her feet didn't move. She couldn't leave. No matter how much she wanted to, she couldn't go anywhere. And she wasn't sure she wanted to.

Eight

There she was across the room, looking like an angel. Angels usually didn't wear red, but why not? The dress had to have been made for her, it fit so perfectly. The top dipped low enough to show a hint of the swell of her breasts. Then it followed her shape and smoothed its way along her midriff before joining the skirt at her waist. His gaze traced the skirt as it followed her curves before ending at her knees. He envied the dress.

There had been a time when he was allowed to follow the body contours that the dress enclosed. Once his hands, instead of just his gaze, had been permitted to trace her curves. His fingers had slowly learned the feel of smooth skin covering the beautiful body hidden beneath the dress. Back then Sheila had allowed him to discover what she liked which became what he liked. He knew how her pulse jumped and raced when he brushed his fingers across the fullness of her breasts; and how his had raced to catch up and synchronize with hers. His body tightened as he thought of what he never forgot.

Jeff thought of the old song lyrics about "across a crowded room," and knowing when you've found what you want, and he finally understood exactly what they meant. If he was lucky, this was his enchanted evening. He excused himself and eased away from the group.

The room seemed miles wide as he made his way,

weaving around the tables and chairs blocking his way to her, speaking to people who spoke to him, but not looking at them, not seeing anyone else, no one but the only person he wanted to see—needed to see.

Don't run, he thought. He obeyed that thought only because he didn't want to frighten her off. She looked like an animal ready to bolt in the next second.

"Dinner is ready," somebody announced from the back, and more people became obstacles as they passed in front of him on their way to the food.

He felt like a fish swimming against the tide. He forced himself to let a group pass before he continued on his quest. What he needed wasn't on the food table. He felt as though he were in a slow-motion commercial trying to reach his destiny. He hoped he ended where the people in the commercials did: achieving their goals. Elation and apprehension swelled in him at the same time. He felt the same way he had the first time he saw her after he realized that he loved her. He wished he could go back to that time. He had been young, but not yet too foolish. He wished he could find an eraser to rub out his mistake that came later.

Finally, after too long, he stood in front of her. He fought to slow his breathing and heartbeat, which acted as if he had just run all the way from Houston. He lost the fight.

Her face had a glow from the red dress or the candles. He didn't know which one. Maybe it was something else altogether. He did know that it wasn't from any feelings for him.

He tightened his hands to match the rest of his body and forced them to not reach out to her, not to cup her face, not to trace the cheeks that lifted to her eyes when she smiled. He kept his hands to himself instead of letting his fingers brush a trail from her ear to the spot under her chin where he knew how to make her pulse jump and race.

He did not permit his thumb to brush over her full lips, to trace the path he used to cover with little kisses until they both needed his mouth fully on hers, covering, tasting, fulfilling a need. He wanted to explore her body with his hands, with his mouth, to discover if his memory was correct or if he had enhanced it over the years. He did none of those things, and it felt as if it were killing him. Instead he tried to be satisfied with just looking.

Candlelight flickered in her eyes, lending a warmth that used to be natural when she looked at him. Natural or not this time, he'd take it. He took a deep breath. He should step back. He should move so her perfume of flowers and spices and promises she couldn't mean, couldn't reach him. This was just another thing that he should do, but knew he wouldn't.

Her stare wrapped with his the way he wanted to wrap her in his arms. Was that longing that he saw in her eyes or just a reflection of his own? Was she as hungry for him as he was for her, or was he expecting too much from this season of miracles? Did she have to stay as he did, or was she looking for a reason to leave him? Over the years he had wanted answers to a lot of questions, but tonight, for the first time in ages, he didn't want the answers.

Words came to mind and lingered for consideration before being replaced by others. He, who his mother swore had read through the big dictionary on the shelf in the living room several times before he got to first grade, couldn't find the right words to make everything all right, to make her stay with him, if only for a little while, to make her want to turn back time with him.

He wanted to kiss away eleven years. He wanted to find a clock that he could turn back to the other side of their split and start over again. He wanted to replace the old memory of her in his arms with a new one. He wanted her back in his arms where she belonged, filling the space that had ached for her for too long. He wanted her, but he didn't know what to say, what to do, to make it so.

"Hi."

One of her students could think of something more clever to say. He hoped her brain wasn't functioning any better than his was so she wouldn't realize how dumb he sounded.

He wanted to touch her hand, rub his fingers over it, circle each knuckle, caress her palm with just one finger, hold her hand close to his chest so she could feel what she was doing to him. Instead he stared into her eyes and hoped that she could see enough love shining there to take the place of the words he couldn't find.

"Hi."

The same word whispered from her as if she had trouble finding enough air, as if it was impossible for her to find the right words, too. That had to be his imagination; his wants clouding the truth. Her stare caressed his face, warmed him more than the huge fireplace in his living room could. Heat coursed through him as her gaze held his as if they were laced together, as if their bodies were touching.

"Hi, Jeff." Malik came back and his words broke into the connection, setting Jeff free. He hadn't asked for his freedom. "I heard you were back."

Malik placed his arm around Sheila's shoulders and severed the ties that remained between her and Jeff. He held his other hand out to Jeff. Jeff stared at it, shook it quickly, and withdrew his hand. He put it in his pocket so he wouldn't remove Malik's arm from Sheila. She hadn't moved away.

"Hi, Malik." He was sorry he had been right when he thought that Carolyn didn't know everything about what was going on in Sheila's life. He tried not to look at the way Malik's arm fit around Sheila's shoulders as if it belonged there. He tried not to imagine where else Sheila didn't mind Malik touching.

"Nice seeing you." Malik turned to Sheila. "Let's go get something to eat. I want you to taste my macaroni before it's gone. I sneaked a look at the table. Everything looks as good as last year, if not better."

"Okay," Sheila said, but Jeff noticed that Malik had to give her a gentle tug before she went with him. The look she gave Jeff before she went with Malik had just enough uncertainty in it to keep Jeff from leaving the party. Maybe things weren't as they looked.

He followed the two of them to the line at the food table. *I'm not running away this time. I'm staying until she tells me to go.* He sighed. He might not even leave then.

He slipped into line behind Malik, sorry that custom dictated that the woman stand in front of her date. He took a deep breath. Her date. Was Malik just her date for the evening, or was there more between them?

Jeff thought of the way Malik's hand had touched Sheila. It had just been there. She hadn't even seemed aware of it. He nodded. Back in the day, he and Sheila had known when each other had been in the same room. When they touched, everything else moved to the back. To say they were aware of their connection was to call winter in Philadelphia a little chilly.

"I heard you were back." Sheila's neighbor, Mrs. Harding, said, as she and her husband moved into line behind Jeff. Jeff turned to talk to them.

"It was time to come home."

"How was Houston?" Mr. Harding asked.

"Big, like the rest of Texas. I drove for three days once, and I still wasn't out of the state."

"I know what you mean. I made the mistake of driving

to Dallas once. Only once. I saw more of Texas than most Texans want to see." He laughed. "A whole lot more than I wanted to see." Jeff laughed with him.

He listened to Mr. Harding's story of his trip and tried to look at him, but the soft shoulders covered by a red dress pulled his gaze. He had to fight to stay where he was instead of moving around Malik and behind Sheila and pressing his mouth to the slender neck almost close enough to touch.

He reached the table. The food probably looked delicious. Tempting aromas probably mixed together over the table. He wasn't aware of it. He had caught a whiff of Sheila's perfume and was trying to keep it from leaving him.

"I made peach cobbler," Mrs. Harding said. "I must have known you were going to be here." She patted his shoulder. "Good to have you back." She laughed. Then she leaned close. "Stop by during Christmas week and I'll have more for you."

"Thanks, I will."

Others leaving the line spoke to him and welcomed him back, too. Many recommended dishes for him to try. He hoped that his comments to them made sense. He had no idea what he said. All of his attention was on the only person here who mattered to him.

Jeff put food on his plate when Malik put some on his own, and hoped he had chosen something that he liked. He shook his head. It didn't make any difference. He doubted if he would taste anything anyway. All of his senses were taken with someone who wanted him to stay out of her life. He frowned. That was what she wanted, wasn't it? But if so, why hadn't she said so at the post office? Why hadn't she just told him to get lost; to leave her alone? Why had she let him put the barrier of the kids he thought were hers between them? Why hadn't she just told him the truth? Was it the truth?

He left the table and hesitated. Then he followed Sheila and Malik to their table.

"Is anyone sitting here?" He stopped beside the chair to the left of Sheila.

"I think it would be better if you sat somewhere else," Malik said as he pointed to chairs three tables away. "I saw empty seats over there."

"I have to talk to Sheila." Jeff set his plate in front of the empty seat, but he didn't sit. "Sheila?"

"Sheila doesn't want to talk to you." Malik put a hand on Sheila's arm.

"Is that right, Sheila?" Jeff hesitated. "I won't take up much of your time." He hadn't begged since he had begged her to come with him to Houston. This was just as important as that other time. "I-I promise. I'll leave as soon as you tell me to."

"I don't know." Sheila shook her head slowly, but she hadn't said no.

For the first time in years, Jeff felt hope bubble up. She hadn't told him to go away. It was only an "I don't know," but it was enough for now.

He pulled out the chair and sat before she could change her answer to a "Leave me alone." He was careful not to touch her as he sat beside her, careful not to brush his leg against hers to add her heat to his. Careful not to scare her away. *Now what?*

"Are you sure about this, Sheila?"

Malik's words hung in the air, and Jeff's breath waited with them. Somebody at the next table scraped a chair against the floor. On the stage, the deejay tested his speaker system. Somebody else eased past Jeff's chair. He leaned forward, but he didn't look to see who it was. It didn't matter. Still Sheila didn't answer. Jeff stared at his plate, afraid that eye contact would make her change her mind, wondering what he would do if she did.

"I'm sure, Malik. It's okay."

Jeff's gaze flew to her, but now it was her turn to stare at the table. She hadn't told him to go. He relaxed and tried to breathe normally.

"I'm going to get some more punch." Malik may have looked at Sheila. He may have looked at Jeff. He could have stared at anything in the room. Jeff didn't notice. He was busy looking at Sheila and wondering whom he had to thank for this first part of his miracle. Then he was wondering what he would say now that she had given him a chance.

"I-I'm sorry for hurting you the way I did."

The words sounded as if he were apologizing for bumping into her. They weren't enough after so big a hurt and so many years. He wasn't even sure he could call them a start. But they were the best he could do. "I can't say how sorry. If I could change things and make it go away, I would."

"That was a long time ago." Her glance slid to him and then quickly away. "It's over. We've both gotten on with our lives."

"It depends on what you mean by 'gotten on with.' " Did surviving with a vital part missing qualify? "I still . . ."

"Hello, Jeff." Dr. Miller stopped at the table. "I was wondering if you'd show up tonight." He turned to Sheila. "Where's Malik? I'm surprised he let you out of his sight, the way he feels about you." He turned back to Jeff. "That young man is crazy about her. Has been for years. Even through high school, when she didn't notice him." He stared at Jeff. "I think Sheila finally realizes what a fine young man he is. It's about time. She could do worse. A lot worse. Malik is dependable. Nothing underhanded about him."

Jeff winced. Dr. Miller should have been a surgeon. He knew how to cut deep and to the spot.

"He . . . He went to get some punch. Dad—"

"That Malik is thoughtful, too. I don't know any young man who is any more thoughtful and considerate than Malik is." His stare still held Jeff.

Jeff looked at him, then slid his gaze away. He shrugged. "You're probably right."

"I know I'm right. Did Sheila tell you that she's head of the math department at her school now?"

"No. We haven't had a chance to talk yet."

"You know she went back to college after you left her. She graduated on time. With high honors, no less."

Dr. Miller didn't say them, but Jeff heard the added words *in spite of what you did to her* in his tone.

"She's doing real well. She could be a principal, if she wants to. Or teach at the college level. With her master's degree that she earned a few years ago, she could go wherever she wants. Even into business. But you remember how she always wanted to teach."

"I remember."

"She did what she said she would do."

"Yes."

"Some people do, you know."

"I know."

"Dad—"

"Right here in Philadelphia where she grew up. She wouldn't have to go anyplace else to get another job. She talked about staying here ever since she was in junior high school."

"Hello, Jeff." Mrs. Miller rested a hand on his shoulder. "It's good to have you back in town. It's too bad it took you so long to come home, but at least you're here now."

"Hello, Mrs. Miller." Her smile told Jeff that she, at least, had no ill feelings toward him. He smiled back even though he didn't feel like it.

"Why don't we sit here?" Dr. Miller set his plate on the table. "There are empty seats." He pulled out a chair.

"Because Justin and Flora Patterson are waiting for us at our table." Mrs. Miller tugged on his arm. "I'm sure we'll be seeing you, Jeff. Come on by for a visit during the holidays." She nudged Dr. Miller when a "humph" escaped from him. "We'll leave you two now."

"You know Daddy," Sheila said after her parents left. She didn't look at Jeff. She shrugged. "He always was protective of me. He hasn't changed."

"I remember."

It had taken a lot before her father had smiled at him. Then he betrayed him by hurting Sheila.

"Was he telling the truth about you and Malik?"

"Sometimes Daddy exaggerates if he thinks it will help." She stared at the table. "It doesn't always help."

"Is there something between you two?"

"Nothing but friendship." She looked over Jeff's shoulder, stared at the table behind him, and finally let her gaze rest on him.

Jeff wanted to pull her close. He wanted to jump up and twirl her around. Friends. Nothing but friendship. And she hadn't pretended that there was more. He smiled.

His gaze met hers and their eyes held steady, suspended, reluctant to separate. She blinked free and stared back at the table.

Because he needed something to do so he wouldn't follow his impulse, he picked up his fork. He dropped it to the table, picked it up again, and looked at his plate. How much would he be able to eat? More important, now that he was with her, what was he going to say?

Now what? Sheila frowned. *Is he just going to sit there and push his food around on his plate? He's as bad as the first few times I sat at the lunch table with him.*

She spoke to a neighbor passing by on the way for

second helpings. This was ridiculous. They had never had this awkward silence between them since the times she used to push him to talk to her. He might as well have sat across the room with Lynette. He had been talking to her. Lynette had a crush on him when they were in high school. Sheila stabbed at a piece of carrot. *I'll bet he would have something to say to her.*

She tightened her mouth. *Why did he come over here? He could have brought one of the thick books he used to read, for all the company he is.* Was he just trying to see if he could get next to her again? Sheila shook her head. This was too much like high school. This time she wouldn't push him. She took a bite of roast beef. She'd pretend that he wasn't here.

Why did he have to smile at her? His dimple was still there. Of course it was. Dimples didn't go away, like some people did. They stayed where they belonged. They were dependable. You could count on them. She frowned. He knew how his smile got to her. Was that why he did it? *Small talk. Make small talk. Maybe about the weather. Or ask how the new house is coming along.* She shook her head. *No, don't mention the house. He might invite me to come see it, and I don't want to.* She shook her head. *I want to but I'm not going to; I'm not ready. I might not ever be.* She frowned. He hadn't asked her. He might not ever. She sighed. Houston. That was a safe topic. They had no history in Houston. She took a deep breath. *Okay. Here goes. The sooner we get through this, the sooner he can get up and leave. Why did he come over? Obviously he didn't have anything to say to me or he would have said it. If he thinks he can come to me and pick up where he left off, he's crazy. Why doesn't he just leave?*

If he left the table, if he went across the room, then maybe the old hurt would shrink back to a size that she could manage. *Houston. That's it. A nice, safe topic. Better than the weather.*

"How was Houston?"

"Lonely without you. And hot even without having you near."

She made the mistake of staring at him. The smile was gone, and heat like an August day burned in his gaze. How did they get there so fast? What happened to making unimportant conversation? She looked away from him before she caught on fire.

"I-I have to get some punch." She scraped her chair back.

"What about that?" Jeff pointed to the cup that Malik had left for her. He tilted his head to the side. The twinkle in Santa's eyes couldn't be a match for that in Jeff's.

Sheila grabbed her cup and drank it as if she were dying of thirst. *Thank you, committee, for small cups.* She glared at him. "I have to get some punch."

She hurried as if she were rushing to something instead of away from something. From someone.

How had they gotten there so quickly? What happened to "Houston is big?" Or flat? Or sprawling? Or even busy? What happened to what he would have said to her father if he had asked the same question? She shook her head as she got to the punch bowl. *Not Daddy. Daddy would never leave the conversation so neutral.*

She picked up a cup, but didn't leave the beverage table. She stood there sipping as if the dentist's chair was waiting for her at the other table.

Please let her come back. Jeff stared after Sheila. The hem of her skirt fluttered slightly, as if trying to keep up with her. *I shouldn't have said that. I shouldn't have told the truth. I should have told her what I told Mr. Harding when he asked about Houston. I scared her off.*

He released a long breath. *Please give me a second chance.* He shook his head. He had just used up his second chance. *Another chance, even though I don't deserve it. Please let her come back,* he thought again.

He stared at the punch table trying to will her to come back. If she didn't return to the table, there was no way he could hope for her to give him another chance.

He watched as five people went to the other table, refilled their cups, and went back to their tables. Sheila was still standing as if she were waiting for somebody to bring out another flavor of punch.

Most people would have given up hope of her returning and left. Most people weren't in love with Sheila. If she didn't come back soon he'd go get some punch for himself.

Finally Sheila turned. She hesitated and so did his breath. Then she started back toward him. She moved slowly, and each time she stopped at a table to speak to somebody, he was afraid she would stay there. He took his first real breath when she passed the last table between them. She didn't sit right away. She stared at him as if she wasn't sure this was where she wanted to be, but she finally sat down in the same chair she'd occupied before.

"You managed." She pushed her potato salad around on her plate.

"What?"

"In Houston. You managed to get along for eleven years. I don't want to hear about lonely." She cut a bite-size piece of chicken, but didn't eat it. "I've read a lot of articles in different magazines about you and your successes. Congratulations."

She darted a quick smile his way, but quickly looked away before he could see the sadness in her eyes.

"You did? You read about me?" He sounded a lot like he had years ago when she told him she loved him. She should have looked away sooner. That looked like hope in his eyes. She shook her head. Her imagination was in perfect working order. Or maybe he just wanted to see how stupid she was.

"You succeeded in what you set out to do. You kept saying that there had to be a way, and you did it. Congratulations on winning that international prize, too. You deserve it. You worked hard for it. I'll bet Switzerland was great. What are you working on now?"

"A way to fix some things. I hope it's not too late."

Sheila took a forkful of food and reminded herself to chew. Then she took another. She couldn't pretend that he was talking about a business problem. She couldn't pretend that he wasn't sitting close enough for her to touch, close enough to discover if he still felt the same under her hands when she touched him. To find out if he felt the same things inside that he used to tell her about when she touched him. Now, when she needed it the most, her imagination was hiding somewhere and refused to help her pretend.

She put another piece of chicken into her mouth and chewed. When her plate was empty enough, she could take it to the trash and sit somewhere else.

"Your dad said you're the math department head now." Safe topic. Now if he could just keep it that way.

"That's right." She nodded as if pleased with his choice of topics. It was better than the one she had started about Houston.

"But you still teach."

"Um-hmm. Three classes a day."

"I guess it keeps you pretty busy."

"Yes."

He watched as she ate a forkful of macaroni and cheese. He didn't want to remember that Malik had brought it. He didn't want to think about Malik. He was just a friend. Sheila had said so. He had to believe that.

"Has school changed much?"

"Not really. The kids are still the same. More things are out there to tempt them than when we were young, but most of them handle it, some better than others. Some ace the test, some struggle and still fail, but most are in the middle."

"Tell me about last week in school."

Her voice hadn't changed: sweet and sexy at the same time. Jeff shifted in his chair as his body remembered the effect her voice had on it. She didn't have to touch him. She didn't have to speak. Just anticipating any action from her was enough to make his pants uncomfortably tight. He was lucky he was sitting. He shook his head. He was grown now. He should have more control over his body. Would reciting square roots help take his mind off where it shouldn't be?

He made himself listen to her go over the past week. He made appropriate comments when she told of how difficult it had been to get the kids back in focus after the Thanksgiving holiday.

"I guess it will be even harder between now and Christmas."

"It always is."

Neither one found more words, but the silence wasn't as awkward as it had been at first. Still Jeff was glad when somebody came over to welcome him back. Too much silence and she might decide that she was finished with him. Again.

Nine

"Okay, folks, time to work off what you just ate." Jack laughed. "Just like last year, the food table looks like a bunch of folks breaking a month's fast came through here." He laughed again. "I got something for everyone here. Let's start with the 'Electric Slide.' That way you don't have any excuse to stay glued to your chair, even if you don't have a partner."

Sheila smiled and stood. She probably thought she had an excuse to put space between them. Jeff smiled back and stood, too.

"Where are you going?" she asked.

"I'm going to Slide with you."

"You know how to do this?"

"I learned a lot while I was away." *Not just dancing, either.*

She shrugged and went to the floor. He followed her. She didn't need to know that it took Eric and his wife an hour to teach him and that he still had to count beats to stay in step.

He followed the pattern, glad that he had to count. He did pretty well until he was behind Sheila and had to watch her bend over. He lost a beat when her skirt draped over her perfectly shaped behind when she dipped toward the floor. He was thankful that it was only one beat before the kick-turn so he was beside her again and not looking and remembering.

The Slide ended and another upbeat song followed. He had exhausted his fast-dancing ability.

"Ready to go back?" He waited for her to nod.

"Come on, Sheila." A man who was a little younger than they were smiled and took Sheila's hand. "Remember this from last year? Let's see how well we remember the steps."

"How could I forget, Tony?"

Sheila looked at Jeff and shrugged. Then she smiled as she went with Tony. Jeff didn't make a habit of disliking people he didn't know, but he was tempted to make an exception in this case.

He watched them start a routine and wondered what took the space inside him where his own rhythm gene should be. If it was math or chemistry, he could afford to dump some of that to make room. He stood watching for a few seconds. Should he add dance lessons to his list of things to do? Would it do any good? Would it make any difference?

Sheila laughed at something the man said. She had forgotten that Jeff was there.

He went back to the table. He hoped the man was just a friend, but it wasn't any of his business if he meant more than that to Sheila.

He sat at the table and watched as she changed partners when another fast song began. As long as she changed partners it was okay. Right? He had to worry only if she kept dancing with the same man. Right? He shook his head. It wasn't any of his business whether she changed dance partners.

He cleared the dirty plates from the table, but that didn't stop him from watching the floor—or rather, watching Sheila. When there was no trace of the food they had wasted, he sat facing the dancing couples, caring and worrying as if he thought he had a right to do so. He frowned. Didn't they get tired of the loud, fast music? Weren't they plain old tired of all the jumping around?

"A little change of pace, folks," Jack announced. "Some old numbers, some not so old, but all to put a holiday feeling inside us and remind us of the coming season."

What now? A rousing version of "Jingle Bells" or some other speeded-up traditional song?

Jeff stood as Sheila came near. Maybe she was tired and ready to sit out a few tunes. He pulled out her chair when the next record started. *Bless Jack's heart.* Luther Vandross singing "A House Is Not a Home" never sounded better. Or truer.

Jeff thought of his new house—lots of furniture but no other people. He eased the chair back to the table and closed the gap between him and Sheila. He never considered that she wouldn't want to dance with him. He held out his hand. She hesitated long enough for Luther to get through the first few words; then she put her hand in his. He led her to the floor slowly, afraid to touch more than her hand for now, taking his time when he wanted to get to the holding part right now. He didn't want to scare her off. Not before he held her close one more time.

He waited until they reached the center of the floor before he turned to face her. Other couples were already moving together by the time he eased her body against his and folded an arm around her. His heart lurched to a stop before it speeded up, trying to recover the lost beats, racing at least double time.

He rested his chin on top of her head and brushed it back and forth, barely touching her. Soft, just as he remembered. He breathed in deeply. The perfume that he also remembered mixed with the shampoo that he remembered and mixed with the feel of her against him that he remembered. He placed her hand on his chest so she could feel what her nearness was doing to him and wrapped his other hand around her back, stroking to make sure that she was really there and that his imagination hadn't summoned her. He didn't need anything else for Christmas.

He glided his hands down her back, tracing muscles as smooth as he remembered, feeling them bunch beneath his fingers as he remembered, aching as he remembered. He lowered his hands and rested them on her hips as he found the places from years ago but as familiar as today. He heard her quick intake of breath and held his, but she didn't move away. Instead she settled her hips against his, melded her soft body against his hardness like two lost parts finding their places. She eased her head against his chest, and Jeff hoped that his racing pulse wouldn't scare her away. He reminded himself to move his feet, to pretend that he wouldn't want to do this whether there was music playing or not.

The last note of the song faded, and he wished it had been a longer disco version playing. He stood still, since there was no music to use as an excuse, but held Sheila cradled within his arms, wondering how long he had before she moved away from him, and aching to have her even closer than their clothes allowed.

He let himself look into her eyes, afraid of what he would see, but hoping to see his emotions reflected by her. She looked as lost as he was. He allowed himself the beginning of a smile.

Another slow song began, and, even though he was lost, he eased her closer and moved to the music again. He closed his eyes and felt the sweet pain of having the return of what he had missed for so many years. Far away he heard people moving away and others taking their places on the dance floor, but he kept Sheila close. He'd hold her as long as she let him.

Jeff touched his mouth to the spot just under her ear. Her pulse jolted before beating as if trying to catch his. He pressed his lips against a spot on her neck, and her heart showed how fast it could beat. She clutched his shirt before her hand brushed across his chest as if looking for something. He felt her release a sigh as her hands stilled as if they had found what they had been seeking, just as he had. He looked down at her, drew her gaze to his, and didn't let go.

At one point, miles away, Jack said something about a song for the real old-timers. He mentioned something about the singer showing the young singers how it was done. At least that was what Jeff thought he said. He wasn't sure. Jeff was too lost in the depth of brown eyes showing smoldering fire, and smooth, sweet chocolate skin more delicious than any candy, and wondering how to find his way out or if he wanted to get out. Then the new music began.

Bing Crosby or Dick Haymes or some other singer from years ago began. Whoever he was, the singer knew exactly what words and tone to use to tell the message. When this song was dragged out every year that he was in Houston, Jeff had turned it off before it could hurt him. Tonight it belonged.

"I'll Be Home for Christmas" began, and Jeff felt every word. The song was about a man in the military who was far away from home during the holidays. Jeff had never been in the military. He had never been away unless it had been his idea, but he felt the ache more deeply because his absence had been of his own doing. No more. He was home to stay.

When the last line, "if only in my dreams," came, Jeff held Sheila a little tighter. Did she realize that he wasn't going anywhere? That he wouldn't leave her again? That he intended to stay forever? He had to make her realize it. He smiled. Surely she wouldn't dance so close to him for so long if she didn't believe him, if she didn't want him as much as he wanted her?

"That's it, folks. Time to call it a night." Jack's voice broke into Jeff's dreaming. He looked around. The lights were on, and he and Sheila were the only ones left on the floor. He took a step away from her, but still held her. She stepped back farther and broke the connection between them—except she still let him hold her hand.

"Same time next year," Jack continued. "I'll be at the Commodore Club on New Year's Eve as always, so if you want to party hearty, get your tickets." He laughed. "I'm supposed to say that the tickets are going fast, but just between us, I have no idea how sales are going." He laughed again. "Have a great night."

Sheila walked back to the table and Jeff followed. He wished he could find a way to take Jack's music magic with him.

"Do you want a ride?" Malik stood at the table holding Sheila's coat. He looked from Sheila to Jeff and back to Sheila.

"I'll take you home." Jeff looked at Sheila. Did she hear the desperation in his voice? The hope in his words?

She stared back at him, held her stare, then blinked. "I think I'd better go with Malik. I came with him." She slid her gaze away from him and gave her full attention to putting on her coat, but Jeff knew she was still as aware of him as he was of her.

He watched her fasten her coat and wondered how he could change her answer. He didn't think of anything.

"Maybe I'll see you around." Then she turned away from him as if they hadn't just spent time inside each other's arms and hearts. Malik shrugged at Jeff and followed Sheila.

Jeff watched until they went out the door. Then he got his coat and went home alone.

"Are you all right?" Malik eased out of the parking lot and onto Germantown Avenue.

"I've been better."

"You two looked like you used to a long time ago." Malik glanced at her before he turned onto Sedgwick Street.

"It felt like it used to a long time ago." She sighed. "Too much like it used to."

"Then what's the problem?"

"I can't go through that again."

"Why should you have to? He's back. He left his business. He bought a house. He's here to stay."

"For how long? A house can be sold as easily as it's bought. How long will he stay?" She sighed. "I think he just wants to see if he can get close to me again."

Malik chuckled as he turned onto Stenton Avenue. "Looked to me like he proved exactly how close tonight."

Sheila didn't say anything. How could she? Malik was right. She closed her eyes. Heat coursed through her as she thought of how perfect it had felt being in Jeff's arms again, feeling his familiar body next to hers, his lips on her face making promises.

She opened her eyes and stared out the window. He had made promises before, but it hadn't mattered. If she let him get close again it would destroy her when he left her again. And he would leave. The question wasn't if, but when.

Jeff parked his car and went to the apartment that he had converted into a lab above the garage. He opened the file on his latest project and sat at the computer planning to work.

Three hours later he was still sitting there, staring at the computer screen. It had gotten tired of waiting for him to do something and had gone dark. He sighed. Even the computer knew he was wasting time. He left and went to his empty house. The song that Luther had sung was right, as Jeff had known all along: a house could never be a home without the one you loved.

He showered and went to bed, trying not to notice how much emptier the bed was now that he had held Sheila again. After he had spent the evening close enough to her to feel her every movement, every breath she took, he was still alone. He had gotten close enough to dream and hope that he still had a chance with her.

He turned off the light. She was right to go home without him. They weren't ready to move to that. Even if all he did was take her home, it was still too soon. He stared at the ceiling even though he couldn't see it in the dark. Still, her refusal hurt.

Jeff spent Sunday unpacking the last of his things, but he couldn't have told anyone exactly what he had unpacked and where he had put anything. He ate the recommended three meals, although he had no idea what the food tasted like.

What was she doing? Did she go to church this morning even though they had been out late? Probably so. Did she join the choir, as she had talked of doing after graduation? He had to find a church. He'd look near home, but he'd find a church where he didn't have to see Sheila and know that she would never trust him enough to let him get close again.

She was probably at her parents' house. He was sure that they still had family dinner on Sunday. It was too important to them to discontinue it. Her brother and his family would be there. He pictured the whole family around the big dining room table, talking about their past week and their plans for the next, offering suggestions when they were asked for, laughing, enjoying each other's company as love settled over them like a protective blanket.

Maybe Malik was with them. *Her family welcomed me. Why not Malik? Malik hadn't hurt her.* Sheila had said they were just friends, but Jeff knew how friendships could grow into something deeper, something stronger— something meant to be permanent.

He went to his lab and answered the E-mails that were worth it, then dumped the junk mail that had accumulated, including his chance to win a million bucks. If winning Sheila back had been one of the possibilities, he would have answered right away.

He had a frantic telephone conversation with Eric and walked him through a procedure that Eric knew as well as Jeff did.

Then Jeff tried to work on his project, but again his brain wasn't functioning enough for heavy thinking. He pulled up solitaire and proceeded to lose every game for the next two hours. He wasn't going to try Scrabble. The way he was going, he'd lose even if he set the computer to idiot level. He closed up the lab and went to the house. Sometimes he did know when to quit.

He walked around the downstairs, moving things around, then putting them in their original places. He moved a couple of books, but put them back where he had placed them when he had unpacked.

He sat at the desk and looked at the clock. Ten o'clock might be too late to visit, but it wasn't too late to call. Pain stabbed through him. It hadn't been too late when they were in high school. Back then he'd call after he got home from work and they'd talk for hours about the time they had been apart—about nothing, about everything.

He reached for the phone, but panic made him pull back. He didn't have her number. How had he let her leave him without giving him her number? He shook his head. He was lucky he had remembered the way home from the party. He shook his head again. No. If he were really lucky, he'd be with her now instead of beating himself up because he hadn't gotten her telephone number.

He opened the phone book and hoped it held magic. He moved his fingers through the Millers. There were pages of them, but no Sheila or even an S. Miller.

He looked at the clock again. Ten o'clock was too late to call her parents. They had been out late last night. What if they had decided to go to bed early? What if they were already asleep and he woke them asking for Sheila's number? He definitely wouldn't get it. Everybody was cranky when somebody woke them up, especially somebody they weren't too crazy about. Dr. Miller hadn't tried to hide how he felt about Jeff.

Jeff stared at the clock as if he expected it to go backward until it reached an acceptable hour. He sighed and grabbed the shopping list from the front of the refrigerator. Two items, neither one critical. He put the list back, but got his coat and gave thanks for supermarkets that stayed open twenty-four hours. They were great for people being crowded by regrets.

Too soon he parked in the nearly empty lot and went inside. He'd go down every aisle. There might be something else that he needed that he had forgotten to put on the list.

He reached the cheese and prepared-meat display case at the end of the store and went back the other way. Maybe he missed something the first time. He was tempted to go through a third time, but didn't. He looked at the two items. He hadn't needed a cart. He started for the checkout line, but decided to go back for one more thing. He went to the fresh-flower department. He looked carefully through the potted plants until he found the kind he was looking for. After picking up and examining every pot, he put one carefully in the top of his basket and went to the customer service desk.

"Are these plants healthy?"

"Yes, sir." She stared at it. "It looks like it to me."

"The freeze didn't touch them?"

"No, sir. They haven't been outside since they left the nursery except when we brought them in from the truck."

"How about at the other end? How cold was it there? Or maybe they spent the night in the truck during the trip here."

"I don't think so, sir. We use the same supplier all the time, and we've never had a problem." She frowned. "If you have a problem after you get it home or aren't satisfied for any reason, just bring it back and we'll refund your money. We want our customers to be satisfied."

"It's for someone else. I don't want to give somebody a plant that dies as soon as I give it to them." He picked it up and slowly turned it around, carefully examining it from all sides as if he knew what to look for or was waiting for the plant to tell him to either keep it or put it back.

"I can understand that, sir. Like I said, if you have any problem, just bring it back. We'll either give you your money back or you can select another plant."

He looked at her. What did he want, a guarantee? A lot of things didn't come with guarantees—even important things.

He got in line behind a man with a full basket. The cashier at the next register told him that she was open.

"Unless you like waiting," she added. He didn't tell her that waiting in line wasn't bad when you had too many hours stretching in front of you before you could do what you had to do.

He got home and put the things away. He stood in the kitchen before he shrugged and went upstairs. Maybe it was just as well. What if her parents refused to give him the number? What if it took until tomorrow for them to decide that he deserved a break?

He took his maybes and what-ifs to bed with him, knowing that they were cold company in a cold bed and no substitute for the company that he needed.

An hour later he got up and went to the room he had equipped as his gym. Maybe working out would help. It had in the past when he had something difficult to work through, but he had never had a problem this important to solve before.

The next morning, in spite of not getting to bed until it was almost time to get up, Jeff woke before eight. He went to the kitchen.

How soon could he call the Millers? He made his coffee, but the aroma didn't calm him as it usually did. The same grounds could have been used every day for the past month, for all the impact the coffee had on him. He took his cup to the table. If the Millers went to bed early the night before, they'd probably be up already, especially if Dr. Miller had to work today.

Jeff reached for the phone but changed his mind. What if Dr. Miller didn't work today? What if this was his day off? What if they didn't go to bed early last night, but instead decided to sleep in this morning?

Eight o'clock was too early to call and beg a favor. He'd wait until eleven. That was a good time. Not too early, but not too late. He frowned. What if Mrs. Miller had somewhere to go and she'd be gone by eleven?

He slammed his cup down. *Enough.* He left the

kitchen, forgetting that breakfast was the most important meal of the day. He was acting like a kid making his first phone call to a girl. He sighed. He felt like it, too.

An hour on the treadmill, a hot shower, and then he'd go over there. He wouldn't call first. It would be harder to shut the door in someone's face than to hang up on them. He hoped. Maybe what he needed to invent was a way to make time move at the pace you wanted. He sighed. He wasn't even sure what pace he wanted: fast to get it over with, or slow in case Sheila had told her mother not to give him her address or phone number.

He jumped on the treadmill still trying to decide, but knowing that the rate of the passage of time was another thing over which he had no control.

Ten

At nine forty-five Jeff pulled on his jacket and left the house. The crisp air jolted him, but it wasn't the reason he hurried to the garage. A new coat of snow lay over everything, as if it were possible to start over—as if the same old stuff wasn't underneath.

He backed out of the garage and drove down the driveway and onto the street. On the side streets, traffic had melted a path through the two inches of new snow to gray slush. The main streets had been sanded and salted, so the only trace left was the white residue left by the combination. It didn't matter what was on the ground. If there had been more than a foot of new snow, Jeff would still be out here, trying to repair old damage that didn't have anything to do with the weather.

He had just turned onto the Millers' street when he realized that he had forgotten the plant. He went back home, got the pot, which was wrapped in a heavy layer of paper, and carefully set it up front with him. It would be warmer up there. He shook his head. Especially since the car was warm from his wasted trip.

He turned down the street again and parked in front of the house. The sidewalk had been shoveled. Did somebody clear it so everybody could go out? He shook his head. They didn't have to leave this way to get to the garage. They would have gone out the back. Maybe they cleared it because nobody would be back until late and they didn't want anyone passing by to slip and fall. He frowned. What if nobody was home? He looked at his watch. It was almost ten-thirty. They could be out. His jaw tightened. If they were, he would wait in the car until somebody came home.

He got out of the car and walked up the steps. He started to ring the bell, but, realizing he had forgotten the plant, he sighed. Then he went back to the car and lifted the plant out. He removed the newspaper he had wrapped around it. The cold air couldn't cause harm in such a short time, could it? He looked at the plant. He should have taken off the shiny blue paper covering the pot. He frowned. Then it would look too plain. He stared at it. He could have bought wrapping paper at the supermarket. And some of those bows. They would have made it look better. There was a drugstore a few blocks away. They probably sold wrapping paper. Mrs. Miller would just take it off, but the plant would look good when he gave it to her.

He rang the bell before he convinced himself to leave for something else. He rang only once. He wouldn't ring the bell again in case Mrs. Miller was still asleep. He didn't want to disturb her. He could come back later. The door opened and ended the first part of his misery.

"Jeff. How nice to see you. Come on in." Mrs. Miller smiled and stepped aside. *Good.* She was dressed. She hadn't been asleep. She didn't have her coat on, so she hadn't been on her way out, either.

"I hope I'm not disturbing you." He looked at his hand and frowned. "Here. This is for you. I hope you like it." He thrust the plant at her even though it looked punier than it had in the store or when he took it out of the car. Maybe he should have bought two. "I hope it's healthy. If not, the cashier said I can take it back."

"A miniature rosebush. It will be all right. Look how

full the branches are, and the leaves are dark and healthy. Thank you." Her smile widened. "I know just the spot for this. Come on in."

He followed her down the hall. The walls were a deep rose now, instead of the creamy yellow that he remembered. He paused in front of the print of an older man teaching a boy how to play the banjo. He smiled. He had always liked that picture. When he first saw it he had wondered how it would be to have a grandfather to do things with. He shrugged. That was a long time ago. The prints of women at an open-air marketplace were still on the wall, too.

His smile faded. He and Sheila had promised themselves that on their fifth anniversary they'd go to Africa and look for a market just like the one in the print. *Maybe it could still happen,* a voice inside him said, but it was so weak that his doubts overshadowed it.

He followed Mrs. Miller into the large living room that he remembered more clearly than his own of that time. He had worked so many hours that he couldn't have spent much time here, yet it was still so clear in his memory.

He stood just inside the doorway, but he didn't go to the couch. He and Sheila used to sit on the couch holding hands, touching, reading the love in each other's eyes. He was glad Mrs. Miller had gotten a new couch.

"Right here." Mrs. Miller drew his attention from furniture memories. "This is where it belongs." She shifted plants around on the wide windowsill and made room for the new one. Then she stepped back. "Perfect." She turned to him. "Do you remember the time you picked two white roses from one of my bushes to give to Sheila?"

"Yes, ma'am." Jeff shrugged. "The bush was loaded, so I didn't think it would matter."

"It didn't. It wasn't the roses I was concerned about;

rosebushes benefit from having the blossoms cut. It was the way you cut them."

"You mean broke them off."

"That was the problem, but no harm was done. I took you out and taught you how to prune rosebushes, and the proper way to cut the blossoms." She shook her head. "Your face stayed frowning the whole time you were clipping, and you would clip only a fraction of an inch at a time."

"I didn't want to mess it up."

"You were so serious about everything."

"I guess so." *That didn't keep me from messing up things more important than rosebushes.* "I still remember how to prune roses." He frowned. "My yard is big, but I don't know whether or not I have any rosebushes."

"You probably do. No flower garden is complete without at least a couple of rosebushes. Come spring, you'll find out for sure. That's soon enough. You can't rush important things." She looked at him for a few seconds. "Come on out to the kitchen. I made a fresh pot of coffee with different beans, and you can tell me what you think of the new flavor. You do still drink coffee, don't you?"

"Yes, ma'am." He followed her. It was strange being here without Sheila.

"Sit down."

She pointed to the table as if Jeff couldn't see it—as if he hadn't spent so much time sitting at it that Sheila had once teased him that they should charge him rent.

He walked over to the chair that had become his usual seat when he came here regularly, but today he just looked at it. Then he sat in the chair next to it.

"Have you eaten lunch yet?" She set a mug in front of him.

"No, ma'am." He hadn't even had breakfast, but he didn't tell her.

"I'll fix you something. I have some baked chicken from yesterday. I can make you a sandwich."

"I don't want to put you to any trouble. I just want—"

"No trouble." She opened the refrigerator and began taking things out. "I baked the chicken with the same spices that I always use, but you used to like it."

"I'm sure it's still as delicious as it always was." He took a deep breath. "You don't have to do this. I only came by to ask you for—"

"Wait until after you eat. Young people are in such a hurry nowadays. Tell me about what happened when you got to Houston."

He told her about how lonely he was at first and how he worked so many hours to escape his empty apartment that his supervisor made him cut back.

"How did you decide to start your own business?" She set a sandwich in front of him.

"My friend, Eric, believed in me. We worked together on several projects. We had been discussing my theory for a couple of years. Actually, I had had the idea since high school."

"I remember you explaining it to us."

"I used to explain it to whomever was polite enough not to yawn or walk away." He chuckled. "Sometimes their yawning didn't make me stop." He shook his head. "Anyway, one day, after being told again why my idea wouldn't work, I got tired of hearing it. I had worked it out on my own time. I had tested it at home with computer simulation, but they wouldn't let me do an actual test. They had decided that it was a waste of time and money." He smiled. "That night Eric and I decided to quit our jobs and start our own business." He shook his head. "It probably would have been smarter for one of us to work." He laughed. "But we decided not to do it halfway. We pooled our savings and cashed in the few shares of stock we had accumulated." He looked at her.

"We didn't have enough to call a portfolio. Anyway, we formed a corporation. Eric would handle the business end and I was the man with the ideas to make the business necessary." He shook his head. "A two-man corporation. Boy, we had guts. Eric's fiancé, Paula, almost broke up with him over it. She didn't talk to him for two weeks." He blinked. "They had planned to get married in a year, and this put their plans on hold." He stared at the sandwich in his hand. "She complained that he hadn't discussed it with her first, that she should have had a say in the decision." Jeff looked at Mrs. Miller.

"A common male problem: not discussing things with the woman in his life."

"Yes." He nodded slowly. "I know."

"But Paula forgave Eric."

"Eventually. I guess their love was strong enough." Jeff stared into space. "Sometimes it is. They've been married for six years now. They have a little boy. I'm Eric Junior's godfather. They're expecting another baby in March." Jeff frowned. *Sometimes people forgive. Why can't this thing with Sheila be one of those times?*

"But your process idea worked." Mrs. Miller brought his attention back before he found an answer to his own question. Maybe there wasn't an answer. Or maybe he wouldn't like it if he found it.

Jeff nodded. "It worked. We rented space in a warehouse in a district that had been forgotten when the industries moved south of the border. For months Eric and I slept in the lab to save on rent." He took a bite of the sandwich. "This is delicious, but it would have been more so back when we existed on yogurt, peanut butter and jelly sandwiches, and determination."

"Determination is important."

"Yes. Our first contract was with a small private company to make machine parts." He smiled. "A few months after the parts hit the market, my old supervisor's supervisor came to see me. He called to make an appointment. I had only heard his name mentioned—I had never been important enough to meet him—and here he was calling to ask for an appointment to see me." Jeff laughed. "He asked me how soon I could see him, and I asked him how soon he could get there."

"I remember how straightforward you were."

"About most things." He blinked. "I try to think everything through better now so I won't make another serious mistake." He didn't have to tell her what mistake he meant; she knew.

"The man was interested."

"The government was definitely interested. He asked me to sell them the formula. They offered more money than I dreamed of ever making. Eric left it up to me. The process was my idea, so the decision was mine." He shook his head. "I couldn't believe I was turning him down all the time I was doing it, but I knew we had something valuable enough to hang on to. And I wasn't going to go back to working for somebody else." He sighed. "The supervisor said he had to check with his boss, and he left. Eric and I spent three restless days second-guessing ourselves. This time, even though he was afraid Paula would try to get us to change our minds, he told her. She was reluctant, but she went along with us. I don't think any of us got any sleep while we waited. Finally, after we had decided that even if we never heard from him again, we could still make a living by supplying small companies with parts, he called to offer us a contract. He called on a Friday. We were ready to quit for the week when the call came." Jeff smiled. "Since then we've developed other processes based on the first." He looked at her. "As they say, the rest is history."

"You can be proud of yourself. You didn't give up. Not giving up is good."

Jeff looked at her. Was she still talking about his company? Giving up wasn't an option with Sheila. He just had to figure out the solution—take it one step at a time, like any other problem. Being here was the first step.

"Here you are." Mrs. Miller set a big slice of sweet-potato pie in front of Jeff. "If I remember correctly, you used to like my potato pie."

"Sheila used to bring me a slice every Monday when we were in high school." He took a deep breath and let the aroma bring up memories sweeter than the pie. He tasted it.

"Well? Is it as good as before, or has your taste outgrown my potato pie?"

"This is better than I remember. I could never outgrow my taste for this. Some things never change." He stared at the pie.

"I don't think we're just talking about pie anymore." She folded her arms across her chest.

"No, ma'am." Jeff set his fork on the plate as if afraid he would break it. "I forgot to get Sheila's phone number from her last night." *I barely remembered my own name after holding her in my arms again after so long.* "I-I checked the phone book, but I couldn't find any listing that might be her. I'm not even sure that she still lives in Philadelphia."

"She does, but her number is unlisted."

"I figured that was it, since she's so crazy about living in Philadelphia. I would have called her school and left a message, but I didn't get the name of her school from her, either."

"She called me after she got home last night." Mrs. Miller took a sip of coffee. "Jeff, she told us not to tell you how to reach her." She shook her head. "I'm sorry."

"I understand." His words had trouble squeezing past the lump in his throat. He had to get out of here. He had to be alone. He didn't want to fall apart in front of anyone.

Mrs. Miller set her cup down. "I don't. I saw you two dancing together. When you were in each other's arms, neither one of you even knew where you were. A couple of times, between numbers, you hadn't even realized that the music had stopped playing. You were in your own world."

"Last night felt perfect." The fresh memory of last night, sweet and bitter at the same time, flashed through his mind. It hurt to remember what would never be again, but he wished the memory had settled down instead of leaving as if something better could take its place. "I thought last night was the renewal of something. I didn't know that, to Sheila, it was the finale." He blinked hard. "I-I guess I hurt her too much for her to forgive me. Some decisions I have to live with. I guess this is one of them." He stood. How could he move when he was dead inside? "I'm sorry I bothered you, Mrs. Miller. You can tell her I came by or not." He shrugged. "I don't think it matters to her." What was he going to do? What could he do now that hope was gone? Did he keep bothering Sheila? If last night didn't mean anything to her, what could he do?

He walked down the hall. If he hadn't looked at the pictures on his way in, he wouldn't even know they were there.

"Jeff, wait." Mrs. Miller touched his arm. "Come back in and sit down." She held his arm and led him into the living room. "What do you do with your time now that you're back?"

"Ma'am?"

"How do you plan to spend your time now that you're not working at your company every day?"

He frowned. What did it matter? Why was that important now? He couldn't spend his time as he wanted: with the one he wanted, the one he needed. "I moved here because I wanted to come home. I thought something was here for me. I still work with Eric, but we set it up so I can work from here." He shrugged. "Moving back home seemed like a good idea when I made the decision." He sighed. "It's a good thing my ideas in the lab are better."

"You don't plan to spend all of your time on business. If you do, you may as well have stayed in Houston."

"No. I'm fortunate to be at the point where my money works for me. I'd have to work hard to spend all that I make." He leaned forward. "Last year I saw an interview with a pro football player who set up a program in his hometown that makes it possible for homeless single mothers to have a home of their own. I met with him and I plan to start a similar program here." He smiled at her. "I lived in Houston for all of those years, but Philadelphia is still home. The player named his program Homes for the Holidays. It operates between Thanksgiving and Christmas." Jeff stared at the print of a family on the wall. "I remember how hard Mom struggled to get the down payment for our home." He smiled. "The only day I missed school in all my years was the day she made settlement. We rode the bus to our new house and for the longest time she stood on the porch crying." His words sounded as if they rubbed against sandpaper on the way out. "Mom held the keys so tightly that she looked like she was afraid that, if she loosened her hand, somebody would snatch the keys away. When she opened the door she walked in as if we were going into a church. We slept on pallets on the floor that first night because our old neighbor couldn't help move our stuff until the next day. I was afraid to go to sleep." He took a deep breath and let it out slowly. "I was afraid that I'd wake up the next day and discover that it was a dream and that we were back in the small basement apartment." He looked at Mrs. Miller. "I want to help others know the feeling of owning their own homes. My plan will include whole families."

"It sounds like a great plan, Jeff." She touched his arm. "I know it will be appreciated. Too many people are homeless through no fault of their own. Three days a week I do a story hour for the kids in the day care at a shelter. I've seen families broken up because most shelters who accommodate mothers and children don't include fathers. The families have to make a choice: separate at a time when they need each other the most, or live on the streets together." She shook her head. "I wouldn't want to have to make that decision."

"We won't be able to provide for all families in need, but we can help some. When I decided to move back here, I made contacts with some corporations. A couple are interested, but only after they see that the plan works. I can understand that. There is only so much money available for charity. They don't want to commit until they see results." His smile faded. "Of course, when I decided to come back home, Sheila was the most important part of my plans." He shook his head. "I guess that's another example of the lack of male communication." He wished he could smile. Instead he shrugged. "I'll find something to do with my time now that Sheila's not . . ." He clenched and unclenched his jaw. "Maybe I should have stayed in Houston. I could have funded the program from there." He shook his head. "No. I'm not giving up. This is too important to me." He leaned forward. "Mrs. Miller, I understand your not breaking your promise to Sheila. I also understand her being afraid that I'll hurt her again. What I don't understand yet, is how to gain her trust again. I have to work on that. Before I can do that, I have to find her and get her to talk with me." He stared at Mrs. Miller, knowing she could see the desperation in his eyes, but not caring. He fumbled in his pocket, finally pulled out a business-card holder, and held a card out to her. "This is in case she changes her mind about talking to me."

Mrs. Miller stared at it before she took it and set it on the coffee table. "Did you ever consider working with young people? I mean junior high kids?"

He shook his head. "I never thought of it."

"How would you feel about it?"

"You mean teach?"

"No, not full-time. I mean tutor. Maybe a few times a week. Maybe at a middle school. A middle school nearby."

"I don't know. I guess I could. I used to help some of the other kids in high school and college with me. I hadn't thought about doing anything like that here."

"You know, Durham Middle School really needs math tutors. The department head told me so. She keeps talking about it."

"Durham Middle School?" He frowned.

"Yes." She nodded and stared at him. "The department head tells me about their need every time I see her on Sundays for dinner here and Wednesdays for dinner at her place."

"She does?" Jeff's frown deepened.

"Jeff, dear, didn't they used to call you 'the Brain' when you were in school?" She stared at the puzzled look on his face. "Did you use it all up in your lab? Or did you maybe work with chemicals that dulled your senses?"

"Sheila? You're talking about Sheila? Sheila teaches at Durham Middle School? The one over on Sedgwick Street?"

"That's the only Durham Middle School in Philadelphia, and unless they moved it this past weekend, it's still in the same place."

"Durham Middle School. Sheila's at Durham." A wide

grin covered his face. "I can go over there right now, can't I?"

"I don't see why not."

"Okay, okay." His head bobbed up and down like one of the little figures some people put in the windows in the backs of their cars. He grabbed her hand and pumped it up and down. He felt like a college kid again. "Thanks, Mrs. Miller." He opened the door but closed it and turned to face her again. "I-I can't thank you enough."

"Jeff, there's no guarantee that she'll change her mind about wanting to see you. She's stubborn. She gets it from her father." She laughed. "And her mother, too."

"I know. I mean I know how stubborn she is. I don't know where she got it." He frowned. "I'm back to square one. I have to convince her. I can be stubborn, too."

"One little step at a time, Jeff—one step at a time." She squeezed his shoulder.

"Yes, ma'am."

"You know, yours wasn't the only decision made that day." Her voice softened. "Maybe you should have gone about it differently, let her know from the beginning what you had in mind, but Sheila made a decision, too."

"Maybe she still thinks she was right."

"Could be. Maybe that's because nothing has happened since then to make her question her decision." She touched his hand. "Jeff, you drive carefully. The school's not going anywhere, and you have a couple of hours before it closes. If you don't make it in time today, the school will be there tomorrow."

"Yes, ma'am." He shook his head. "But I can't wait until tomorrow." He turned away, but turned back and gave her a quick hug. "You won't be sorry. I won't hurt her again; I promise."

"I'm not the one you have to convince."

"I know." He nodded. "I know."

He left. He got to the sidewalk, went past his car, and

had to come back. He took a deep breath and tried to slow his heartbeat. If he couldn't find his car parked right in front of him, how did he expect to find the words to make Sheila change her mind?

Eleven

A few snowflakes floated as if, after an exhaustive dance, they were the only ones with enough energy to move. Jeff looked at the heavy gray sky. Or maybe they were the intermission distraction. He wouldn't say it to anyone, but he didn't care if the snow didn't stop until they had a foot of accumulation. He grinned. Or two feet. He was going to see Sheila. His grin widened. He hoped Mrs. Miller found everything she wanted under the Christmas tree. His smile faded. What he wanted wouldn't be under a tree, but he hoped he got his Christmas wish anyway.

Jeff turned on the radio. Was it too soon for them to play Christmas carols? He pushed the scan button. It was searching through the stations for a second time when he stopped at the end of a familiar tune. The deejay announced the next set as an uninterrupted hour of oldies. Jeff laughed when a song he used to listen to when he was in college came on. Oldies. His music was now considered oldies. He sighed. He and Sheila had played music as they studied, as they held each other, as they swore their love for each other, as they promised forever together. He hadn't known then that forever was such a short time.

A song about never-ending love came on. He started to turn it off, but changed his mind. It was possible. It could still happen to him and Sheila. He felt the same about Sheila; it had just taken him years to realize that love doesn't go away like people do. He had to believe that she still felt the same way about him. This was a season of miracles and dreams coming true, wasn't it?

He parked across the street from the school, took a deep breath, and walked to the concrete step worn down in the middle from years of so many footsteps. If concrete didn't last forever, how could anger? He went up the steps two at a time and pulled open the heavy metal door painted the same red as the school doors where he had attended middle school.

The smell of dampness from the hundreds of wet shoes that had walked up the front steps before him mixed with the smell found in every school. Pine cleaner? Board erasers? Chalk? Did they still use chalk and chalkboards, or had dry boards and markers replaced them? He took another deep breath. Paper? Paper had a smell. Salt dragged in from the sidewalks on shoes coated the floors and steps. It had a smell, too. He let out a sigh. He didn't smell the perfume that was her signature, but he hadn't expected to. A sign posted on the wall just inside the door instructed visitors to report to the office.

"Can I help you?" A man sat at a desk at the top of the stairs in the corridor. Did they still call them non-teaching assistants, or had somebody finally come up with a term that included everything that they did?

The man stared at Jeff, but Jeff was still trying to decide. Should he ask for Sheila? She was probably in class. He shrugged. Even if she wasn't, she had already made it clear that she didn't want to see him.

"I need to speak with the principal."

"Are you a parent?" Sheila wouldn't even talk to him. How could he be a parent? Was he old enough to have a kid in middle school? Life was passing him by, and he was stuck with a bad decision from years ago.

"No, I'm not."

"Turn right at the top of the stairs. One of the secretaries will help you."

This office looked the same as the school offices that he remembered from long ago: crowded with one too many desks, every surface covered with papers, and not enough people to handle the work.

Hanging on the wall to the side was a shelf unit with a built-in series of boxes. This was something that every school had, too. In the age of e-mail, schools still found the old way of distributing messages to staff worked the best. His gaze found Sheila's name and held there. He'd leave a message, but she'd just add it to the recycling basket.

"Can I help you?" A woman came over to the high counter forming a wall between the working part of the office and the rest of the room.

Jeff introduced himself and asked to see the principal. No, she wasn't expecting him; yes, he would wait. What if she told him to come back tomorrow? Or the next day? What would he do if Sheila came in while he was waiting? What would she do?

"I'm Mrs. Watkins." A woman who didn't look much older than he was smiled at him. "How can I help you?"

"I'm Jeff Hamilton." He held out his hand. "I understand that you're looking for math tutors."

"We certainly are. Did you read about it in The Express?"

"No, Mrs. Miller told me."

"You mean Miss Miller?"

Jeff let out a slow breath. He found it easy to answer her smile with one of his own. He shook his head. "No, Mrs. Miller, her mother."

"You know the Millers?"

"Yes. I used to know them well." *If I get my wish, I'll get to know them well again.*

"Come into my office so we can talk. I'll tell you what we need, and you can tell me what you have in mind." She turned to one of the secretaries. "Please ask Miss Miller to come into my office when she has a chance. Tell her that it looks like her prayers have been answered." She motioned to Jeff.

"Have a seat, and tell me about yourself."

Jeff began telling her his background. He emphasized everything that he thought would keep her from sending him away.

"I thought your name sounded familiar," she said when he told her about his work in Houston. "Please forgive me for not making the connection. Your move back has been reported several times in the paper and on news broadcasts. I guess I never thought you'd come here."

"There's nothing to forgive. My work in Houston has nothing to do with Philadelphia, and every news report is full of different people. I'm interested in trying to give something back." *The only connection is that I severed any connection that could have been.* Even though he was hoping to gain something, that wouldn't take away the benefit of the kids' having a tutor.

She asked a few more questions and wrote down a few things. "I don't want to push my luck, Mr. Hamilton, but maybe after the first of the year you would be willing to talk to the kids in an assembly about your work?" She laughed. "We grab every chance we get to make our students aware of possibilities open to them. It isn't often that they get an opportunity to meet someone as successful as you."

"I'd be glad to talk to them. I'll try not to bore them." *You might have a battle with Sheila about my being around long enough to reach that point.* He was glad Mrs. Watkins was the principal and Sheila the teacher instead of the other way around.

A few minutes later they had finished talking. Mrs. Watkins leaned back in her chair and smiled at him.

"I'll rush the security check through. I know Miss Miller will be glad to hear that we have a tutor." She frowned. "I'm surprised that she didn't mention that you were coming in to volunteer."

"I didn't tell her. I thought I'd surprise her." *Shock* was a better word to use.

"We've been concerned about the kids who need more than we can give them in their regular classes. Our teachers work hard, but it's impossible to meet the needs of the students who need more help without holding back those who are ready to move on." The door opened. "Come on in, Sheila. I have good news."

"What are you doing here?" Sheila stood just inside the door. Her red blouse reminded him of a red dress and dancing and getting lost in each other's arms. The temperature in the small office suddenly felt as if somebody had turned the thermostat up ten degrees. He took several deep breaths and hoped they would cool him down. Her hair was pulled back from her face again. Did she ever wear it down? Her eyes looked as heated as he felt, but he remembered passion wasn't the reason for her look. She was angry. He shook his head. *Angry* wasn't a strong enough word.

"You know Mr. Hamilton?"

"I know him." She looked at Jeff. "What are you doing here?"

"I'm your new math tutor."

"No. You can't be. Find something else to do with your time."

"Is there some reason why Mr. Hamilton shouldn't work with our students?"

"No." Sheila shook her head. She still stared at Jeff. "Maybe it would be better if you volunteered at another school."

"You don't need a tutor?"

"I didn't say that."

"We need a tutor desperately," Mrs. Watkins interrupted. "I don't understand you, Sheila. Ever since we lost the tutors when DAB left the area, you've been complaining about how much the kids need math tutors. You said that we could cut down on the number of students failing if we could find tutors to take the places of the tutors we lost. I agreed. One who appears to be more than we could hope for walks into my office, and you want to send him somewhere else?" She frowned. "Is there something about Mr. Hamilton that I don't know?"

"We used to know each other."

Jeff felt his stomach tighten. How could she describe what they had as "knowing each other?" She made it sound as if they never got closer than speaking. She swept aside the fact that they had broken each other's hearts.

"The fact that you know Mr. Hamilton is a plus. If you're willing to vouch for him, we don't have to wait for security clearance before he can begin." She laughed. "We need him right now. Besides, I don't want to take a chance of his changing his mind."

"Slim chance of that happening."

Jeff stared at Sheila, daring her to turn him down. He saw her struggle between her personal feelings and the needs of the kids. He saw her sigh, and he knew the kids had won. He breathed, only now realizing that he had been holding his breath. He had won, too.

"Okay." Sheila wasn't happy about this, but *okay* was good enough. "But only because the kids need this."

Jeff smiled. He hoped she would discover that she needed this, too.

"Good." Mrs. Watkins nodded. "Do you want to take him to your room so you can work out the details now, or do you want to wait until tomorrow?"

"We may as well do this now. I have a tutoring group coming in today. He can see what it's like. Maybe he'll decide that it's not what he thought it would be and take his good deed somewhere else." She sounded as if she didn't think that was a possibility. She always was an intelligent person.

"Sheila, don't make him change his mind. You know how long we have needed this. At least once every week you remind me of that. People aren't beating down my door to volunteer. I have exhausted my possible sources and twisted so many arms that my hands hurt. We need Mr. Hamilton."

"I know." Sheila sighed and glanced at Jeff. "Come with me."

"Gladly." Mrs. Watkins didn't know that his need for the chance to get close to Sheila again was greater then the school's need for tutors.

Jeff followed Sheila down the hall with mixed feelings. He was glad that she wore a full skirt that only hinted at the shape of her hips, and sorry that she wore a skirt that only hinted at the shape of her hips. He closed the gap a bit so that all he could see was the French twist at the back of her head. He didn't want his body to show his feelings to everyone who passed by. His body hadn't reacted like this since . . . since . . . since last Saturday when he held Sheila against him. Saturday. This was the way she had worn her hair on Saturday. In college she wore it like this when she wanted to seem grown-up and sophisticated. Regardless of her hairstyle, he knew it was only part of her outward appearance. Inside she was still the sexy, sensual woman that he loved then and now.

Sheila stopped suddenly in front of a classroom and Jeff almost walked into her. He caught a whiff of her scent and regretted his quick reflexes.

"Come on in." She stepped inside, hesitated, and went over to her desk. She dragged her chair out, but didn't sit. She pinned him with her glare. "What brought you here?"

As I told Mrs. Watkins, I heard that the school needs math tutors." He walked closer. Only the desk stopped him from getting close enough to touch her. *That's why she put it between us.* He forced air out of his lungs. *One little step at a time.*

"All schools could use tutors. Why did you pick this one? How did you find me?" She tightened and loosened her grip on the back of the chair as if she were kneading bread, as his mother used to do. Or strangling somebody, as Sheila obviously wanted to do to him. Jeff was glad it wasn't his neck she was holding within her graceful hands. He stared at her. It would almost be worth it just to have her touch him.

"I heard about your need." He stared at her.

She took in a swift breath at his use of the word *need.* Jeff let his hopes rise a little. If she didn't care, she wouldn't react like that. Maybe her need was waiting for her to realize that it still existed.

"My mother told you where to find me, didn't she?" She crossed her arms over her chest. "I asked her not to, but she did anyway. What words did you use to turn my own mother against me?"

"She didn't tell me that you were here. She only said that there was a need for math tutors at this school."

"Same thing." She moved back. If the windowsill hadn't been there, would she have kept going away from him? The answer was a no-brainer.

Jeff leaned forward, but moved back when Sheila took a step to the side. He frowned. Did she think he would hurt her? "Why?"

"Why what?"

"After Saturday night, I thought we were . . . Everything was . . ." He shrugged.

"You thought we were what? Back together like before? Everything was the way it used to be? You thought I'd let you hurt me again?" He saw her swallow hard. "The way things were between us Saturday wasn't anything new. I know how I responded to you." She stared at the desk. "It was always that way between us." Her words sounded as if they had to fight their way free.

"Then you admit that you felt something, too."

"I can't deny it. But it's not enough." She shook her head. "It wasn't enough for me before and it's not enough now." She looked at him and dared him to disagree. "Our love was never as strong as I thought it was."

For a few seconds Jeff didn't answer. Was she right? Was he sure that she was wrong? "It could be now. We were kids, just learning. We could make it work. We're not the same people that we were back then. Our feelings are the same, though. And our love is still between us." He stared into her eyes, looking for the old spark, for some sign that she agreed with him. He didn't find it, but he went on. "I love you, Sheila. I never stopped. When I close my eyes I see you. Each night I imagine how it would be if things had ended differently, if things hadn't ended at all. I dream about holding you in my arms as we fall asleep after making wonderful love. I ache to wake up in the morning with you still in my arms." He stared at her as if willing her to see his dreams.

The bell clanged and shook their stares apart. Sheila stepped back from the chair.

"Don't. Don't talk like that." She shook her head. "You come back expecting to pick up where we left off. Expecting to find me waiting for you to get tired of your project and come back to me. Well, it's not going to happen. Dumb Sheila has learned some common sense." She blinked.

Jeff thought he saw tears in her eyes, but she passed

him before he could make sure. He wasn't sure he wanted to know. He didn't try to touch her even though she was close enough for him to feel her arm beneath his hand. He stared at her, but all she showed him was her back.

"I-I have to get something from my office." Her words had to get around her to find him. She fled from the room as if she didn't know there was a rule about no running in school.

Jeff watched her go. Would she come back? He stared at the doorway as if that would make her return. He sighed. He had forgotten about Mrs. Miller's advice about taking small steps. He had forgotten everything except how much he loved her. Had he scared her off for good? He had to turn in his brain badge and get a dunce cap.

A group of students standing at their lockers stared at Sheila. She slowed her pace and her breathing and hoped that her heart rate would do the same. She quickly wiped her eyes before she got to another group. She spoke to kids as she passed them. She thought she remembered to smile, and was glad she didn't have to say more than "Hi."

"Do we have tutoring today?" Every Monday Tyrik asked the same question. Sheila forced a smile as she gave the same answer, trying not to wish that today the answer was no; making herself remember that Tyrik and others needed tutoring in order to pass math and move to the eighth grade.

She responded to other kids who reminded her that they'd be there as soon as they finished at their lockers.

She frowned. She hoped her comments to them made sense. She made her hand steady enough to get the key into the lock.

What am I going to do? She closed the door and leaned against it. *Why did he have to come here? Why did he even have to come back? I was doing fine with him away from me.*

She tried not to think of how what Jeff had just said had described her own feelings. She lifted her chin. She had managed without him. She had learned to cope. She was doing just fine. Her life was in order. And then he had to come back and upset the balance by uncovering feelings she had buried eleven years ago. Almost buried. How could something neglected for eleven years spring back to life so easily?

She thought about last Saturday. It had felt like old times; being close enough to feel his strong chest under her hands, letting her hands prove that, yes, he was back, and she was in his arms, and this was not another one of her dreams. Saturday night had been as if no time had passed since the last time he had held her and she had melted against him, wanting to remove the barrier of clothes, needing the feel of only him under her hands.

Her body heated from memories and ached for new ones. Her hands itched to touch him, and her breasts tightened with longing.

She shook her head and straightened. *Not again.* She would not let that happen to her ever again.

She moved to her desk. He'd be here only until he found a dream somewhere else that was bigger than his dream with her. He'd leave her again until he got bored and came home. Why didn't he move right to his next dream? Why did he have to come home in between? Home. He had bought a house, but only because of his mother. Sheila understood that. If not for that, he wouldn't have come back to Philadelphia. She was just an afterthought—something to occupy him until he got bored. This would never be his home. Men like Jeff didn't have homes. They had projects and programs that took them all over the place. They finished one and moved on to the next. She sighed. Houston must have really been something to hold him for eleven years.

She got a folder from her desk, took a deep breath, and looked for the strength she needed to face him again. She sighed. This was only day one. If she was lucky, this novelty of his would wear off soon and he'd find something else. She swallowed. It was already too late for her. She was already hurting all over again.

She made her way past the students who were still in the hall talking, joking, probably wishing they were grown; not knowing how much being grown could hurt.

She went back to her classroom, but stopped outside the door. She listened to the kids talking and tried to make herself immune to the deeper, familiar voice talking with them.

She took a deep breath, tried to put a shield around her heart, and went inside.

Twelve

Jeff looked at the kids facing him—or rather, whom he was facing. He was thankful for his height—and that he hadn't done anything to make them mad. Had kids been this angry when he was young? He took a few deep breaths. He was the adult here. He could handle this. He was here to help them—if they let him.

They stood in a loose group around him. There were about twenty but they seemed like fifty. They held their backpacks as if they didn't intend to stay. But they didn't leave. As long as they were there, he had a chance of reaching them. If he could reach them, he could help them.

"Okay. What do you want to know?"

"Who are you? You a teacher?"

"No, I'm not a teacher. I'm Jeffrey Hamilton, and I'm here to help you with math."

"Where's Miss Miller? She's our teacher." A girl taller than most of the boys glared at him.

"Yeah. I saw her in the hall. How come she didn't tell me she wasn't gonna be here today? Why she send you?" A boy added his glare and frowned at Jeff.

"Yeah. Why she cut us loose like that?" Another girl stood just inside the door, as if not sure she was going to stay either.

"If she ain't coming, I ain't staying." Another boy

added his voice. The others muttered their agreement. The twenty now seemed like a hundred.

Jeff let his gaze touch each one. They were just kids. Some of them were as big as some adults, but they were only not-so-sure-of-themselves kids, and they wanted their teacher, not some stranger.

"Let me take this one step at a time." He frowned. That was what Mrs. Miller told him to do, but he hadn't followed her advice. He shook his head. "I am not taking Miss Miller's place. She'll be here. She had to get something from her office." *At least that's what she said. She might have just used that as an excuse to get away from me because I came on so strong.*

"How come you doing this? You don't know us."

"Good question." He wouldn't tell them that the main reason he was here was to be near Sheila. Would he be here if she wasn't? He wasn't sure he wanted to face that question yet. "I was told that you guys are having a little trouble with math. I happen to like math."

"You like math? No way. How can you? What are you? Some kind of a nerd or something?"

"You can call me a nerd if you want to, but I like working with numbers."

"Why? I don't get it. I don't get numbers, either." Some of the anger was gone from the young man's face. His glare had eased into a stare.

"I'm not sure." Jeff shrugged. "Numbers always make sense. They're logical. They never change. If you do a math problem, the answer is either right or it's wrong."

"That's why I don't like it." The tall girl set her book bag on a desk. "I like to be able to make choices. With words more than one can be right."

Several of the others agreed.

"Looking at all of those numbers gives me a headache."

"You got that right." The young man with the stare set his book bag on the second desk.

"You Miss Miller's boyfriend?" Another girl frowned at Jeff. "Is that why you're here?"

"Miss Miller and I . . ." Jeff looked around. Every pair of eyes was focused on him. "Miss Miller and I went to high school and college together."

"You're her boyfriend," the girl, who had left the subject of math behind, added. She nodded. "That's why you're here. Boys do all kinds of things to get next to a girl. Men are probably the same way."

Barely a teenager and this girl had it all figured out.

"I like Miss Miller. She's cool."

"Yeah. She don't get mad when you don't get something right away. She takes as long as you need."

"You got a nice girlfriend, Mr. . . ." The boy frowned. "What you say your name is?"

"Jeffrey Hamilton. And Miss Miller is not my girlfriend." *But I would like for her to be. Again.* "What's your name?"

"Tyrik." He held his hand out.

Jeff looked at it. Did kids shake hands or slap five or what? He offered his and let Tyrik decide. He smiled when the boy looked at it before he took it in an old-fashioned handshake.

"Anybody want to tell me what you're working on?"

"Trying to pass math so we can go to eighth grade."

They all laughed. The glares and frowns were gone. The girl near the door moved into the room and set her book bag on a desk. The others did the same. Relief raced through Jeff. Sheila would never let him stay if he chased away her group.

This is ridiculous. Sheila took a deep breath and went into the classroom. If she stayed out here much longer it would be time for the kids to go home.

"Hey, Miss Miller, where you been?"

"Yeah. We thought you dissed us."

"You got a cute boyfriend."

Sheila glared at Jeff.

"I told them that I am not your boyfriend." *I didn't tell them that I hope that changes soon.*

"Kendra, if you spent as much time on your math as you do on other things, maybe you wouldn't have so much trouble with it."

"Yes, Miss Miller."

"I thought we might break up into two groups. I can keep some of you in here and Mr. Hamilton can take some of you into the room next door." She looked around. "How does that sound?"

"Not good." Her gaze swung to Jeff when he spoke. "All of the kids want to be in your group. They don't know me. They thought you abandoned them during the time you were away from them just now. A whole hour would be distressing. You can't . . . you can't. . . ."

"Dis us." Tyrik stepped forward. "You can't dis us. Mr. Hamilton is a stranger." He glanced at Jeff. Sheila saw the looks they exchanged. Tyrik, who had never smiled in school before, decided that now was the time.

Sheila frowned. *Sometimes male bonding is not so great.* "You can't leave us with him," Tyrik finished.

"Yeah. My mom signed the permission slip for you to tutor me. She wouldn't like it if you let some strange man work with me. You don't know what my mom is like when she gets upset." Kendra smiled as if she had just aced a test.

"Your mom signed the permission slip for you to stay after school for tutoring. The slip didn't have my name on it. She didn't mind when the tutors from DAB worked with you. Why would she be upset now?"

"She . . . I . . . We—"

"I think if a parent expects a certain person to work with her child, that person should work with her child."

She glared at Jeff. Then she looked at the other kids. "My mom expects you to be my tutor, too."

"So does mine."

All of the students were certain that their moms would insist that Sheila had to be their tutor, and they made that point clear to her when she looked at each one.

"Fine." Maybe that was best. If she had left them alone with Jeff much longer they would have taken over the school if he suggested it. Who knew what would happen if he was alone with them on a regular basis? *It's my own fault. If I hadn't been such a coward and run away, I could have divided them before they got to know him.*

"Why don't you start the session?" Jeff offered. "I'll walk around and help when they reach a problem area."

"Okay." She didn't look at him. "Sit down, kids. We've wasted enough time."

"We were here on time, just like you said, weren't we, Mr. Hamilton?"

"Yes, you were."

Agreeable Jeff. "I know, Carla. Take out your math books, but we won't start with them."

"Do you know that Mr. Hamilton likes math?" Kendra sat at the desk closest to Jeff. "He must be good at it if he likes it."

"I know." *I know he's good at a lot of things. Things like kissing and. . . .* She shook her head. *I know too much about Mr. Hamilton.*

"He likes math and you like math. Is that why you all got together? Because of math?" Tyrik slid into a seat.

"No, that's not why we got together," Sheila said. Jeff cleared his throat and Sheila stared at him. "I mean, we're not together. The only reason he's here is to help you." She didn't believe that and she was saying it. Why should they believe her? "Are we going to do math today?"

"Yes, ma'am."

Sheila slowly let out her breath. Some of her tension hitched a ride out.

She took papers from the folder that had allowed Jeff to get close to the kids. It hadn't taken him any longer with them than it had with her. Maybe that was what he should work on. If he could figure out a way to bottle that appeal and market it, he'd make another bankful of money.

"Do you want me to hand out those papers?" Jeff broke into her thoughts. He started toward her.

"The kids can pass them." Sheila tried not to see the start of a grin on Jeff's face as he stopped four desks before he reached her. She handed the papers to Amina, who took one and passed them on. Sheila looked as the last student handed the extras to Jeff.

Sheila watched as he came toward her as if giving her a chance to get away. For all the noise the kids made, she and Jeff could have been alone in the room. If she could, she would move back. If she only could.

Why didn't she turn away? Why did she just stand there as he came close enough for her to see the weave of his sweater, the beard that had grown since this morning, the cleft in his chin?

He stood in front of her and she took a deep breath. It was supposed to clear her mind. Instead it let in the scent of shampoo and aftershave and lost dreams. Jeff reached behind her as if in slow motion, put the papers on the desk, and backed away. The hunger in his eyes was stronger up close. Was her own hunger feeding it?

"Do you want us to do the first one now?"

Sheila nodded even though she had insisted that she couldn't hear their brains rattle when they did that. They certainly couldn't hear her brain, either. It was obvious that she didn't have one. "Yes."

She wrote the first problem on the board. They had spent last Monday on the concept of negative numbers, and everyone seemed okay with it. She hoped that this week it was still with them. "Who's ready?" She smiled when she turned and saw most of the hands up. She watched as Jeff moved to one of the kids who still looked puzzled. This was what she expected the session to be like.

She wrote more problems on the board and told the students to work on them. Then she walked to the student closest to her and checked his paper. Early in her teaching she had learned that, no matter how many times you gave the students a chance to ask questions, some wouldn't unless you were standing beside them. She answered a question before she moved to the next desk.

Once she bumped into Jeff, who was working his way around the room. She spent more time with the next student, trying to get her mind back on math and off the problem of why contact with him disturbed her if she didn't still have feelings for him.

She went back to the board and wrote a problem that covered the next step. She gave the kids a chance to get started. Then she made the mistake of looking at Jeff.

He stood between two rows of desks staring at her. Even from there she could see the hunger still in his face. Heat flowed through her. If the room had been twice as long, it still wouldn't have helped. Why did he have to look at her like that? Why did he make her feel that, more than anything else, he wanted *her*? How could she almost believe him—want to believe him—when she knew what would happen if she did?

"Is this right, Mr. Hamilton?" Jeff continued to stare at her a few seconds longer. "Mr. Hamilton? Can you tell me if this is right?" He looked at the girl sitting at the desk beside him, freeing Sheila.

Thank you, Kendra. How could a look hold her so tightly? Sheila forced her attention to the reason she was there.

By the time the session was almost over, she was confident that the kids were ready to move on to their next problem area. "Let's spend some time on what you did in class today. Do the first two problems of your homework so we can make sure you won't have any trouble tonight." She let them get started, then walked among the desks near her. Jeff did the same with those near him. She left enough space between them so they wouldn't bump into each other, but several times their gazes managed to do just that.

"Great job. A few more sessions and some of you won't need us anymore. Kendra, I think you're almost ready. After Christmas you might not need us at all."

"I think I'd better stay." Kendra nodded and looked at Jeff. "I don't want to fall behind again."

Sheila looked at the girl. She shook her head. Already she had fallen under Jeff's spell. Sheila knew the feeling. "We'll see. Okay, kids. See you next time. We'll work with fractions." The kids groaned. "And decimals." The groans got louder. "Come on. You acted the same when we started with negative numbers, and now look at you. You can do it." She turned toward Jeff, but her glance found the bulletin board behind him. "Thanks for coming."

"My pleasure."

She felt heat flood her face. She looked at him. His look told her that it was obvious to him.

"I'll see you next week."

"Aren't you leaving now?"

"I have to go to my office."

"I'll come too."

"It's not necessary."

"I need to talk to you."

Don't talk about need. Please don't talk about need.
"Talk to me about what?"

"Things. Do you want to wait until we get to your house? Or would you rather come to mine?"

"I'm not going to your house."

"Then we'll make it yours."

"No, we won't." Sheila looked around. Not one student had left. Every other day they almost trampled one another trying to leave. "We can talk in my office." She turned away from him. "Are you kids going home or are you planning to spend the night?"

"What did he do to make you so mad, Miss Miller?"

"He probably forgot to do something or showed up late for something. Women don't like to wait." Tyrik said it, but the others agreed.

"Good-bye, kids. Find some business of your own to mind." They left, but anyone who saw them would think they had been forced to leave in the middle of a good movie. Maybe she should have let them come with her.

She walked down the hall as if to make sure anything in her way was scared off by the noise. She unlocked her office door. It was good that the key was so strong.

"What is it? What do you want?" As soon as she stepped inside the room, she whirled to face Jeff.

He had to bite his tongue to keep from stating the obvious. "Do we start at the same time on Wednesday?"

"You couldn't ask me that in the classroom?" She dropped the folder on the desk as if it were to blame for her situation.

"Come with me for a cup of coffee. Or rather, I'll have coffee and you can have tea. Or we can both have hot chocolate. With those tiny marshmallows that you love."

"I'm not going anywhere with you."

"Okay." He pointed to a small table in the corner. "We can stay here. You have a hot pot. Why don't we share a cup now?"

"I'm not sharing anything with you." She took her coat and purse from the closet.

"You mean not again."

Sheila dropped her purse, picked it up, then dropped her coat. "Go away, Jeff." She pulled on her coat before he could get close enough to help her.

"I did once, and I've been sorry ever since."

"Don't start."

"We never finished."

Sheila took a deep breath, but she didn't look at him. "Pull the door shut when you leave. It will lock itself." She held her breath as she left, but he didn't try to stop her.

She went down the hall close enough to a run to have been stopped if she were a student. She sighed. When she was a junior high student she had never heard of Jeffrey Hamilton.

Jeff stared at the doorway. Her footsteps got quieter until they disappeared. Still he stood staring, hoping that she would come back even though he knew it wasn't going to happen.

Had it gone well, or not? Was it what he had expected? He tried not to be disappointed. When he showed up he had been afraid that she would turn him down. He shook his head. But he had been hoping that she would soften a bit toward him. He smiled. She still cared. She could fight it all she wanted, but the hunger and desire in her eyes told him the truth. His body tightened at the memory, but his smile widened. He still had a chance. There was plenty of time for a Christmas miracle.

Thirteen

On the way home, Jeff made a detour to the florist's shop. He couldn't decide between cut flowers and a plant, so he chose both. He scrawled *Thank you* on the card and gave the clerk the delivery address.

That evening he received a call.

"Thank you for the flowers, Jeff," Mrs. Miller said, "but it wasn't necessary."

"If I thought you had space, I would have sent you one of every arrangement they had."

"So things went well?"

"She didn't throw me out, although she wanted to. You'll probably get an angry phone call."

"I already did. She ended the conversation when I asked her why she was so angry."

"Thanks again. I can't tell you how much I appreciate it."

"One step at a time, Jeff. Don't push too quickly."

"Yes, ma'am. I'll try to remember."

Saying that was easy when he was away from Sheila. The hard part would be when he was in the same room with her.

On Tuesday Jeff had his own one man unpacking marathon. He emptied the last boxes and put them out for trash pickup, but he still had a lot of day left over when he finished. Wednesday seemed a week away.

He went to his lab, but all he did was waste perfectly good time. He made a few phone calls from the numbers Carolyn had given him. He arranged for somebody to come measure his windows for drapes, but nothing took enough of his time and attention.

His whole day had been spent doing things that didn't require much thought. When he finally went up to bed he was glad he wouldn't have to account for his time. His mind was on yesterday and reaching toward tomorrow. Today was just in the way.

He got out of bed before the sun had pulled itself above the wall around his place. He had breakfast and went to his exercise room. Regular school hours didn't end until one forty-five.

Three hours later, noon still hadn't shown up. Jeff pulled on a sweatshirt and went to the backyard.

Crisp air welcomed him. Anybody who was sluggish this morning had only to step outside. He grabbed the snow shovel from the back porch and walked down the salt-covered steps.

The bushes and plants looked as though somebody had used a whole case of artificial snow on them. It would be spring before he could see what was planted. No problem. He had enough patience to wait for that.

The walk looked as if the snow had almost run out when its turn came to be covered. The sun the past few days hadn't left much for him to do, but surely he could find enough to shovel in that huge yard to fill the space until it was time for him to go.

He cleared the brick walkway as if somebody was expected to walk along it. It ended at the play gym. Jeff leaned on his shovel and smiled.

Snow covered the canvas top and must have filled in the floor, but the fort was still at the top of the seven steps leading up to it. He knew there were seven. He had counted them and wondered why seven and not six or eight.

A gust gave the swings a push, as if trying to tempt somebody to come play. The slide and seesaw wore coats of snow. Two rings still hung from the top bar beside the rungs stretched like a ladder laid from one end of the set to the other. His mother had had a fit when she had seen him hanging from a middle rung by his legs.

The set looked so much smaller than he remembered. He looked as the rings clacked together and then separated. What was he going to do with this?

He walked slowly back to the house, but he couldn't find any snow left to shovel.

He went inside and made some appointments for tomorrow, ate lunch because it helped fill the time, then sat down to wait. He knew he was more anxious than the kids for the school day to end.

Finally, as if reluctant to do so, time came for him to leave.

"Hello, Mr. Hamilton," Mrs. Watkins said when he signed in at the office. "I understand it went well on Monday."

"Yes, it did." If Sheila thought it went well, who was he to disagree?

"Thank you again for helping the kids. I know you must have a busy schedule."

"I'm glad I can help." *I'm not as busy as I want to be.*

Jeff left the office. Should he be glad that Sheila said the tutoring went well?

"Hey, Mr. Hamilton. What's up?" Tyrik stood outside a row of lockers. They looked as if somebody spent a lot of time making them look new.

"Nothing. How about you?"

"Nothing going on. You working with today's group, too, huh?"

"Yes."

"Miss Miller is all that today. She is every day, but today she looks like she's got an appointment or something. Wait till you see her. She's wearing a green silk blouse the color of the cotton candy they sell in bags. You ever see that? You know what I mean? She's wearing a dark green skirt to go with it." He frowned. "I don't know how ladies can wear skirts in the winter. Their legs ought to get cold, don't you think?"

The last thing he needed to do was to think about Sheila's legs when he was out here where everybody could see his reaction to that thought. He imagined warming her cold legs with his hands. He shook his head. *Change the subject before somebody notices.* "How was your math class today?"

"It was okay." Tyrik suddenly found the floor interesting to look at. "See you next Monday."

Jeff made his way through the kids beginning to crowd the hallway. Maybe by the time he got to the classroom he would have forgotten all about Sheila's legs. And maybe when he left the school he'd find a sunny beach and the seashore waiting outside for him, too.

He leaned against the wall outside Sheila's classroom. Her voice was as sweet through the door as it was when he was in the room with her. He smiled as her "okay" came to him. She used it a lot. Would that ever be her answer to a question that he asked her?

The kids' moving noises reached him before the kids

did. He kept himself from rushing past them so he could see her sooner.

"Don't forget."

Her voice was moving toward him. He felt as though he were back in school waiting for her in the lunchroom. He made himself wait, enjoying the sound of her voice, anticipating seeing her.

"Short quiz tomorrow," she continued as the kids filed from the room. "Make sure you . . ."

The rest of her sentence got lost when she saw him.

"Hi." Tyrik was wrong. Jeff loved cotton candy, but it never looked as good as this. He stared. And it never tasted as sweet as he remembered Sheila tasting.

"Hi." Her gaze found his face and settled there. Then she frowned and pulled away. "Come on in." She stepped back into the room, making sure he had plenty of room without having to get close to her.

The room must be empty, since no more students came out. Jeff didn't look to see. He was looking at something more important than a room.

"I missed you."

Sheila's gaze flew back to him. Her eyes said the same thing to him that his words said. *Why can't she admit it?*

"Hi, Miss Miller." A girl walked into the room. She looked from Sheila to Jeff. "I heard about you. Ain't you Miss Miller's boyfriend?"

"That's not what Miss Miller says." Jeff's gaze still held Sheila's for a few seconds more. Then he smiled at the girl.

"Have a seat, Donna." Sheila's voice sounded as if she were trying to make his smile go away. She didn't succeed. "How was math class today?"

"It was okay." The girl shrugged. "I had a little trouble."

"We'll see if we can clear things up for you."

"Hi, Miss Miller." A boy tall enough to dream of a pro basketball career came in and slouched into a seat. "What's up?"

"Your math grade if you keep working hard. Did you finish the problems I gave you last time?"

"Yes, ma'am."

"Any trouble?"

"No, ma'am." A wide grin covered his face. "I passed my math quiz. We got the papers back today."

"That's great, Fred. Congratulations." She held her hand up to him and received a high five.

Other students drifted in and took seats. They each looked at Jeff and then at Sheila. Jeff waited for the question again. He wasn't disappointed.

"He your boyfriend, Miss Miller?"

"Miss Miller says I am not her boyfriend." Jeff grinned at Sheila, who glared at him before she looked at the students.

"Class, this is Mr. Hamilton. He is kind enough to volunteer to tutor you."

"I am not Miss Miller's boyfriend." Jeff looked at Sheila. "I'm just clearing up any misconceptions that they might have."

"How long you gonna stay? You gonna leave us like Miss Stewart and Mr. Green did?"

"Who?" Jeff frowned.

"They were tutors from DAB." Sheila set her mouth in a straight line. "The kids had just gotten used to them when they left."

"I'll work with you as long as you need me and as long as Miss Miller lets me."

"They said they would be here as long as we needed them, too, but they left."

Jeff took a deep breath. "I might have to leave town from time to time, but I'll always come back."

The kids seemed satisfied. Sheila wasn't showing any belief in his words.

"Let's review from last week."

She distributed papers and wrote a problem on the board. Then the session went the same as the one on Monday had.

The kids left and Sheila moved toward Jeff. "Thank you for coming." She gathered her things and put them into a desk drawer.

"My pleasure. Come with me for a cup of coffee."

"I don't think so."

"I want to discuss the kids." He watched as personal battled with professional. He decided to give professional some help. "Don't you think it would be helpful if I know a little about the kids? There's more to them than trouble with math, you know."

"I know."

"Do you want to go to your office?"

"No." She folded her arms across her chest.

"You can trust me." He smiled. Maybe it was herself alone with him that she didn't trust.

"There's a little restaurant on Mt. Airy Avenue." She told him the name.

"Good. I'm parked right across the street. I'll go with you while you get your coat."

"You can wait for me at the door."

"Promise you won't slip out the back?"

"Yes." She stared at him. "And I keep my promises."

Jeff watched her walk down the hall. He couldn't argue with her on that. She didn't use the words *I promise,* but she had kept the one about not having him in her life anymore. He let out a hard breath. She was going to the restaurant with him. The only reason was to discuss the kids, but he'd take what he could get.

* * *

Sheila jerked open the closet door and took out her coat. She couldn't turn him down. He did need to know more about the kids. She frowned. All through her education courses in college they emphasized that "we teach students; we do not teach subjects. We need to know the whole child, not just the problem areas." She pulled on her coat. She believed that, darn it.

She shut the closet door and leaned against it. She had told that to Jeff every time a professor had told it to the class. He had saved it until he could use it against her. She closed her eyes. *I do not want to go anywhere with him.* She sighed. *But I want to be alone in my office with him even less.*

She went back to the front of the school. No matter how long she took, she knew he'd be waiting for her.

"I'm in the parking lot."

"I thought we'd go in my car."

"You thought wrong. I'll meet you there."

"It's been years since I've been in that area. What if I get lost?"

"Who's fault is that? If you get lost, I'll see you on Monday." She didn't look to see his reaction. He never forgot anything. She wouldn't be lucky enough for him to get lost.

"That wasn't so bad, was it?" Jeff leaned his elbows on the table. He had drunk enough coffee to float home and had eaten a piece of cake that he didn't want. He smiled. It was worth it.

"No." Sheila smiled at him. Then she took it back as if she had just remembered that he didn't deserve a smile. "I think I told you enough to help you with the kids." She stood.

"Yes." He wished she had given a clue on how to help him with her. He stood, too.

"See you Monday." She never looked back.

Thursday morning Jeff met with the Homes for the Homeless coalition, which included directors of shelters, city officials, and other organizations involved in working with the homeless. Carolyn's boss had offered them space at her realty office for the meeting.

After introductions, Jeff explained what he had in mind.

"I'm looking for families who are about ready to move into a home. They should have steady jobs and should be saving for a down payment. Their income doesn't matter. I'll provide the rest of what they need. The initial funds will be in the form of a grant, but they will pay mortgages based on their income. Instead of to a bank, they'll pay it to the company. That money will go to add houses to the program."

"So you're not talking about giving them houses."

Jeff was glad he had asked them to wear name tags. He was terrible with names. "Mrs. Anderson, I've found that people appreciate things more if they work for them."

"That's true." Reverend Logan nodded. "The Lord helps those who help themselves. Folks take better care of something they have to work for."

"They won't just move in, either," Jeff continued. "Before they take possession of the house, they'll be involved in small repairs—the kind homeowners expect to do. They'll also do final cosmetic touches such as painting. Professionals will teach them the basic skills they'll need. We'll furnish the homes. It might not be what they want, but it will be new furniture." He thought back to his mom's first house. "They don't need to start off in debt to keep from having an empty house."

"Do you have any plans to help them hold on to this house? Some of the homeless had homes but lost them," Reverend Marks said.

"Many times that wasn't through any fault of their own." Mrs. Turner leaned forward. "They get laid off or a company cuts back or moves out of the area and they're out of a job. The old 'last hired, first fired' kicks in. They were barely making it when they had a paycheck coming in. They couldn't afford to set money aside for an emergency. Every penny went for day-to-day living. An emergency happens and they fall behind. They're out in the street."

"I'm aware of that. We'll have counselors to teach them how to budget what they make. Not just for mortgages and utilities. I mean all household expenses, including transportation to and from work and making food choices at the supermarket."

"Maybe we can make them see that fries from a potato are as easy as frozen and a whole lot cheaper."

"Yeah. And a real breakfast is cheaper than chips and soda, not to mention more nutritious."

"I'll need help from your organizations in determining that part of the program."

"Our Neighbor to Neighbor program can set up workshops to cover that sort of thing. We have something similar in place now, for whomever feels the need for it. We can accommodate your people with no problem," Reverend Marks said.

"Thank you, Reverend Marks; we'll count on you for that." Jeff looked around the table. "What I need from you first are suggestions for a board to oversee the program. The idea is mine, but I need regular input from others who have experience in something like this. I've never done it before. I know all of you are busy and the last thing you probably need is to belong to another committee, but I do need you. If you can't sit on the board, I hope you can suggest someone who can. If some of you want to think about it, that's fine. Meanwhile, I need a list of potential candidates for the program so we can get things rolling as soon as possible." He distributed his business card. "This is my home office number. You can reach me there. We'll have to add a secretary right away. I could use suggestions. Maybe one of you has someone you can recommend. Next week I'll find an office for us. I don't expect this to be as simple as I first thought." He smiled. "Few things are."

"Is this just for single mothers?" Sister Catherine had been quiet until now.

"Definitely not. We won't deny someone admission to the program because a husband is in the picture."

"Good. Most shelters aren't set up for families, so they have to separate."

"I think I can serve on your board. We really have a need for something like this." Reverend Marks laughed. "Maybe I can find a few hours to add to the twenty-four allotted to me each day."

"Look for some for me, too," Mrs. Turner added.

Others agreed to serve on the board.

They discussed a regular meeting time. It took a while, because everybody had full schedules. Jeff worked his own around late afternoon on Mondays and Wednesdays. After they finally found a time that everybody could fit into their schedules, Jeff dismissed the meeting.

He tried to contain his enthusiasm during the drive home, but he couldn't. He had been thinking about starting this program for a long time. Now it looked as if it would work, and after this meeting he had a better idea of how he was going to proceed.

After he got home, he stayed up past midnight working

out the details. He was tired when he fell into bed, but not too tired to think—and then dream—of Sheila.

Jeff spent Friday looking at properties. The real-estate agents wanted to go with him, but he insisted on going alone. This was one time when it was smart to judge according to outer appearances. He refused to consider houses in deteriorating areas. If this plan was going to work, the new homeowners would need to be living among homeowners who took pride in their homes.

He visited neighborhoods he hadn't known existed. His idea was to find scattered sites in stable neighborhoods. Once he decided upon the recipients of his grants, he'd consider any houses that they had in mind. He start looking at the insides of houses next week.

That evening he met with his new accountant to incorporate the program and work out the financial aspect. He almost didn't have time to think about Sheila.

Jeff was almost home when snow remembered that this was its time. Large flakes drifted down as if too fat to go fast. This was not what they used to call serious snow, but it was enough to cover the ugly gray mess left from the last snowfall.

Jeff had just taken off his coat when the phone rang.

"Hi, Jeff. I'm calling to invite you to dinner on Sunday."

"Dinner, Mrs. Miller?" Jeff tried not to let this surprise allow hope to grow inside. *Maybe Sheila asked her to call.* "Are you sure you want me to come? What about Sheila? Did she ask you to invite me? What about Dr. Miller?" He wanted ignore to his own questions. He wanted to say yes before she changed her mind, but he didn't want to put her in an awkward situation.

"Sheila doesn't know. She doesn't decide who gets invited to this house. As for my husband, I think it's time you two cleared up your unfinished business, and I told him so. He agreed that you two should talk." She chuckled. "I'll act as referee." She hesitated. "I didn't stop to think that maybe you have other plans."

"I don't have anything to do. If I did, I'd change my plans. I'd love to come, if you're sure it's all right."

"See you on Sunday. Make it about two-thirty." A smile crept into her voice. "That way you and Bob can get the fireworks out of the way before everybody else gets there. By the way, I'm making sweet-potato pies."

"My mouth is watering just thinking about them." He hesitated. "I-I'm looking forward to coming. Thank you for inviting me."

"Sometimes even miracles need a little help."

"This one needs all the help it can get."

Jeff hung up. He laughed. If he knew how, he'd turn cartwheels through the whole downstairs and up the steps. Then he took a deep breath. What was he going to do until Sunday? He sighed. Use the time to figure out what to say to Dr. Miller.

On Saturday Jeff went furniture shopping. He needed to furnish some of the empty rooms. Five rooms of furniture didn't make a complete fit in a twelve-room house. More than that, he needed to help the time move along.

"May I help you?" a salesman asked. Jeff looked around at living room furniture placed in room settings. He frowned. "I'm just looking." One thing he definitely didn't need was living room furniture. He walked on.

"Are you looking for anything special, sir? Is the furniture for a boy or a girl, or do you want something for either?" The salesman laughed. "Or both?"

Jeff looked. He was surrounded by rooms for children. A white set with gold trim was to his left. A bed with a pink-and-white spread and a matching ruffled canopy stood against a wall. A doll in a fancy pink-and-white dress with lace at the edges sat against a small pink pillow, waiting for a little girl. He wished he could say both. "No, I'm just looking." He'd love to be able to say that he needed a set for his daughter. This would be perfect. He sighed. Before he could have a daughter, he needed a wife. That was the order he wanted to follow. And he didn't want just any wife. He wanted Sheila.

He quit wasting salespeople's time and went home to his sparsely furnished house. He had a lot of empty rooms, but furniture wasn't the most important thing missing from his house. All the furniture in the world wouldn't make up for the missing Sheila.

Fourteen

Jeff made appointments to see office space. His fax machine had been busy while he had been wasting time at the furniture store. Several résumés from people recommended by members of the new board lay in the basket. He was confident that he'd find a secretary among the group.

He made arrangements to look at office space, checked his E-mail, and talked to Eric. He still had too much day left over. Even after tomorrow came, he had to wait until two o'clock before he could leave. He went to his gym room to see how much time he could use up before he collapsed from exhaustion.

Sunday came at its regular time, and each hour took its usual sixty minutes before it made room for the next. Finally the clock had mercy on him and reached two o'clock.

Jeff decided to wear his blue shirt. It had brought him luck at the party. Maybe it had a little left for today.

He went to the garage, but went back to the house to make sure he had locked it. Then he had to go back to make sure he had turned off the coffeepot. Finally he drove down his driveway.

He made himself slow down as he went to pick up

the cake he had ordered from the bakery. An accident would only add to the time before he could see Sheila.

He parked outside the Millers' house. He stared at the house, took a deep breath, and got out of the car. Before he could see Sheila, he had to face Dr. Miller. He carefully got the cake and went up the steps.

Mrs. Miller opened the door before the chimes died down.

"Come on in, Jeff. Good to see you."

"I'm a little early."

"That's all right. Give me your coat." She looked at the cake box. "What's this?"

"I didn't want to overdo the flower bit, so I brought a cake instead. I know it won't compare with your sweet potato pie, but it's something different."

"You didn't have to bring anything."

"I know, but I—"

"So. You did show up. I was wondering if you'd have the nerve."

"Bob, be nice." Mrs. Miller lifted the top of the cake box. "Look what Jeff brought."

"Are you trying to buy me off?"

"I know that's impossible."

"Just so you realize it."

"Come on in. I'll put this in the dining room." She looked at her husband. "Play nice while I'm gone."

"I don't know what to say. I'd say I'm sorry and that I didn't mean to hurt Sheila, but neither of those is enough. I know that no words can take away the hurt that I caused."

Dr. Miller stared at him. "Marie invited you, so you may as well come on into the family room."

Jeff followed him.

"Don't just stand there. Sit down."

Jeff sat on the edge of the chair. He felt like a kid sent to the principal's office.

"If I had it to do over, I would do things differently."

"Hindsight is always perfect." Mrs. Miller came in and sat beside her husband.

"You hurt her so bad."

"I know." Jeff stared at the carpet. "The job with the space program was important to me. I had always dreamed of it." He shook his head. "I don't know if I would have gone if I had known that it meant losing Sheila." He shrugged. "I figured that after she had time to think about it, she'd change her mind." He sighed. "Then I came home for Mom's funeral and Sheila introduced me to her fiancé."

"Bill is a nice guy," Dr. Miller said. "I thought he'd be the one to make her happy." He stared at Jeff. "Sheila broke the engagement a few weeks after you left again. He's married to somebody else now. They have a son."

"She wouldn't have been happy. Neither would he." The grandfather clock in the hall tried to fill the silence left by Mrs. Miller. "If something is not meant to be, it won't be, no matter how much you want it." She turned to her husband. "Don't you agree, honey?"

"She was hurting so bad for so long. It took a long time before she got over it. Now here you come back to hurt her all over again."

"I won't hurt her again. I love her."

"Be honest, Bob. She never got over it. She tries hard. Sometimes she goes for a long time looking happy, but then the pain shows in her eyes and I know she's remembering. We can't shelter her from this. She has to work through it for herself."

Again the clock took over the conversation. It added chimes to fill in empty spaces, trying to cover up for missing voices.

"Do you still play chess?"

"Not for a long time."

"Maybe I can beat you."

By the time the door opened, Jeff had lost two games and was working on the third.

"I know you're in here, because I smell the food."

Jeff knocked over the bishop he had been moving. It moved the knight out of place. It didn't matter.

"I hope it's ready. I'm starving." Sheila moved to the doorway of the family room. She had one arm out of her coat and looked as if she had forgotten how to take out the other arm. "What are you doing here?"

"Hi, sweetheart." Her mother kissed her cheek, but Sheila still stared at Jeff. "I invited Jeff to dinner."

"You didn't mention it at church."

"Give me your coat." Mrs. Miller slipped Sheila's coat the rest of the way off and folded it across her arm as if afraid Sheila would try to put it back on. "I guess it slipped my mind."

"Nothing ever slips your mind."

"First time for everything."

"It's your house. You can invite whomever you want." She glared at Jeff, then started from the room.

"Where are you going?"

"To help out in the kitchen like I always do." She looked at her mother. "That didn't slip your mind, too, did it?"

"Don't show off in front of company. Everything is just about finished. I'm just waiting for your brother and his family."

"I'll wait in the kitchen with you."

After a staring war they both left. Jeff hoped Dr. Miller didn't want to finish the game. He hoped even more that Sheila wouldn't come out, get her coat, and leave. He swallowed. If anyone left it would be him. This was her family. He was the outsider.

* * *

Sheila barely let her mother reach the kitchen. "Why did you do it, Mom? You knew I didn't want to see him. It's bad enough at school, but here . . ." She shook her head. "Why?"

"I don't know that you don't want to see him. I don't think that you know that either."

"Dad is playing chess with him. He's acting as if nothing ever happened. I don't understand you two."

"If you don't care about Jeff, you shouldn't mind that he's here. Just ignore him. If you can." She touched her daughter's arm. "Sheila, don't keep lying to yourself. It's impossible to make yourself like or dislike somebody." She sighed. "The feelings between you and Jeff went way beyond the liking stage."

"That was years ago. I'm not letting him hurt me again."

"I don't think that's what he has in mind."

"He didn't have it in mind before either, and look what happened."

"Do you intend to stay stuck on what happened so much that you're not open to what might happen?"

The door opened before Sheila had a chance to answer. It was okay. She didn't have an answer. She went to the door. She had never been so happy to see her brother before.

"Auntie Sheila, Auntie Sheila." Tonya and Tammy grabbed Sheila.

Jeff was glad the girls were there. They put a smile on Sheila's face, and she looked more like his Sheila. He stared at her. He had a long way to go before she was *his* Sheila again.

"Are you family?" Tonya—or was it Tammy—asked Jeff once they were seated at the table.

"No. I'm just a friend." Jeff smiled at the girl.

"Are you Aunt Sheila's boyfriend?" asked Tammy.

"Yeah, are you?" Tonya's question echoed her sister's.

"No." Jeff wanted to add "not yet."

"Too bad. She needs a boyfriend so she won't be lonely," Tammy said.

Mrs. Miller cleared her throat, Robert laughed, Cynthia snickered, Jeff stared at Sheila, and Sheila glared.

"Tammy, I am perfectly happy alone. Everybody doesn't need someone. Some people are happy alone."

"Don't you want to get married someday and have kids?" Tammy pushed.

"Yes, I do."

"Don't wait too long or we'll be too old to play with them," She wouldn't let it go.

"Eat your dinner, girls. Stop pestering Aunt Sheila." Robert couldn't keep the laughter out of his voice. "Maybe she's waiting until you girls are old enough to baby-sit."

"How old do we have to be to baby-sit?" Tonya took the lead.

Everybody laughed. Everybody except Sheila.

Jeff looked around the table. He felt as if he belonged again. It had been a long time, but he remembered. He listened to the conversation, content to just be a part of this once more. It might be his last chance. Sheila was sure to try to talk her mother out of inviting him again. He'd enjoy this time.

"How are you making out with the plans for your program?" Mrs. Miller brought Jeff into the conversation. Everyone listened as he explained what had happened so far—even Sheila.

Robert suggested a site for an office. "I don't know if it's what you have in mind, but you might want to take a look."

They were still discussing the program when Sheila

and her mother put the desserts on the table. Mrs. Miller gave Jeff credit for the cake.

"You must have talked to Dad. He raves about this cake to anyone who will listen," Robert commented.

"No. I remember how much he liked it."

"I said he was trying to butter me up." Dr. Miller stared at Jeff.

"It must have worked." Robert laughed. "He's still here."

"The cake didn't have anything to do with it." Dr. Miller took the plate from Sheila. "I'm glad he brought it, though."

Laughter skipped around the table.

"Want to come ice-skating with us, Mr. Hamilton?" Tonya asked.

"Yeah, every Saturday afternoon Aunt Sheila takes us ice skating at Penn's Landing. Want to come?" Tammy leaned forward.

"Do you know how to ice-skate? If you don't, me and Tammy can teach you."

"I'm sure Mr. Hamilton has a busy schedule for Saturday." Sheila stared at him.

"Not at all." Jeff stared back. I'm free all day Saturday." As soon as he got home he'd reschedule whatever he had planned. He looked at Tammy. You never could tell where your help was coming from. "Yes, I can ice-skate. Your Aunt Sheila and I used to go every chance we got."

The other adults at the table divided their stares between Jeff and Sheila as if a tennis match were in progress.

"Do they ice skate in Houston? Do they have ice skating rinks?" asked Tonya.

"Probably so, but I never went skating there. I never seemed to have time."

"Maybe you forgot how to." Sheila looked as though

she thought he wanted an out. She must be out of her mind.

Before he could answer, Tammy answered for him.

"Daddy said you never forget how to do something like that."

"I think your daddy is right. We'll see on Saturday."

"You can ride with us," Tammy offered. "Aunt Sheila has room." None of the pictures he had seen of Cupid got it right; they didn't look anything like these two little girls.

"I'm sure Mr. Hamilton would like to drive his own car. He might have somewhere to go afterward."

She hadn't refused to let him go. He might as well push his luck a bit farther.

"I don't have anyplace to go afterward. It doesn't make sense to take two cars. You know how hard it is to park down there. Besides, we want to do all we can to save fossil fuel."

"What's fossil fuel?" Tammy asked and frowned.

Jeff was glad they had changed the subject before Sheila could push her separate cars idea. Now all he had to do was come up with an explanation in terms the girls could understand.

He started but had to back up until he got to a point where Tonya and Tammy understood the words. They had seen fossils in the museum, and a public television channel had done a special on dinosaur fossils. Jeff made a mental note to send the channel a generous donation. When he got to the fuel part and people's dependency on it, the girls were still with him.

"If we just turn off lights, that saves fossil fuel?" asked Tammy.

"That's right."

"And the TV, too?" Tonya asked her own question.

"That's right."

"And the radio?" Tammy asked.

"Um-hmm."

"And our Game Boy?" Tonya was not to be outdone.

"They use batteries," Tammy said.

"But fossil fuel is used by the factory that makes the batteries," their father added. He turned to Jeff. "I'm going to keep my fingers crossed. I've been trying to get through to them about saving energy. Looks like you did it." He laughed. "When we get our next electric bill, we'll throw a party with the savings and you can be the guest of honor."

"You're on."

Robert and his family left first. After kissing him on the cheek, the girls promised to be careful about fossil fuel and made him promise not to change his mind about going ice-skating with them. Jeff promised. He wanted to tell them that he wasn't the one they should be worried about. He was glad Sheila couldn't back out. She wouldn't disappoint the girls.

She got her coat from the closet. He followed her. "How do you want to do this on Saturday? Do you want me to drive to your house?"

"No. I don't want you to come to my house."

Her answer was so quick. Jeff frowned. She couldn't be afraid of him, could she? "You can come to me, then." She looked as if she were searching for a third choice.

She sighed. Finally she shrugged. "Okay."

She got as far as the door when he called her back.

"Now what?" The look she gave him was as sharp as her words. He tried not to let it hurt that she was so anxious to get away from him.

"You don't know how to reach me." He fumbled in his pocket, trying to find his business card before she found a way to explain to the girls why she had to back out. He didn't bother to ask for her phone number. Once she had been glad to give it to him. Now she'd just be glad to keep him away. Finally he found a card and handed it to her. "My phone number and the address in case you forgot how to get to the house." He stared at her. "That was a long time ago."

"Yes, it was. We were different people back then."

Several times when they were home from college, they had gone to the Wilsons' house in Sheila's car to give his mother a ride home.

"Give me a call when you're on the way."

She stared at the card as if she had to decide whether or not to take it. Finally she did and he could breathe again.

She put the card into her pocket and left without looking at it or him again. He smiled. She hadn't left early. And he would see her three times next week.

"Doggone those girls." Sheila frowned as she pulled away from the curb. "I love them, but right now . . ." She shook her head. "I have to talk to Robert and Cynthia. Those kids read too many fairy tales about happily ever after." She turned onto Stenton Avenue. "They even have me talking to myself."

She swallowed hard. There had been a time when she had believed in happily ever after—when she thought she had found her Prince Charming, more handsome than any picture in a book of little kids' stories. She sighed. Then she had learned, the hard way, the difference between fantasy and reality.

It was bad enough that she had to face Jeff on Mondays and Wednesdays. Now, thanks to Tonya and Tammy, she had to see him next Saturday, too.

She drove into a spot in the parking lot. If only things were different. If only she were brave enough to take a chance. If only she could see into the future before she risked her heart again. If only there were a way to make "if only" come true.

It was a given that he would ask her to skate with him. He'd put his arms around her and she would have to do the same with him. That was the way it was done now. Couples didn't skate side by side the way they used to a long time ago. Sheila was grateful for modern conveniences and considered many changes to be for the better. Skating close with someone you were still trying to get over wasn't one of them.

She didn't want to think about being close enough to Jeff to feel his heartbeat. She didn't want to imagine being in his arms again. She didn't want her mind to settle on how his muscles would bunch and contract beneath her hands as they skated in movements as synchronized as other, more intimate movements between a man and a woman.

She got out of the car and unbuttoned her jacket. Maybe the cold air would ease the tension that the things she would not think about were causing. Her breasts tightened and ached. The cold air had nothing to do with it. Neither could it be blamed for the heat that settled in parts of her body that ached for Jeff's touch.

She went into the apartment. Why didn't he hurry up and leave again, as she knew he was going to do? Why was he still here, causing her to remember things she wanted to forget?

Fifteen

Monday morning brought precipitation that couldn't decide if it wanted to be rain or snow. The sun hid behind thick gray clouds as if it didn't want to have anything to do with anything. It was beautiful. He was going to see Sheila again today. And on Wednesday. And again on Saturday.

Many times he had been told that he was lucky he hadn't set his heart on being a singer, but this morning he sang during his breakfast. He paused his singing during his workout and smiled instead. The only problem he had to figure out was how to go slowly with Sheila and be content with talking when what he wanted more than anything else was to skip the words and get to the showing. He wanted to take her in his arms and try to make up for the eleven years of loving they had missed. He set the treadmill incline up another notch and increased his speed. Maybe going faster would make his imagination slow down. His smile crept back. Or maybe not.

His singing came back during his shower. He stopped only when he had an interview with a woman who wanted to clean for him. Mrs. Miller had recommended Jean Marshall, a member of her church. He could have gone with an agency, but he wanted the person doing the work to get all of the money.

He hired her and she agreed to start tomorrow and come every Tuesday and Thursday. Jeff watched her leave. He hoped she was as good and trustworthy as Mrs. Miller said. He wasn't in any frame of mind to make judgment calls this morning. He was going to see Sheila in—he looked at his watch—in too many hours. He shook his head to try to clear it. He had some work to do and it was too important to mess up.

He visited the suggested office spaces and decided on the one that Robert had recommended. It was the right size and close to the bus stop. One of the back rooms was large enough for his committee meetings, and the other was perfect for his office.

He signed the lease to start next week, made arrangements to have the space cleaned and prepped, and went back home. Then he started the process of finding a secretary. He tried to force his mind to stay on each résumé and not on a soft face with a smile that could make him forget his own name, but every now and then Sheila's smiling face came back as if promising him another chance.

When that vision came, he stopped what he was doing and let himself believe that this Christmas held magic for him. After her face faded, he got back to work more hopeful than before.

By the time two o'clock came, he had completed more paperwork and had been sitting watching the clock for twenty minutes. He smiled. He was probably the only person who watched the clock because he wanted to *go* to work.

"Hey, Mr Hamilton. What's up?"

Jeff stood in the hallway outside the classroom door, trying not to look as eager as he felt. "Nothing much, Tyrik."

"Ask me the same thing." Tyrik looked as if someone had told him that he could have an excused absence for the rest of the week.

"Okay. What's up?" Jeff smiled at him.

Tyrik pulled a paper from his notebook. "Look at that. That's what you helped me with. Fractions. I got all the fraction problems right."

"Congratulations, man." He offered a high five.

"Now I got a new problem. I don't understand the new stuff we started today."

"We'll fix that. You didn't understand fractions, either. Now look at you."

"Yeah. Now look at me." He grinned at the paper.

"Hey, Mr. Hamilton, I still got trouble." Amina came up to him with Kendra. "I thought I knew how to do fractions, but I messed up on the quiz. I need you to go over it again."

"Me, too." Santos frowned. "I don't see why I need this. They got calculators to do this stuff. At home I don't even have to cut a cake. My mom makes sure that the slices are even."

Jeff looked at the kids gathered around him. Today they looked like kids who needed his help.

"We'll see what we can do to help you guys."

One of the kids said something, but Jeff didn't hear it. His eyes were using all of his attention. He watched as Sheila came closer, and reminded himself that she was coming to tutor the kids, not to see him.

"Hi." She stopped when she reached him, but only because he was standing beside the door. He didn't care why she stopped. She was here. She tried not to look at him, but failed.

"Hi, Sheila." He wanted to ask her if she had missed him at least a little. He wanted to know if she had had trouble thinking about anything else after they left yesterday and during today except that they were going to be together.

"Wait till you see my math paper." Tyrik held out the same paper he had shown to Jeff.

Jeff smiled at Sheila. He didn't care that he had to share his time with her with twenty kids. At least not for now. She was here and so was he.

They went inside and Sheila started reviewing fractions and percentages. From their comments, many of the kids still had trouble with them. Jeff walked around checking and helping where needed.

He had to be content with the "hi" Sheila had given him in the hall, because she didn't say anything else to him. She spent her time in the half of the room where he wasn't. When she went to the chalkboard, she wrote a word problem. The kids started to groan before she finished. Jeff smiled. Kids hadn't changed. If he didn't know better, he would think these were the same kids in seventh grade when he was a student. He had always liked word problems. They were like puzzles. But he never told that to the other kids. They didn't call him "the Brain" for nothing.

"We have a few minutes. Let's look at probability." Sheila explained the concept and the kids asked questions.

"You mean if I flip a quarter ten times and it comes up heads every time, there's still a fifty-fifty chance the next flip will be heads again?" Carla frowned.

Jeff wasn't sure that he wanted details about probability. What was the probability of him and Sheila getting back together? What were the chances that he'd ever get close enough to her to hold her in his arms, to feel her soft curves pressed against his hard body? What was the probability that they would love each other as completely as they had promised would happen when they ready? He was more than ready. He had been before he came home; he just hadn't realized how much until he saw her.

He made his mind back off from the image of Sheila wrapped in his arms, of him inside her. If he didn't, every kid in the room would see how ready he was.

He moved to the desk farthest from Sheila. Did the time factor have anything to do with their love probability? Were his chances less in proportion to the number of years that he didn't see her? Did the years of neglect have a negative or a positive effect? Had they made their love diminish or expand? Was there a way to factor in hopes and wants? They should count for something.

Jeff was still working on his own probability problems when Sheila asked for everybody's attention. Didn't she realize that she had his all along, even when they weren't together?

"Great session, everybody. See you next Monday. If you need to see me before then, you can find me here after classes."

Jeff wished she were talking to him. He let out a hard breath. Maybe it was just as well that she wasn't. If she tried to satisfy his need—which he hoped was her need, too—neither one of them would get anything else done.

"Come have a cup of something with me. Anything. I want to talk with you about . . . about the kids." He felt his hope peep out a bit.

"We already did that." She hadn't said no right away. She looked as if she were considering it.

His hope crept out a bit more. "I know, but I have some more questions. And we didn't talk about all of the kids. You name the place," he added. "It doesn't matter." He wouldn't suggest her house or his. She wasn't ready for that. Yet. "I really think it would help if I knew more about the kids."

"The weather is so bad." She glanced at the slanting sleet that was coming down as if it had just started.

"We'll go to a place where we can park near the entrance. We won't get too wet. I'll let you off at the door."

Her face told him about the battle going on inside her. He hoped his side won. He wished he could think of words to reinforce his side.

"I guess you're right. It would help the kids if you knew more about them." She sighed as if it were a chore.

He looked for somebody to high-five with. He settled on smiling. "Where do you want to go this time?"

"Smoky Joe's is nearby."

"Good. I know where it is. I'll meet you out front."

"I think we should take separate cars."

"I don't want you to get wet. I can bring you back here for your car."

She shook her head. "No sense coming back here."

That was what he had expected her to say, but it didn't stop him from being disappointed. *Stop. She's going somewhere with you. Just the two of you. Take it.* "I'll see you there."

It wasn't hard leaving her because it was for only a few minutes.

"Tell me about Santos. And Amina."

They were seated in a booth at the side. If he dared to, he could stretch his legs a little and touch hers. If he were dumb enough to try, he could easily reach her hands across the table. He could see if they were warm or if she was still looking for the perfect gloves. He could hold her hands and warm them the way he used to.

If he wanted to, he could look into the strip mall across the street. If he didn't have something better to look at.

He stared at her face, looking for signs of forgiveness

and wondering if she could see how he still felt about her.

"Don't look at me like that." Her words sounded as if she had trouble finding enough strength to push them out. *Good.*

"Like what?"

"You know." She stared at him as if she could see how he felt. "Like you used to when . . ." She took a deep breath and looked at the mall as if she intended to go shopping later, or was thinking about going now. ". . . when there was still something between us; when we thought we were in love."

Jeff stared at her. How could he make her see that there was still something between them? Not just a "something." It was love. They both felt it. It hadn't gone anywhere. It had waited for both of them to find it again. A lot of time had passed, but it was still there, waiting for a chance to spring back stronger than ever. All it needed was for both of them to give it a chance, for her to admit that it still existed.

"I can't help it, Sheila." He shook his head. "You know I could never hide my feelings. Especially for you—from you." She looked as if she wanted to leave. He looked for something to make her stay. "I'll try, okay?" He almost touched her hand, but didn't. "Tell me about the kids. Maybe if I know a little about them, I can find a way to help them understand the math concepts better."

Sheila hesitated. Then she gave him a little information about the background of each student and where she thought they first ran into trouble.

"They have trouble with the same concepts that most students do. These kids just need more time on the problems before they move to the next step."

She finished and Jeff wished they had more than

twenty kids in each class. He knew his time was over when she looked at her watch.

"I-I didn't realize it was so late."

"Almost dinnertime. Want to grab a bite to eat while we're here?" He didn't expect her to say yes, but he was disappointed when she didn't.

"No. I'd better go on home."

"Yeah." Jeff didn't ask if somebody was waiting for her to have dinner. He didn't want to know.

He didn't go home. He went shopping for office furniture. He didn't have as much trouble concentrating on what he was doing. He had new memories of Sheila, but she might be making newer memories with somebody else.

Tuesday he contacted the applicants interested in the job of secretary. Three of the résumés sounded promising, and he started with them. He made arrangements to interview the prospects on Wednesday morning. The furniture would be in place the next day.

He leaned back in his chair and put his hands behind his head. Wednesday afternoon he'd see Sheila. He shook his head. *Man, you're worse than when you first noticed her back in high school.* He smiled. He didn't care.

He checked his E-mail and talked Eric through the latest crisis. Maybe he had left too soon. He shrugged. It was done. He had business he had to straighten out here. Unfinished business. He shook his head. Sheila wasn't business. He had never been as emotionally involved with business as he was with her.

Wednesday he hired a secretary and explained her duties, moved some files into the office, did more paperwork, and wondered why time was reluctant to get to two o'clock. Finally, at five minutes to two, he gave up. So he'd wait a little longer outside her classroom.

He tried, during the whole tutoring session on percentages and probabilities, to think of an excuse to get Sheila to go out with him for coffee—or anything—again today. What was the probability of that happening again? It didn't seem as high as Carla's fifty-fifty. If he could think of a good reason, would it increase his chances? Did probability have anything to do with a situation like this? He failed to think of an excuse so that he could test it.

The session ended and they left, she eager to get away from him, and he reluctant to see her go. He wouldn't see her again until Saturday. Saturday.

On the way home he turned to a station playing Christmas songs. When the one about New Year's Eve came on he didn't let himself think about spending it with Sheila. They hadn't gotten close enough again for him to hope for even Christmas together. "You're All I Want for Christmas" started playing, and he wished he could sing it to Sheila. He wished he could imagine, if he could sing, that Sheila would listen and believe him and sing the same words back.

Was there a song about Christmas wishes coming true?

Sixteen

Saturday. Beautiful Saturday was here. Jeff got out of bed as if he were late for an appointment instead of hours early. Anticipation rode his treadmill with him, as if he needed its company instead of that of the woman he was determined not to lose a second time.

He fixed breakfast for one and sat down, looking forward to the time when Sheila would be sitting with him. He didn't look down until his fork scraped against his empty plate. He smiled. He hadn't tasted a single bite. He leaned back and folded his hands behind his neck.

He had accomplished a lot this past week, but he still had a lot more to do. The office was open and the secretary was working. He had looked at houses, but he still had to look at them inside to see if they were acceptable. The new board agreed that, because he wanted some families in their new homes by Christmas, he would select the first ones himself.

He let out a hard breath. There was one part of the program that he wasn't looking forward to: he had to screen and interview the candidates for the houses. He intended to have five families in homes by Christmas and five more soon after. A lot more would have their hopes denied. He shook his head. He had to focus on the ten.

When he told people of his timetable, several of them

had told him that he was being too ambitious, that he needed to be more realistic about the amount of time it took to make a program like this operational. Jeff smiled. If he had listened every time somebody told him that, he'd be . . . Where? Right here in Philadelphia working at one of the refineries, drawing a decent salary and married to Sheila? A frown moved onto his face.

Eric and Paula were expecting their second child. They had already asked him to be the godfather again. If he had stayed in Philadelphia, would he and Sheila have children? Was the trade-off of staying here instead of having his work in Houston so bad?

He'd have a lot less money, but it was never about money. That wasn't why he left. He thought he'd find something he was looking for somewhere else. He couldn't even define it. How did he expect to recognize it when he found it?

If he hadn't gone, there'd be no program. He couldn't afford to fund it if he had to work for somebody else. He shrugged. Someone else would have come along.

He tried to put the houses he would visit in a logical order, but he was short of logic this morning. He continued because he had to do something to help time move along. He expected to have to make a lot of changes in the order when he could think better—when his mind wasn't spending more time and energy on what he was waiting for instead of what he was supposed to be doing.

Sheila was coming at one o'clock, but Jeff had been ready since he got up. He started to put on his coat to wait, but changed his mind. If he did, she wouldn't have a reason to come in, and that would mean that much less time he had to be with her.

He jumped up when the buzzer sounded, announcing that somebody was at the gate. He ran to the intercom as if he were afraid that Sheila would change her mind.

He buzzed her in and then rushed to the door as if he were a kid waiting for somebody to bring him a present. He smiled. She wasn't bringing a present; she *was* a present. He tried to be casual when he opened the door, but failed. He didn't care.

"Are you ready?" She stood as if poised to run if he said the wrong words.

"Come on in."

"I don't think—"

"Cool house, Mr. Hamilton." Tammy moved in front of Sheila. "Can we see inside?"

I have to make sure I get her the biggest of whatever she has on her Christmas list.

"Sure, come on in."

Sheila shook her head, but she stepped in after the girls.

"This is a big house. Do you live here by yourself?" asked Tammy.

"I do for now. I hope I have a family to share it with someday." He stared at Sheila. "I want a wife and children. This is too much house for me."

"Why not just get a smaller house?" Sheila's stare challenged his.

"It would be a lot more fun having a wife and family to share this one—a wife to love, kids with her." Jeff met her challenge. He watched as hunger on her face pushed her anger out of the way.

"Maybe you'll have girls like us. We could play with them," Tammy said.

"Yeah," Tonya said. "I don't think Aunt Sheila is ever gonna get married."

"Don't give up on her; there's still time. She could still have kids."

Maybe it was his imagination, but he thought he saw her hunger get stronger. Was she thinking about how kids were created and imagining creating one with him? He let himself think so.

"She doesn't even have a boyfriend. How can she have kids if she doesn't even have a boyfriend? Do you have a girlfriend?" Tammy wouldn't let it rest.

"I'm working on it. I have someone in mind." It wasn't his imagination that he saw desire flare up in her eyes.

"We . . . we should be going. The . . . the longer we wait the harder it will be to find parking."

"Last week we saw a whole lot of empty spaces. Remember?" Tonya's wide eyes stared at Sheila.

Jeff laughed. Sheila glared at him.

"There might be a special program going on in that area. We need to leave now."

Jeff got his coat and followed them out. He didn't mind leaving. He was going with Sheila.

Jeff followed the girls to a bench facing the ice. Skaters were spinning, racing, circling in groups, or just trying to make it across the ice. Jeff hoped he wasn't going to be in the last group.

"Be right back." He went to rent skates. He thought about buying a pair, but he decided to wait and see how today went. Sheila might not invite him to come with them again, and then the skates would just be proof of his failure.

He took his skates to the bench where Sheila and the girls were waiting, sat down, and put them on. He hoped it wasn't a myth that skating was like riding a bike: once you knew how you never forgot. How could he hope to hold her while they skated together if he couldn't stay on his feet?

"When we grow up, we're going to skate in the Olympics and win medals," Tammy predicted.

"Yeah," Tonya agreed. "We'll be the first twins to win

gold medals." She smiled. "We're gonna tie, so they'll have to give medals to both of us."

"Then we'll stand and pledge allegiance while they play the national anthem." She stood straight with her hand over her heart.

"Watch." Tammy skated a few feet from the bench and did a spin. Tonya followed. "We need a lot more practice first, though."

Jeff watched them. Then he scanned the ice. A few of the skaters looked barely old enough to walk. He took a deep breath. If kids could do this, he could, too.

"See you later." Sheila smiled at him. Any other time he would be happy to see her smile. Right now he was just worried about staying upright. He watched her skate away from him. She turned and skated backward, waved good-bye, and skated across the ice.

Her heavyweight sweater and slacks weren't tight—not nearly as tight as his pants were becoming on him. He shook his head. If she knew how often she made his thoughts center on her and what he wanted to do with her—to her—she'd make sure she was never within his sight again. He squirmed, but never took his gaze off her. She stopped at the girls and bent down to tell them something. She was across the ice, but the sight of her rounded, tight behind shot heat through Jeff, and he nearly exploded. Skating wasn't the only way to get warm at the skating rink; sometimes what you saw and your imagination were all that was needed. His hands itched to brush across her cute bottom—slowly, as if touching it for the first time, as if afraid it would disappear from him.

Sheila did a spin with the girls. He had forgotten how graceful she was. And how she could fill a sweater. She raised her arms over her head, and he wished she would slow down so he could take his time looking and wishing he were allowed to mold her breasts to his hands the way he remembered. A couple skated past and, in order to keep from splintering, Jeff forced his gaze from Sheila and to them. He watched them move as synchronized as a pair of ballroom dancers. He and Sheila had once moved together like that—sometimes on the ice.

He hadn't come to watch. He wasn't going to miss this opportunity to hold Sheila in his arms, even if it was full daylight and they'd be in view of everybody and he had to limit his hands to her hands and her back.

He stood carefully, but held on to the back of the bench. Eleven years was a long time to expect knowing how to skate to stay in his mind. Remembering how to ride a bike was easier. You were seated and you got to stay seated. You had real brakes. And everybody wasn't watching you. He could do this. He took a deep breath and left the safety of the bench.

After one lap around the rink during which everybody—including a little kid who looked like she was a year old, and a man who looked like he was one hundred and one—skated past him, Jeff found in his memory the directions for how to skate.

Halfway into his second lap he went over to the girls. He smiled as he pulled his feet together in a stop. It was true, it was just like bike riding.

"Hi, Mr. Hamilton. We saw you. We have to tell Daddy that he was right about remembering how to skate." Tammy skated a little circle in front of him. "Want to go around with us one time?"

"Sure, ladies. It will be my pleasure." They giggled as Jeff took their hands and they circled.

"Let's go over to Aunt Sheila. She's all by herself. She probably needs some company." Tammy pulled him in that direction—not that he needed any pulling.

"Good idea."

"I bet she's lonely." Tonya pulled his other hand. He

smiled. It was a good thing they were pulling in the same direction.

They reached Sheila just as the announcer called a couples-only skate.

"I couldn't ask for any better timing." He stared down into her eyes.

"Are you sure you're up to this?"

"We'll wait for you on the bench." Tammy and Tonya held hands and moved across the ice. Jeff barely glanced at them. Sheila seemed as if she hadn't even heard them.

"I'm always ready for an opportunity to hold you in my arms."

"It's been a long time." She stared at him.

"Too long. We need to do something about that." He held out his arms, and she moved a bit closer. Not long ago she had found a mint somewhere. He wished she would share it with him. Sunlight slanting over his shoulder gave her face a golden glow. He took a deep breath. Maybe the sunshine didn't deserve all of the credit.

"I'm talking about ice-skating." She sounded as if she had raced around the rink a dozen times without stopping.

"I'm not." He slipped his gloves into his pockets, then eased hers from her hands. "I want to touch you."

"Yes."

He eased her against his body, and his muscles remembered how to fit themselves to hers. She nestled close, as if her body remembered, too. She brushed her hands against his chest, and he wished he had worn a less bulky sweater. Her hands stopped searching and rested side by side. His heart leaped out to meet the hand settled over it and sped faster than any music.

They were in the second circuit before she eased her head against his chest. He smiled and placed his chin on the top of her head. Then they moved around the rink as if only a minute had passed since they were last in each other's arms like this. His leg muscles bunched and stretched, and hers followed as if she knew his moves before he did.

Too soon the music stopped. Jeff had no idea what the song had been, but it was perfect, except that it was too short.

Jeff still moved as if the music played on. If he kept moving, maybe she wouldn't notice that it had stopped.

"We'd better go to the girls." The words slipped out, but Sheila didn't move away as soon as she said them. Did she really sound sorry the song had ended, or was his imagination kicking in again?

"Yes." He didn't move.

She eased away a little bit, but gazed into his eyes. A frown marred the smoothness of her forehead. Jeff reached to smooth it. Her breath caught, but she let him glide his finger over her forehead. She didn't step away, so he traced one eyebrow and then the other. Still she stood close, so he allowed his hand to stroke down the side of her face. She didn't leave him, so he dared to trace a finger around the mouth that he ached to touch with his own. She gasped but waited, so he feathered his finger first over the fullness of her lips and then back along the crease. She moaned his name, and her warm breath against his finger shot heat through his body as if a stack of wood were inside waiting for this spark.

He lowered his head toward her slowly so she could move hers away if she wanted to, but he hoped she wouldn't. He almost made it when she skated back a step, leaving room for reality to appear.

"Let's go to the girls." She didn't sound as if she wanted that any more than he did.

Jeff held her hand, because that was all she would allow him to touch now. They glided over to the bench. A few seconds more and he would have . . . He tried to let deep breaths cool him. A few seconds more and everybody would be trying to ice skate in water. His need for her was stronger than ever.

He tightened his hold on her hand and she didn't pull away. They reached the bench before she eased her hand from his.

"That was beautiful. You looked like the ice-dancing couples in the Olympics, and they practice all the time," Tammy said.

"Yeah. They been skating together forever and this was the first time for you, but it didn't look like it. Maybe you should try out for the Olympics. You could win gold medals when we do," Tonya added.

"Maybe we'll think about it." Jeff smiled at them.

"Want to go around one more time with us, Mr. Jeff?" Tammy asked.

"Mr. Jeff?" Sheila questioned Tammy.

"Yeah. We decided that Mr. Hamilton is too long." Tammy looked at Jeff. "Is that all right?"

"That's fine."

"You and Aunt Sheila looked perfect together," Tonya smiled dreamily.

"Yeah. You look like you belong together—like in a fairy tale about ice-skaters." Tammy's smile was just as dreamy.

"Maybe that's because we do belong together." His stare dared Sheila to disagree.

She stared back at him, but she didn't deny it. Then she looked at the girls. "You'd better go before the music ends."

"I'll be back," Jeff told her. "Hold my place for me. I'd like to pick up where we left off." He stared for a second longer before he let the girls pull him onto the ice.

* * *

Sheila watched as they skated away from her. It had felt too right being in Jeff's arms for her to deny it to herself. If only she could believe that things could be all right between them; if only she could turn back time and see if she could make it come out right this time.

She shook her head. He'd still go to Houston and she'd still stay in Philadelphia. Neither one would give up the plans they had made. She sighed.

But it was wonderful to get lost in his arms once more. Today felt even better than at the party. She sighed. She got warm just thinking about it. If she let her mind stay there, she'd have to take off her sweater. She still loved him. And she wanted him more than ever. They weren't kids anymore, but her love had survived all these years no matter how much she had tried to ignore it, forget it, deny it.

Maybe she should forget about the past and deal with the present. Jeff was here now. He didn't have any real reason to come back unless it was because of her. He had bought a house and started a community project that needed him. Maybe he really was back to stay forever. Eleven years had passed, but the same amount of time had passed for her, too. Maybe he still loved her as much as she loved him. He definitely wanted her as much as she wanted him. He had made his feelings obvious since he got back. She had seen it in his eyes even when he thought she was married.

She had made a comfortable life for herself. She couldn't complain. A lot of people were worse off than she was. She smiled.

Still, I wouldn't mind a little Christmas miracle about now.

Seventeen

The four of them skated together, and Jeff and Sheila skated with each of the girls, but Jeff and Sheila didn't skate alone together again. Jeff was disappointed, but he had to admit that it was for the best. He wouldn't have been satisfied with holding her close and just skating. If she had let him kiss her, he still wouldn't have been satisfied. He wanted more; he needed more. He had needed more when they were younger. So had she, but they had managed to hold off. They had decided to wait until they were sure they were ready to deal with everything that went with sexual intimacy, and that was best for them at the time.

They were older now, able to handle all that went with being as close as a man and woman could get to each other. And he was way past ready. He shook his head slowly. A heavy sigh escaped him. He wasn't sure if Sheila wanted anything with him anymore. She was fighting against it every chance they got to be together. Had his chance come and gone before he realized how badly he needed it?

"Time to go." The sun was spreading pink lines across the sky over the river when Sheila called an end to the day. Everybody was ready. Even the girls were half-hearted in their protest.

"Today was fun." Tonya hugged Sheila and then Jeff.

"It's always fun with you, Aunt Sheila," Tammy added, "but it was more fun with Mr. Jeff here with us. You have to come with us next week, Mr. Jeff."

"Yeah, you have to come." Tonya looked up from changing from her skates to her boots. "Right, Aunt Sheila? We want Mr. Jeff to come next week."

Sheila didn't even glance at the girls as she kept busy adjusting her boots that she had already put on. "Mr. Jeff is a very busy man. We can't expect to take up so much of his time. I'm sure he has plans for next Saturday."

"My only plans are to come with you." He hesitated. "If that's all right with you." He looked at her and let his gaze wait for her to see it.

She glanced at him, then back to her skates. She stuffed them into the bag. "You can come if you want." She looked across the rink, then at the girls—everywhere except at him. "Let's get in the car."

"Yea." The girls sounded like they were practicing to be cheerleaders. They bounced in circles over to the car as if they were jumping on pogosticks.

"What's all of that for?" Jeff opened the door for them.

"We had a lot of fun with you. We had a partner to skate with just like the big kids." Tammy grinned.

"Yeah. Did you like having him with us, Aunt Sheila?"

Jeff decided to push his luck. "Yeah, did you, Aunt Sheila?"

"It was all right."

He laughed. He could live with that—especially since her body had told him exactly how "all right" it was.

The girls chattered away during the ride back to his house and he listened. What if they were a family? What if he and Sheila were going home from taking their kids ice-skating? You made choices and you never knew what effect they would have on your life years later.

They took Kelly Drive up to Mt. Airy, and Jeff promised to bring the girls to feed the geese that had taken up permanent residence along the Schuylkill River. The only stipulation he made was that Sheila had to come with them.

He had never wished for heavy traffic before. He had never seen the drives so empty. They reached his house too soon. Before Sheila could say good-bye, he turned off the engine and got out.

"How about some hot chocolate? We always had hot cocoa with marshmallows when we used to go skating. Remember?" He dared her to deny that it was fresh in her mind. He opened her door and stared at her.

Her eyes widened and she swallowed hard. "I remember."

He could tell that she remembered how the chocolate wasn't the only thing that had heated them up back then. The same memory still held heat for him. He had to find a way to replace the old memory with a new one. "Come on in."

"We'd like that. Can we help?" Tammy unfastened her seat belt and scrambled out.

"Yeah, Mommy lets us help make hot chocolate."

"Sure. Give me your coats."

He hung them up and waited for Sheila's, but she looked as if she wasn't sure whether she was going to take hers off. He held out his hand. Finally she slipped her jacket off and handed it to him. *One step at a time.*

"Come on. Let's get to work. We have some cooking to do." He led them to the kitchen.

"Is this rock?" Tammy patted her hand along the countertop.

"Yes, it's called granite."

"But it's smooth. I never saw a rock so smooth." Tammy rubbed across it.

"Yeah. Even at the shore the rocks are a little bit rough. And they're little." Tammy leaned closer to the counter.

Jeff explained about quarries and the smoothing process. Then he got out the things they needed.

"Where are the little envelopes?"

"We're going to make real hot cocoa. It's more complicated than the cocoa in cnvelopes, so I really need your help." The girls moved closer to him.

Sheila watched as he handed them what was needed. He was patient as he answered their questions as they measured and mixed. They even got a short story about cocoa. He let them taste the powder when they asked to. Sheila laughed with Jeff at the looks on their faces when they put the bitter cocoa on their tongues and agreed that they'd better use a lot of sugar.

Jeff would make a great father. If things hadn't gone bad between them, they could be here with their kids. Sheila didn't pull her thoughts away from that possibility, as she might have done even a few weeks ago. She didn't question the reason why she didn't, either.

"Do we have marshmallows? We like lots of marshmallows."

"Of course we have marshmallows. You can't make a decent cup of hot chocolate without marshmallows." The girls giggled.

"Daddy said we use so many marshmallows that we don't leave much room for the hot chocolate."

"We like it real sweet." Tammy put four marshmallows into her mug; then she passed the bag to Tonya, who did the same before passing the bag to the grown-ups.

"We like sweet things." Tammy said, and Tonya nodded. They stirred their cocoa, then tasted it.

"I like sweet things, too." Jeff dropped a couple of marshmallows into his cup and held the bag out to Sheila.

She wrapped her fingers around it, but he didn't let go. Finally she looked at him.

"I like some sweet things better than others." He wasn't talking about food, and Sheila knew it.

Sheila quit tugging on the bag. She looked as if she had forgotten that it was there. She let go and Jeff took the bag.

"Do you still like it the same way?" He smiled as she gasped. Her gaze darted to the girls, who were busy talking and giggling. Then she looked back at him. He smiled. "I mean the cocoa, of course. Do you still like three marshmallows?"

"Yes." She took a deep breath. He held her stare as he dropped the marshmallows into her cup slowly, as if he wanted each to melt before he put in a new one.

Sheila blinked free and pulled her mug closer to her. She tried to ignore the drops that sloshed over the sides. She took her hands away, took a deep breath, and tried again. This time she managed to keep the cocoa in the cup.

Jeff had refilled the girls' mugs and emptied his own and Sheila was still stirring hers. "It's going to get cold."

"Huh?"

"Your chocolate isn't hot anymore."

"Oh." She drained her cup. "I think we'd better—"

"Come see the house."

"We'd better go."

"Just look at the downstairs."

"Can we? Please, Aunt Sheila?" Tammy tugged on Sheila's hand.

"Yeah, please?" Tonya pulled Sheila's other hand.

"Yes, please, Aunt Sheila?" Jeff smiled at her as he added his plea to those of the girls. "It won't take long."

"I'm outnumbered."

She followed him into the living room and den. He commented on some of the furnishings and she tried to listen to his words instead of how her body was reacting to the sight of him. His backside held as many memories for her as his front. She shook her head. Almost as many memories. She tried to breathe normally, but his arm muscles showed where they were whenever he picked up a piece of art and let the girls hold it. He had a lot of artwork. And they had to hold each piece. Sheila wasn't sure if she was glad or unhappy about that. The girls asked a lot of questions, especially about the African masks and statues. Jeff answered all of them. Sheila was glad the girls were with them. She didn't want to think about what might happen if she and Jeff were alone in his house with her mind asking for new memories to add to the old ones.

"That picture looks a lot like Sunday dinner at Grandma and Grandpop's." Tammy pointed to the painting on the living room wall.

Jeff smiled and nodded. "That's what I thought, too. That's why I bought it." He took their hands. "Come on. I want you to see something." He took them to window and pointed to the bird feeder. "The birds are probably in bed by now, but you have to come back sometime and see how many come to eat." He looked at Sheila. "Maybe Aunt Sheila will bring you to see for yourselves."

"Do you really live here all by yourself?" Tammy looked from the yard to him.

"I do for now."

"Don't you have any family?" Tonya's face held concern for him.

"Not anymore."

"Don't you get lonely?" Tammy touched his arm.

"Yes. Sometimes more than others." He looked at Sheila. He knew she could see the hunger in his eyes. He thought he saw a bit in hers, too.

"That's okay, Mr. Jeff." Tammy patted his arm. "You can borrow us. Mommy and Daddy won't mind sharing."

Jeff smiled at them. "That's very nice of you. I'll take you up on your offer real soon."

"We really have to go. I want to get home before that stuff freezes. We have had more snow this winter than we've had in years."

"Okay. I don't want you to have an accident."

He helped them on with their coats and watched them leave. They were still in the car in the driveway, but he missed them already.

He went to the kitchen to find something for dinner. How many hours until he could see her on Monday?

He had just finished in the kitchen when the phone rang.

"Hi, Jeff. I just realized that we didn't make it clear last Sunday that we expect you to have dinner with us tomorrow, too. Am I too late with my invitation?"

"Absolutely not, Mrs. Miller." Jeff leaned against the wall. He could barely talk, his smile was so wide. "You could have called after everyone was seated at the table and it still wouldn't be too late."

"How is Durham Middle School's new math tutor getting along?"

"The department head didn't ask me to leave yet. I think she's resigned herself to having me there. She would have preferred someone else—anyone else but me—but the kids need a tutor, and I'm the only one who applied for the job. As for me, I love my new job. The pay is nothing to talk about, but I couldn't wish for any-one better to work with." They both laughed.

"She didn't forget to pick you up for ice-skating, did she?"

"Tammy and Tonya wouldn't let her. If the girls want a couple of real stars for Christmas, I'll see that they get them."

"Did you remember how to skate, or did you have to watch?"

"One lap around, and it was as if I had been on the ice just the day before." He sighed. "The nice man played a couples-only skate, and Sheila didn't run from me." His whole body tightened and ached at the memory of exactly how much she hadn't run away. "The girls invited me to go with them again next week. Sheila didn't say no to that, either."

"Must be the Christmas magic kicking in. The big day is not that far off." She hesitated. "Maybe she finally came to her senses and realized that some things are important enough to risk giving them a second chance."

"I hope that's it, but I want this magic to last beyond Christmas. Forever might not be long enough."

"Seems like you're giving it time. Keep doing what you're doing. It's working. Remember: If it ain't broke, don't fix it, don't change horses in mid-stream, and all of those other clichés that apply."

"Yes, ma'am. Should I bring a chocolate cake again?"

"To quote you, absolutely not."

"Won't Dr. Miller be disappointed?"

"Probably, but he doesn't need it. That man would eat nothing but sweets if I weren't around to watch."

"I don't mind getting it."

"No. Then he'll expect you to bring it every week." She paused. "You do realize that this is a standing invitation, don't you?"

"I do now. Thank you. I'll see you tomorrow afternoon." He hung up. Yes. The urge to turn cartwheels came back. The only reason he didn't give in was because he never learned how back when the ground wasn't so far down.

Instead of risking breaking his neck, he closed his eyes and smiled. He didn't have to wait until Monday. He'd see Sheila tomorrow.

It was hard, but he pulled his thoughts away from tomorrow. He had a lot more work to do on the project. Except for when he wanted it to, time was racing as though it were a stone going down a steep slope.

He called to make sure that the furniture for the new houses needed only the final approval. He felt like a juggler at the circus. He had to coordinate houses, new owners, and whole roomfuls of furniture, and he had only about two weeks to do it.

When he turned off the light in his office, it was after midnight, but the piles of families and potential neighborhoods had been matched. The application form asked the families which neighborhood they preferred. Everybody listed at least one, but they all said that they would live anywhere if it meant having their own home. Still, Jeff tried to find homes close to their first choices.

On Sunday morning Jeff shoveled the new coating of snow that had fallen during the night. He didn't complain; he had a lot of paperwork to do, but he was glad for some physical work.

He smiled. He could think of a different kind of physical activity that would be most enjoyable. He shoveled harder. His mind stayed on that track as if it were stuck.

He and Sheila in his bed, in her bed, on the carpet in front of the fireplace; he and Sheila anywhere as long as she was in his arms holding him the way she used to, loving him the way they had promised to do when they were ready. He and Sheila making love.

He ran out of walkway. Would they come and take him away if he started on the street? He went back inside before he found out. That was just what he needed: to be locked up somewhere for observation when he should have been sitting next to Sheila.

He sifted through the potential houses again and sorted them according to real-estate companies. Then he made arrangements to look at the first group after he went to school on Monday, and at other groups on Tuesday and Wednesday. Thursday he'd meet with the final families. By the end of the week, he hoped to have selected at least four houses for the program. If he didn't have five, it was okay. The fifth family wouldn't know.

He had conference calls with the board members to keep them informed of the progress and to discuss the families that he had in mind.

The director of one of the shelters suggested that they postpone the first official meeting until the first of the year.

"It seems more hectic than usual." She laughed. "Of course, it seems that way every year."

Most of the others were relieved to wait until after the holidays to meet. He had to reassure Reverend Marks, who asked if Jeff was sure that he wanted input from others rather than doing it all himself.

"I need all of you. I wouldn't have known where to start. You folks supplied names, neighborhoods, even furniture stores that would give us discounts. I definitely needed that, not to mention the network of workshops that our families need. I'll need your help in making decisions about the next families to be included, also. I picked the easy ones. The next will be harder. Don't quit on me."

Jeff hung up after the minister promised to remain on the board.

Finally it was late enough to go to the Millers' house. He remembered what Mrs. Miller had said about the cake, but he stopped at the bakery anyway. It would have been different if Dr. Miller had a medical reason to cut back on sweets. Everybody should be able to eat at least a little of a favorite dessert. He smiled as he put the cake into his car and drove to the house. Mrs. Miller would see to it that her husband didn't eat too much cake. And she would forgive Jeff for bringing it.

How would Sheila act? Did she know he was coming? Would she act as if the feelings between them hadn't come through yesterday? Would she act as if yesterday had never happened? He took a deep breath and went up the steps. She couldn't. She wasn't that good an actress.

He rang the bell and hoped he wouldn't witness Sheila's attempt at acting.

"Hi, Mr. Jeff." Tammy opened the door as if she had been standing in the hallway. "Grandma told us you were coming. We've been waiting for you. Didn't we have fun yesterday?"

"Let Mr. Jeff get into the house." Sheila came into the hallway. Had she been waiting, too? "Let me hang up your coat."

She didn't look as if she were sorry that he was there. Jeff handed his coat to her, and she didn't pull away when their hands accidentally touched. He let his gaze explore her face. She didn't look as if she had even tried to forget yesterday. Was magic at work or only acceptance of the inevitable?

"Hi, girls, Sheila." Was it yesterday that he had seen

her? It seemed like longer than that. How had he stayed away from her for eleven years?

"Everybody's in the family room. Come on in. I have to help Mom finish in the kitchen."

She didn't move. She didn't head for the kitchen; she didn't lead him into the family room; she just stood gazing at him as if she were back in his arms as she had been yesterday. That was okay. He was back there, too.

"Are we going into the room or what?" Tammy reminded him that he and Sheila were not alone. He didn't say so, but he'd rather have the "or what." He could think of a lot of pleasurable things to do that didn't involve going into a room with other people.

Tammy tugged on his hand, eliminating the "or what" possibilities. He handed the cake to Sheila and smiled. She moved as if she didn't want to leave him. It wasn't his imagination.

He sat and tried to discuss football with the others, but his mind was in the kitchen. He got up and went to find Sheila. The idea of women being the ones to finish preparing a meal was outdated. It was time to change it.

"I knew you would bring a cake." Mrs. Miller smiled at him.

"You're not angry about it?"

"A cake isn't important enough to get angry about." She kissed his cheek. "Thank you."

"What can I do to help?"

"We've got everything covered. You didn't have to come out here."

"I thought it was time to break tradition."

"The fact that Sheila is out here doesn't have anything to do with your decision, does it?"

"It has everything to do with it." His gaze locked with Sheila's.

Mrs. Miller looked from one to the other. "Let's get this food on the table before you two set my kitchen on fire. Jeff, you can take the breadbasket and butter. Sheila, if you think you can find your way to the dining room and can manage without dropping it, you can take the platter with the chicken." She looked at them again. "Come on, you two. You can stare at each other later. The food is getting cold."

Jeff managed to walk behind Sheila when they left the kitchen. He caught a whiff of her perfume. He could see the sensitive spot below her ear. He still wasn't close enough.

The girls chattered about ice-skating, and Jeff thought about one ice dance in particular. His leg brushed against Sheila's. She didn't move hers away.

"You should have seen Mr. Jeff skating with Aunt Sheila. They looked like the couples in the Olympics. I told them they ought to try out."

"Yeah. They can win gold medals, like me and Tammy will."

"What's so funny?" Tammy asked when everybody laughed.

"The idea of me and your aunt Sheila in the Olympics."

"Wouldn't you like to skate in the Olympics? Wouldn't you like to win a medal?"

"I'm happy just to skate with her." Jeff looked at Sheila, who looked back at him.

The conversation stopped.

"It's like that, huh?" Robert asked.

"I hope so."

"If you two stop looking all moony-eyed and pass the food, we can eat before the game comes on," Dr. Miller said. "Please pass the potatoes. Marie won't let me have dessert until I eat my dinner, and I understand that you brought another chocolate cake this week."

"What does 'moony-eyed' mean?" Tammy asked.

"You'll find out when you're older," her mother said.

"A whole lot older," Robert said.

They finished and went back to the family room. They watched the game, and comments flew with each play.

Jeff had no idea who was winning, and he didn't care. Sheila was sitting beside him. He didn't dare hold her hand—not yet. He tried to be satisfied just feeling the length of her leg against his. From time to time she reacted to a play and the pressure on his leg increased, which caused the pressure on his body to increase. He had to work hard not to moan whenever that happened; still, he was sorry when the game ended. If Dr. Miller hadn't mentioned the win, he would have had no idea of the outcome. He was working on an outcome more important to him.

He left when Sheila did and walked her out. A cold wind that only winter could bring was blowing, but he wished her car were parked farther away.

"Today was great."

"Yes." She pulled her hood farther up on her head.

"But not as great as yesterday. I only felt your leg against mine today. Yesterday the whole length of our bodies was touching."

The color that spread over her face wasn't caused by either the weather or the wind.

"I have to go." She held her keys, but she didn't unlock the door.

"Me, too." He stared at her mouth. He didn't even remember where his keys were. And he didn't care.

He lowered his mouth to hers. She waited for him. Then she tilted her face up just a little, just enough.

He brushed his lips across hers and pulled back. He'd have to be satisfied with that for now.

"See you tomorrow."

"Definitely." He opened the door for her and waited for her to get in. "Drive carefully."

"You, too."

"How many hours until tomorrow?"

She laughed at his question and drove away.

He was serious.

Eighteen

Jeff awoke Monday morning, but he didn't jump out of bed as he usually did. He folded his hands behind his head and smiled. This morning the lonely bed didn't remind him that Sheila had slept somewhere else last night. For the first time since he had come home, he allowed himself to believe that maybe, just maybe, there was a chance that he and Sheila had a future together.

Yesterday at her parents' house it had seemed as if they were back in college. The conversations showed that everyone was older: talk of children and grandchildren, discussions of jobs held instead of jobs planned for the future. Yesterday it had felt as if he belonged again.

Sheila had been softer toward him; forgiveness seemed to layer over her words and the way she acted toward him. She hadn't seemed uneasy or awkward. She hadn't shifted away when his leg brushed against hers at the dinner table and again when they were sitting on the couch. She might have even allowed him to lace his fingers through hers, if he had dared to try. He shook his head. As much as he wanted to, felt a need to, he hadn't tried for fear of losing the progress he was making.

His body tightened. He still felt a need, and not just to hold her hand. He wanted her—all of her. He wanted to trace his finger down her face and circle the dimple in her cheek.

First he'd use his finger to mark the way; then he'd follow the path with his mouth, his tongue tasting her sweetness. Next he'd stop at her ear and draw the lobe between his teeth and release it slowly. Whenever he used to kiss her ear, she would moan and tighten her hold on him. He needed to see if it still had the same effect on her. Then he would see if her breasts were still a perfect fit to his hands, if the tips were still as sweet.

His pajama bottoms were loose when he went to bed last night. This morning, after his fantasy with Sheila, he felt as if, while he was sleeping, somebody had slipped in and exchanged them for a pair two sizes smaller.

He forced himself to get up when he was tempted to stay and let his fantasy continue. Sweet as it was, it didn't satisfy his need. He wanted the real thing, not an imitation created by his imagination. He got dressed.

It didn't have to stay a fantasy. It could be a preview of what would come between them. He hoped it would happen soon. Now that he let himself believe that it was possible to get back together with Sheila, he was impatient for it to happen. He sighed. Little steps were almost impossible when you were ready for giant leaps.

He went to his office to weed out applicants for the last time. He had planned to place four families before Christmas, but changed his mind. Some of the families were equal in need and readiness, so he took the coward's way out: he decided to expand the initial group to include five families. He'd find a fifth house.

He placed the other applicants who seemed eligible in a file for the next group. The board could help with those. He probably should have let them help with these first ones, but he was determined that at least some of the families would have their homes for Christmas, and if he and the board had to juggle everybody's schedules, it would never happen.

He stopped for lunch and then started screening the houses on paper. The mechanics were time-consuming; he had to shuffle all of the houses and families to get a better fit, but he would rather have to find another house than to cut a family.

He called the realtor to confirm the time and place of their first visit that afternoon.

By the time he stopped work to go to school, he had only to visit the homes he thought would fit the program, decide on a few of them, and make offers. After going through his file another time, he was confident that he'd find the houses he needed. With three visits scheduled, he hoped to find more than enough houses to meet his requirements for the first group. He'd narrow the choices depending upon who accepted his offer first.

He nodded as he left the house. Things were moving ahead of the timetable he had set. He wouldn't meet with the families until he had the houses. He didn't want to risk having to tell anyone that they couldn't have a home after all. He smiled as he backed out of the garage. By the end of the week he expected to have closing dates for the houses. Unless something went drastically wrong, five families would celebrate Christmas in their new homes. On Friday he expected to schedule the meetings with the families for Monday. They could carry over to Tuesday, if necessary. He'd work around their schedules.

He frowned as he turned onto the street. At least his timetable for the program was ahead of schedule. His personal life was another story. He was impatient with the progress—or he should say lack of progress—with Sheila. She seemed to have thawed toward him, but things weren't moving fast enough. He shook his head. That wasn't true about a timetable. He was impatient, but he hadn't set a schedule concerning Sheila; he had decided that however long it took, it didn't matter as long as they ended up together. He sighed. He did wish, however, that things would move faster. It was hard accepting a thaw when he wanted a meltdown. He pulled out some patience.

He wasn't going to let disappointment crowd him. He was on his way to see Sheila. That counted for a whole lot. He hadn't seen her since yesterday. He smiled.

He was already happy when he waited outside the classroom for Sheila, but he had enough room for more happiness to come in. He was talking to some of the kids when he saw her coming down the hall. She stopped to talk with a couple of students along the way, and took time to look whenever they showed her something. If she had to stop on the way to him, he was glad when she had her side to him. Then he could admire the way her gray skirt draped over her hips, the way her long-sleeved blouse fell away from her breasts before the edge of the blouse disappeared inside the waistband of her skirt. The blouse and skirt were a loose fit; his imagination was tightening them close to her body. It was also tightening his pants. He took a deep breath and thought about cold and blizzards. Adolescent males thought they were the only ones capable of reacting this way. He was glad he was holding a file folder. He lowered his hands in what he hoped was a casual move, until the folder was in front of the lower part of his body. Still he watched her come closer. He had never before realized how much he could welcome discomfort. His smile widened.

Finally she was there, standing in front of him. Her deep pink blouse added a warmth to her face. Jeff knew he wasn't responsible for the glow, but he wished he were. Maybe soon he could be—would be.

"Hi." He stuck his free hand in his pocket so he

wouldn't touch her. They weren't at that point. At least not yet. He smiled at her.

"Hi." She smiled, and he knew she was glad to see him—almost as glad as he was.

"Did you forget the key, Miss Miller?" Tyrik reminded them that they weren't alone.

"No." Sheila laughed as she opened the door. "Let's see how much you remember from last Monday."

Jeff watched as she went to the board. She hadn't been talking to him. He didn't have to reach back in his memory to Monday. He had only to go back to yesterday and there was no chance that he would forget it.

She wrote a few percentage problems on the board. Then she walked around the room as the kids worked, but not as she had last Monday or even on Wednesday. Today she didn't stay on her side of the invisible line dividing the room. Today, when she found herself near Jeff, she didn't rush away. Today, when she was close enough and their gazes met, she smiled at him instead of wishing he'd go away. When they brushed together— which wasn't often enough—she murmured an "excuse me," but she didn't seem in any hurry to break contact. Still, Jeff felt that she moved away too quickly; moving away from him at all was too quickly.

She looked at him as she walked back to the board. Today she was reluctant to put that much space between them. At least that was the way Jeff saw it. He believed her reluctance was real; his imagination couldn't have created it.

She reviewed the lessons of the past week and answered any questions the kids had.

"Anything else?" She looked around the room. The kids all shook their heads. "That's it, then. See you next week, same time, same channel."

Jeff watched the kids leave. Sheila was still there with him when the last one left. She stood behind the desk.

He took a deep breath and walked up to her, but he didn't get as close as he wanted. He couldn't get that close—not while they were in a public place.

"I know it's short notice and you're probably busy, but do you want to go with me now to look at some houses? For the program, I mean." He stared at her, willing her to agree to go with him. It didn't work.

"I can't. I have other plans."

"I thought so." He shrugged and hoped his hurt didn't show too much. "See you on Wednesday." He managed a slight smile. Even that was hard.

"I can go tomorrow, though, unless you're busy."

"Tomorrow? Yes. I mean no. I mean I'm not busy. I have to look at some more houses in the morning, but I'll be free by the time you get out of school. Or do you mean later than that? If you do, I can wait for you." He took time to breathe. "I can go whenever you say. You call it."

"After school is fine." She laughed. "Just now you sounded like you used to when you were excited about a new idea."

"There's no new idea involved here, just a long-overdue old one, but I can't begin to tell you how excited I am at the possibility."

"You know snow is predicted for morning." She stared at him. "There's the possibility of school being closed."

"They wouldn't dare do that to us."

"I hope not."

"You do?"

"Yes." She nodded.

"I have four-wheel drive."

"That's good to have in the winter."

"I can come to you even if you can't get to school."

"Yes, you can." A softness crept into her words. "I'd like that."

The bell rang and Sheila looked at the clock.

"I have to go." She came from behind the desk and stopped in front of him. "I'll see you tomorrow." She still held him with her stare.

"I'll be here." Jeff saw trust in her eyes. It wasn't big, but it was there. Hunger was keeping it company. What was the rule about kissing in school? Did it apply to faculty, too? What about one faculty member and a volunteer? Heat grew inside him. He leaned closer to her.

The heck with it. What would they do? Suspend them?

He closed the rest of the space and stood with the whole length of his body touching hers. Heat built. He didn't know if it was coming from her or from inside him. He didn't care. He lowered his mouth to hers and brushed his lips slowly, barely touching, across hers. Then he forced himself to step back.

She looked as sorry as he felt.

"Tomorrow." He touched a finger to his lips and then to hers. Then he did the hardest thing he had done in a long time: he walked away from her.

Sheila watched him go. Was she making a mistake in considering getting back together with him? She shook her head. She was way beyond the considering stage. It was no longer a question of if, but of when. She closed her eyes. Heat flooded her face. Man, he could still kiss. If his kiss had been deeper or longer they would have found a new use for her desk. She got just as lost as she always did when he held her, when he kissed her. She shook her head. He hadn't even been holding her. Only their lips had touched. Only their lips. And their bodies.

There wasn't anything "only" about Jeff. She wanted his arms around her more than she ever had. She wanted him to kiss her until she forgot where she was, who she was, that she was anything except the woman who loved him. She wanted him to love her until her need for him was satisfied. She wanted to explore his body to see if it was as glorious as she remembered. She formed her hands into fists, hoping that would make the ache to touch him go away.

He hadn't been back long, but it was beginning to seem as if he had never gone away.

She sighed and left the room, got halfway down the hall, then went back for her folder. She got as far as her door this time before she realized that the key was back in the classroom. She laughed. *I've got it bad. I don't know yet whether that's good or not.*

She went home trying to decide how she felt about not being able to go with Jeff tonight. Would they have just looked at houses? Was she ready for more than that between them? Maybe it was good that she had a meeting this evening. It would give her time to decide exactly how fast she wanted this relationship to go. It was a given that it was going somewhere.

She'd see him tomorrow. She shook her head. No way was that enough time for her to think about anything.

Sheila was going with him tomorrow. Tomorrow. He should ask her to go to dinner with him afterward. No, he should make dinner for her. No. It was too soon for that. It might scare her off. They'd go out to dinner. That was it. He'd call her and make sure she didn't have plans for later.

He let out a hard breath and slapped the steering wheel. He still didn't have her phone number. He turned around and went back to the school. He pulled into the lot, but it wasn't necessary. Only two cars were parked there, and neither was a blue Pontiac. First thing tomorrow when he saw her, he'd get her phone number. He shook his head. Second thing he'd get her number. First thing he'd do was kiss her—just a little kiss because the kids would be around, but he would kiss her.

He drove to the house where he would meet the real-estate agent, Nancy Crane. It would be a struggle, but he had to keep his mind on homes for other families and not on the possibility of having Sheila in his own home. At least not right now.

Later that evening Jeff stood outside the last house he was scheduled to see. After he was assured that the wiring, plumbing, and roofing had been inspected and certified and the houses were free of lead-based paint, he made offers on two of them.

"I'll let you know for sure," Nancy said, "but I'll be surprised if the owners don't accept your offer. These two houses have been on the market for quite a while. I'll let you know tomorrow. If it's okay, as soon as I hear I'll go ahead and schedule the settlements. I got a lot of cooperation in pushing through the title search and other necessary paperwork when I told them about the program. If you find your other three houses in the next day or two, let me know. We'll see if settlement can be done on all five at the same time."

Jeff searched for a station playing Christmas carols. He had several to choose from. Christmas was in the air, and more and more people were grabbing it. After being with Sheila today, he was feeling a bit Christmasy himself.

He called the family he had matched with one of the houses. Mr. Williams had been laid off from a refinery for a year and had just gotten a comparable job. His wife had been working two jobs trying to support the family, but with his unemployment, they had fallen behind in their bills and lost their apartment.

"I know it's late, Mrs. Williams, but I thought you wouldn't mind. I'm calling about your request to be included in the Homes for the Homeless program. I'd like to meet with you and Mr. Williams sometime on Wednesday, if that's convenient for you."

"Did we get rejected? Are you calling to say we've been cut? I know we're not out on the street, but we can't keep staying here with my mother. She loves us and she took us in, but with us and two of our kids, this little three-bedroom house is about to burst. Our other kids are staying with my sister halfway across the city." She hesitated. "We really do need a house. If there is anything else we have to do to—"

"Mrs. Williams," Jeff interrupted, "your family hasn't been cut from the program." He hesitated. He was about to break his own rule: don't promise until you have the house. *What the heck.* It was Christmas. He took a chance. "I think we found a house for you."

He had to hold the phone away from his ear, but he laughed. She sounded as if he had told her that she had won the lottery. She was laughing and crying at the same time.

"We got a house." It sounded as if a party were suddenly in full force around her. "You all hush now. I can't hear Mr. Hamilton." She laughed. "I don't know who's happier, us or my mother. You don't know how hard we've been praying for this. Our church's prayer band has been at work since we fell on hard times. Wait until I tell them that our prayers have been answered." Her voice broke at the end. She sniffed before she continued. "When do you want to see us? We can come anytime."

"I don't want anyone to miss work. You tell me. The time doesn't matter."

They scheduled the appointment for Wednesday night after Jeff assured her that he'd meet them at eight o'clock, since that was the earliest both of the Williamses were available. He called the Martin family next and got a similar reaction. Millie Martin had been recommended by the director of the shelter. She and her three children had been living there since their apartment building burned down. She was in the process of trying to save enough for the security deposit and the first and last months' rent needed to move in. She didn't want to stay in the shelter until her name made it to the top of the list for subsidized housing. She was trying to find her own way out.

She cried as soon as Jeff told her why he was calling. They scheduled a meeting for Wednesday after she got off from her job as a receptionist. She was still thanking him as he hung up.

Jeff smiled. He needed to thank the families for the joy they gave him. He had a better understanding now of why it was better to give than to receive.

Two down and three to go.

Jeff had barely hung up when the phone rang.

"Nancy Crane here. Congratulations. You are now the owner of not one, but two houses."

"You work long hours."

"I'm at home. I've been trying to reach you, but your phone has been busy. I didn't want you to have to wait until tomorrow for the good news. I know how important this is to you. First thing tomorrow I'll schedule the settlements."

Jeff thanked her and hung up. Sometimes even an amateur could juggle successfully.

He tried to do some more work, but quit when he realized that he'd just have to redo it all tomorrow. He smiled. Tomorrow. He was going to see Sheila again tomorrow. His smile widened. Not just see her: she was going out with him. He shrugged. It was only to look at houses, but if he didn't mess up, maybe she'd go to dinner with him afterward. Maybe after that . . . He shook his head. *Don't anticipate too far. It's dinner. That's all.* He smiled. *For now.*

Nineteen

Tuesday morning Jeff got out of bed and looked out of the window. Just enough snowflakes were falling to remind anyone who might have forgotten that it was still their season. He wondered how many people besides him were glad that this hadn't been declared a snow day from school.

He frowned. He'd better not relax just yet. Before he made his coffee, he turned the television to the Weather Channel. Sometimes schools closed early if the snow or ice was bad enough. He smiled. Nothing more expected, just what was coming down.

He left the television on while he ate. He'd check back again after his workout.

He met with Sam, another realtor, and made offers on three of the houses with the understanding that he had to go to settlement on the same day as he closed on the others. Sam called the current owners, who accepted Jeff's offer right away. They all agreed to be available whenever the settlements were scheduled. Some people were as eager to get rid of houses as others were to buy them.

As soon as he got home Jeff called Nancy and told her about the houses.

"I was just about to call you. I scheduled the settlements for next Thursday. I also told them about the possibility of your closing on three other houses. The title abstract company officials agreed to shuffle their schedules to accommodate you and Sam. They can be hardnosed at times, but I think the combination of your program and the holidays gave them a little Christmas spirit."

"I don't care what the reason, I appreciate it. I'll be sure to let them know."

"Looks like you'll make it a merry Christmas for five families. Thanks to you, you won't be the only one home for Christmas."

Jeff got the files and made calls to three other families who had been praying for a miracle. There was nothing like celebrating Christmas in your own home. He sighed. It was even better if you had somebody to share it with.

He looked at the clock. Maybe, if things went the way he hoped, he'd have someone to help him celebrate his first Christmas in his new home.

He put on his coat. It was time to go meet Sheila. He shrugged. Almost time. He'd wait in the car. That way he wouldn't get her in trouble by kissing her in front of whomever happened to be in the hallway when he met her.

Finally, but on time, Sheila came out of the school and walked down the steps. He sat in the car and watched her. He shook his head. It was amazing. He knew she was beautiful, but each time he saw her she was more beautiful than he remembered.

He stepped out of the car. Her face seemed to light up when she saw him. He smiled. It might be his imagination at work, but what was the harm in believing that it was true?

She didn't rush, but neither did she act as if she was sorry she had decided to go with him. She held his gaze as she came closer. When she was a few inches away, she stopped.

"Hi, Jeff." She touched his arm.

"Hi, beautiful." Color flooded her face, but she didn't break the connection. She licked her lips, as if she were getting ready for his kiss. He didn't intend to disappoint her. He brushed his mouth across hers. She didn't move away, so he brushed back the other way.

"I-I think we'd better go. If we're going. Unless you intend to stay here."

"My intentions have nothing to do with standing out here in the open barely touching you."

She took a deep breath as if she were having as much trouble keeping control as he was. *Good.*

"Where are we going?" She stepped back as if moving away from him wasn't her first choice.

He wished he could answer "to my house to make sweet love" or "to your place to make sweet love." The where didn't matter. The important thing was what they would do when they got there.

Jeff opened the car door for her and Sheila got in. Taking it slow was hard. He tried to control his breathing as he walked around to the driver's side. That wasn't the only hard thing he had to contend with. Did she know what she did to him?

Once he was seated, he turned toward her. "Before we go anywhere, I need something very important from you."

"What's that?"

"Do you know I don't have your phone number or your address? What if there's an emergency after school is out and I have to reach you?"

"What kind of an emergency could that be?" She smiled up at him, and he remembered when that used to happen often. He missed it. He had to try harder to make it happen again regularly.

"Maybe I'll need to hear your voice to tide me over until I can see you again. Maybe I'll need your reassurance that I'm not just dreaming about you, as I have been for too long; maybe I'll need proof that you are really back in my life."

"Oh. I . . . Oh." She blinked and seemed to search for an answer, but gave up to try to find enough air just to breathe.

"I-I guess, if that's the case . . ." She fumbled in her purse. "I-I have a notepad in here somewhere." Her purse wasn't that big, but she was having trouble. Jeff glanced at her. She looked as if she had forgotten what she was looking for. He kept from laughing.

"Look in the glove compartment."

"I know it's in here somewhere." She continued to rummage in her purse.

"Sheila." He touched her arm. "There's a pad in the glove compartment."

"Okay." She glanced at him and frowned.

"Don't you want me to have it?" He didn't want to consider that possibility.

"No. I mean yes. I mean I don't mind giving you my number." She stared at him. "I'll look in the glove compartment."

Jeff smiled as she wrote on the pad. She handed him the paper, and their hands touched longer than necessary. Neither of them complained. Jeff wouldn't have minded if their hands stayed together. He didn't think she would mind either. He let go so he wouldn't be so distracted that he forgot where he was going.

He drove her to see the first house. The street was as clean and the neighborhood looked just as stable as when he had first looked at the property.

"Tell me about the family who will live here," she said as they got out. A neighbor across the street waved at them. They waved back and walked up the steps to the stone rowhouse. *She probably thinks we're planning to live here*. This house was a lot smaller than his, but he'd give up the other place in a heartbeat if that were the only way to have Sheila with him. *Patience*.

Jeff told her about the Williams family.

"If the inside looks as nice as the outside, they'll love this house." She stared off. "But then, I guess if you don't have a home of your own, any house looks good."

They looked at the other four houses, and he told her about the families who would live in them.

The houses were all in West Philly, and not too far away from one another, but by the time they got back to school it was late enough for Jeff to bring up the subject of dinner. He hoped she was too hungry to refuse. If not for food, maybe she was hungry for spending more time with him.

"Come to dinner with me. We can go to my house and I can fix something."

"I . . ." She started to shake her head.

"Or we can go to a restaurant." He watched her so closely that he felt he could see the second she changed her mind.

"A restaurant will be better."

"Okay." Jeff allowed himself to breathe again. "Any suggestions?"

"Do you want soul food?"

"What I want has nothing to do with food, but if I have to settle for food, soul food is good."

"Behave yourself." Sheila shook her head, but it didn't mean no. She told him how to get to a little restaurant on Mt. Airy Avenue.

Jeff drove the whole way trying not to wonder if she would ever answer yes to coming to his house.

"Jeff, you have a great program," Sheila said after they had been seated. She smiled. "I'm not surprised, though. When you set your mind to something, you make it happen regardless of the difficulties in your way."

"I hope that's true." He stared at her. She stared back. Then their food came, and she looked away from him.

"Tell me more about the program. What happens next?"

The rest of the meal was spent discussing Jeff's plans. He hadn't had Sheila's approval in mind when he started the program, but he was glad to have it.

"How about dessert?" *I'll stuff myself if it means spending more time with Sheila.*

"I can't hold another bite." She patted her stomach. "It's time for me to go home." She smiled. "Tomorrow's a school day, you know."

"Yes, I know." As he motioned to the waitress, he noticed that he and Sheila were the only people left in the restaurant. He looked at his watch. The place was supposed to have closed ten minutes ago. He added a generous tip to the bill.

As they drove to get Sheila's car, he tried to console himself with the fact that he'd see her again tomorrow.

"I'll follow you home." He got out of the car.

"Not necessary." She stood beside him.

"You're sure?" He moved closer, until only their coats stopped him from getting closer still.

"I'm sure." She leaned against him—only slightly, but enough to let him hope.

"Okay, then. You'd better go." He put his hands on her shoulders.

"Yes. I'd better." She placed her hands against his chest, but she didn't push.

"Yes." Jeff lowered his head, and she raised hers until their lips met. Then he pulled back. He wanted more than a kiss from her. He stared at her. Then he lowered his head again. If that was all he could have right now, he'd take it.

They both pulled back at the same time and walked over to her car with his arm around her. She fumbled with her keys. He took them from her so he could help. He didn't do any better. Finally they somehow got the door unlocked. He didn't touch her again; he didn't dare.

He watched her go. The only reason he could was that he knew he'd see her tomorrow.

Jeff made sure that he had all the paperwork he needed to meet with the families. He'd meet with everybody except the Williams family at six o'clock. The general things would be discussed together. He'd meet with them individually to discuss the financial aspects.

He tried to find enough to do to keep busy until it was time to go to school. At some point in his life he might wish he had back all of the time he had wished away. He smiled and looked at the clock. But not today.

He left early as usual. He waited outside the classroom for her, not trying to understand why, when he had just seen her last evening, it felt as if a year had passed.

The tutoring session went fast, and too soon Sheila was telling the kids good-bye. Tyrik stopped beside Sheila.

"I wish we could have dinner together, but I have to meet with the families at six o'clock and another at eight." Jeff looked at Tyrik and then back at her.

"Tyrik asked for some more problems to work on."

"I got a test on Friday. I want to make sure I don't mess up."

Sheila stared at Jeff and shrugged. "I have to get them from my office."

"Oh. Okay." He looked at her mouth, but quickly tore his gaze away. Not in school. He sighed. That was a dumb rule. Who could he see about changing it?

"I'm not sure if you got a school calendar. Next

Wednesday is a half day for students. We have report-card conferences."

"No two days of tutoring next week?"

"No, just Monday. I thought I'd let you know in case you want to make other plans."

"Only one day of tutoring?"

"That's right."

"Whose idea was that?"

"Jeff, it was that way when we were in school." She stared at him. "Call me when you get home tonight."

"What?" He frowned. Did she really say what he thought she said?

"Unless it's too late. I'm still allowed to get calls late, you know."

He knew. Oh, yeah, he knew. "I will." He stared at her and took a step toward her. Then he remembered Tyrik. "I-I'll call you."

He walked away from her while he still could.

Jeff's meeting with the families went well. The only reactions he got while he explained everything was sniffling, which was out of place with their smiles.

It was after ten o'clock when he got home. The phone rang before he had a chance to take off his coat.

"I thought you decided not to call, so I decided to call you."

"No, you didn't think that."

It had been a long time since he had spoken with her over the phone. Her voice was just as sexy and tantalizing as when she was with him. Maybe more so. Now he didn't have her to look at and distract him. He could concentrate on her voice and imagine her whispering in his ear.

"You're right. No, I didn't." She left a space in the air as if she wasn't sure how to fill it. "I don't want to keep you."

"That's too bad."

"How did your meetings go?"

"They went well. I think five families won't get much sleep tonight. If they are anything like my mother and I were, they're afraid they'll go to sleep and find out that they were dreaming."

"Yes." She left more space.

Jeff waited for her to fill it. He knew she hadn't asked him to call just to ask about the meetings. He wasn't sure he wanted to know what her reason was. What if she was calling to say that she found another tutor and he didn't have to come anymore? What if she told him that too much time had passed and that they needed to back off? He hoped and waited.

"I wanted you to call because . . . I asked you to call to ask you . . ." She took a deep breath. "Do you want to come over for dinner on Friday?" When he didn't answer she continued. "Maybe that's not such a good idea. Forget I—"

"What time?"

"What time what?"

"What time do you want me there?"

"Where?"

"Your house for dinner." He laughed.

"Is six o'clock okay?"

"Anytime is okay." He laughed again. "I'll see you then." He hesitated. "I hope you have sweet dreams." He didn't add "of me." He didn't want to scare her off.

Sheila hung up but didn't move. She hoped she wasn't making a mistake. She smiled. It seemed too right to be a mistake.

Twenty

Friday-morning sunlight showed up, and Jeff had an excuse to get out of bed. He tried not to look at the clock every half-hour, but he failed. He was glad he had something besides empty hours waiting for him, but wished something would take him right up to dinnertime.

Eric called, but for once his voice wasn't filled with panic. They had a new contract, and the plant was retooling to begin filling the order after Christmas.

"Paula is fine." Eric said when Jeff asked. "She thinks she's starting to look as if she swallowed a melon, but I told her that she's just beautifully rounded with our child." Eric sighed. "Man, you have no idea what you're missing. To see your child growing inside the woman you love . . ." He sighed. "It's too awesome to explain. It really gives you proof of miracles. March is too far away."

"If I get a miracle of my own, I'll find out exactly what you're talking about."

"You and Sheila?"

"Got it in one."

"You're back together?"

"I don't want to jinx things, but it looks like it. She invited me over for dinner tonight." He hesitated. "If things go the way I hope . . . Well, let's just say that next year this time we might have a Christmas miracle of our own on the way."

"That's great, man. You deserve it."

After he hung up Jeff thought about the conversation. It was the first time he had dared to put into words what he had been hoping for.

He left for the closings, ready to play a part in somebody else's miracles.

After the closings, each new homeowner, laughing and crying at the same time, made him promise to come for dinner during the holiday week.

Jeff watched them go. Then he went home to wait for the next part of his own miracle.

At five-thirty he quit pretending that he was doing anything worth spending time on, and pulled on his coat. Sheila lived only fifteen minutes away, but she wouldn't make him wait until six o'clock before she let him in.

He drove to her house trying not to expect anything more than dinner with the woman he loved.

"Good evening." Sheila smiled at him and his hope grew. "Dinner is ready." She stepped back to let him in.

"Yes, it is, and good." He shut the door, but never took his gaze from hers. Her breath caught as he took the steps necessary to close the space between them.

"The cold is clinging to your coat." She leaned into him.

"Let's see if we can warm it up." He brushed his mouth across hers. "It's working," he murmured before his lips found hers again. He made himself step back. Too fast. She invited him for dinner. He didn't want to scare her off. He shrugged out of his jacket and held it out.

She frowned at it as if not sure what was expected of

her. He smiled. She was just as lost as he was. Maybe they could find their way together.

"I'll just put this on the chair."

"Oh. No. I'll . . . I'll hang it up." She reached for it, but stopped when her hand brushed against his. Jeff kissed her forehead and wrapped her hand in his. Boyz II Men were singing their tight harmony and filling the living room. Jeff let his coat fall onto the chair. He needed both of his hands.

He drew her into his arms, glad for the music as an excuse, but thinking that he didn't need it. What he did need was in his arms, and her need seemed as great as his.

He pulled her closer, and she adjusted her body to fit his, her soft parts against his hard parts, just as it was meant to be.

He kissed a path down the side of her face until he found the hollow at her neck. He pressed his lips against her skin, and her pulse jumped as if the only thing keeping it from escaping were his kiss.

His hands drew circles on her back until one left to find a better spot. His lips found hers at the same time his hand found her breast.

Her mouth opened in a gasp and his tongue tasted its way inside. Peppermint. He loved the taste of peppermint.

He drew back his head and touched his lips to the corner of her mouth. His fingers found the already tight point of her breast and brushed it to a pebble hardness. She moaned and he caught the moan with his mouth.

They no longer pretended to move to the music. Instead they stood together, moving slightly to a rhythm only they knew.

Jeff kissed the swell of her breast above the low neck of her dress. Then he pulled back and took a deep breath.

This was too important to rush. They had time. All night. The rest of their lives.

He looked into her eyes and saw a reflection of his own need, his own desire.

"I want you," he whispered in her ear as his hands moved restlessly up and down her back. "I've wanted you for so long."

"I want you, too." She kissed the side of his jaw. Her hands brushed across his chest and found the hard buttons. Jeff moaned as her lips replaced her hands.

Slowly he eased the zipper down the back of her dress, giving her enough time to change her mind but hoping she wouldn't. His mouth found hers again as her dress formed a pool around her feet. Still tasting her mouth, his tongue dancing with hers, he eased her half-slip off to join the dress.

She eased him away and worked at the buttons on his shirt until they broke free of the buttonholes. She leaned her head back and smiled at him as she pushed his shirt down his arms to join her clothes. She unfastened his pants, but he stopped her from pushing them off.

"Not yet. We've waited too long to rush this." He smiled at her. "And if you touch me there it will be over, and we just got started." He eased her hips against him and his hardness found her soft mound. He wrapped his hands around her and brushed them against the sides of her bra. "I always did like lace." He traced the edge along the top with his finger and felt her breast swell up to meet his hand. He replaced his hand with his tongue and her fullness met it. He fumbled with the clasp at the back, and Sheila helped him free her. Her breasts, a little fuller than he remembered, still fit into his hands perfectly. He brushed his thumbs across the tips, and Sheila groaned as she leaned into him.

He bent his head and drew one swollen tip into his mouth. She whispered his name and arched her back. At some time her hands had found their way around his neck, and now she tugged his head closer. He let his tongue circle the tip before he pulled his mouth away.

"No." Sheila pulled at his head.

"Shh. It's all right."

He lifted her into his arms and headed for what he hoped was the bedroom.

Light from outside streamed onto the bed as if to make sure he found it. He smiled at the turned down covers, kissed her again, and laid her on the bed.

"Don't go." She reached for him when he stepped back.

"I'm not going anywhere." He kicked out of his shoes. He slipped something from his pocket before he shed his clothes. Then he went back to her.

She opened her arms to him. He pressed a kiss on one breast before he pulled back.

"One second," he said, as she tried to keep him from leaving. "Want to help?" He held up a blue foil packet and tore off the top.

"I-I don't know how." Her eyes widened as she stared at his arousal. Quickly she stared at his face. "Help me."

He guided her hand to him. "I won't break," he said as she barely touched him.

"Okay." She took a deep breath. "Will it fit?"

He laughed. "Right now I'm not sure, but I hope so."

"Okay." She took another deep breath. "Like this?" She tried to position the protection, but had to start over.

"I'd better do it or we won't need it." He rolled it into place. "Next time will be your turn."

He straddled her and positioned himself between her thighs. Then he kissed her eyes, her cheeks, the side of her neck; everywhere except her mouth.

"Please," she whispered. Her hands grasped his shoulders. His hands told him that she was ready. He eased himself against her moist softness and stopped when he met resistance.

"You waited for me." He eased inside her when he wanted to rush. She gasped, and he swallowed her gasp with his kiss. He waited until she began to move against him, inviting him in further. He slowed until her legs closed around him. Then he thrust the rest of the way.

He held her while she held him tightly inside her. Then, as if following some signal, they moved together in the way men and women have moved together since the beginning of time.

Together they climbed the highest peak and flew off, soared into nowhere, and floated back to reality.

Still inside her, he wrapped his arms around her, afraid she would vanish as in a dream.

Sometime later he found the cover and threw it over them. Then he closed his hand around her breast and drew her close. He kissed her and she moved closer. Her hand brushed along his length, paused at the part that had brought them pleasure and moved back and forth.

"Insatiable," he murmured against her cheek. "That's okay. So am I." He prepared himself; then they traveled together on another love journey that was different, but brought the same pleasure.

Sunlight had replaced the moonlight when Jeff next opened his eyes. His smile met Sheila's. "You aren't a dream." He brushed the hair back from her forehead.

"Neither are you." She rested her hand against his chest. "We never did have dinner."

"We just skipped right to dessert." He touched her cheek. "Better than any food."

"Yes." She traced a line along his jaw.

"You waited for me." He kissed her. "Thank you."

"I never met anyone I cared enough for." She stared

at him and he saw her love for him shining there. She glanced at the clock on the nightstand. "I'll give you first dibs on the shower."

He kissed her. "We could share."

"If we do, we'll never leave in time to meet the girls." She hesitated and looked at the blanket before she got out of bed.

Jeff smiled at her. "No need to be self-conscious. Not after last night." He watched as a warm glow spread over her body. He felt her body react. "Go take your shower before we have to call the girls and disappoint them."

Sheila scurried into the bathroom. Jeff propped himself up against the headboard.

He had been dreaming and hoping for this forever. Now that it had happened, it was better than he had ever imagined.

After a hurried breakfast of coffee and yogurt, they went to get the girls.

Jeff tried not to look at his watch to see if enough time had passed so they could leave. He smiled when he caught Sheila doing the same. Finally it was time to go. They dropped the girls off and headed to Sheila's.

Jeff kissed her as soon as they got inside.

"Wait." She sounded as out of breath as he felt. "I worked hard cooking yesterday, and you're going to eat."

Jeff cradled her in his arms. "Okay, as long as I can have dessert afterward."

"You got it." Jeff chuckled at her choice of words. "I mean you can have it." He laughed. She smacked his arm. "I mean it's a deal."

He was still laughing as he followed her into the kitchen.

"Can I help?"

"You can help by staying away from me." She looked

at him. "If you come near me, the leftovers will be left over again." She smiled. "It won't take long."

"I hope not. I'm ready for dessert. I've been ready since this morning."

"Don't look at me like that. You make me forget everything." Her voice got husky. "Everything except you."

"Keep talking like that, and we'll both go to bed without dinner."

Jeff ate. At least he must have. His plate had been full when Sheila set it on the table, and it was almost empty now. He was sure it tasted delicious, but it couldn't compare with the taste of the dessert that he had in mind.

He stood and she stood, too. Their stares met. Then Sheila blinked free.

"I'll just . . . I'd better put these things away." She put the serving bowls into the refrigerator.

Jeff stacked the dirty dishes and put them in the sink. "Do we have to wash them tonight?"

"No." Sheila shook her head slowly. "I don't see why they can't wait."

"Me neither." He walked toward her. She met him halfway. "Time for dessert." He wrapped his hands around her shoulders.

"The same as yesterday?" She brushed her hands across his chest.

He felt his body tighten in response.

"No, sugar. It's never the same. It's always better than the last time."

They walked into the bedroom arm in arm. As if in a race, they undressed each other. *Maybe one day we'll be able to do this slowly,* Jeff thought. Then he didn't think at all; feelings took over as he began to fulfill his promise of better.

* * *

"I have to get up," Sheila said the next morning from within Jeff's arms.

"What's stopping you?" Jeff slowly ran a finger down her bare back.

"You are." She lightly pinched the hard center of his chest. His whole body tightened.

"I'm barely touching you." His hand molded to her rounded behind and opened and closed gently. He smiled as she eased closer to him.

"Do you have any more of those things?"

"One more. I thought I had more than enough, but I guess I underestimated you." He kissed her. "Us."

"I still have time."

Later Jeff left with her as he promised to meet her at her parents' house for dinner. He watched her drive away, then headed for the mall. He hoped he'd find what he was looking for at the jewelry store. If he did, he wouldn't wait until Christmas to give it to Sheila. It was already eleven years too late. He wouldn't let another day pass.

Twenty-one

Jeff went to three jewelry stores before he found the perfect ring. A large heart-shaped diamond in the center was flanked by three slightly smaller diamonds on each side. He let the saleswoman wrap it before he slipped the box into his pocket.

Should he give it to her in front of her family or call her aside? Maybe he should go to her house and give her the ring when she went home to change. He smiled. He'd better not do that. If he did, they'd miss dinner again. His body tightened at the memory. He promised himself a cold shower when he got home, but he doubted if it would help. He knew from experience that cold showers were greatly overrated.

He smiled all the way home, planning on going to Sheila's again. Maybe they would go to his house this time. His smile widened. He didn't care where they went as long as they were together.

As soon as he walked into the house, the answering machine light caught his attention. He listened to Eric's panic-filled voice. Then he called him back on his cell phone as instructed.

"I know this is bad timing, but I'm here at the hospital with Paula. She almost miscarried." Jeff heard Eric take a deep breath and let it out.

"Is she all right?"

"They . . . they stabilized her, but she has to stay here. Her doctor said she needs complete bed rest until the baby is big enough to survive. She should be all right, but he didn't guarantee it." He let out several heavy breaths. Jeff waited. "I was afraid I was going to lose both of them. I don't know what I'd do if that happened. We're still not sure about the baby."

"They'll be all right. You guys had nothing but praise for Dr. Steel the last time."

"Yeah. That's true." Eric hesitated. "I know things are just starting to smooth out between you and Sheila, but—"

"I need to come there and oversee the start-up of the project."

"You know how much time it takes to get something new up and running. I hate to leave Paula for that long. Dr. Steel says she needs to stay calm, and you know how Paula can be, especially when she's worried."

"You need to be with her." He asked a question, but he already knew the answer: "How far along is the project?"

"Too far to quit unless we want to shut down completely and start up again from the beginning later."

"We can't shut down for that long. If we do, the company waiting for the parts will have to close down and so will we. A whole lot of people would get a layoff notice for Christmas."

"I'm sorry, Jeff. Maybe I can be on-site enough to keep things going. Paula will understand."

"What about Eric Junior? I know you're good, partner, but you can't divide yourself three ways." Jeff closed his eyes. "I'll catch a flight out as soon as I can."

He sat beside the phone and pulled the box from his pocket. Then he took a deep breath and picked up the phone again, but hung up without making a call. He couldn't do this by phone.

* * *

He parked in the lot beside her car. Any other time he would consider himself lucky to catch her at home. This wasn't any other time.

He got out of the car and went up the steps. He didn't want to think about how this reminded him of that other time.

"Hi." Sheila smiled and brushed her lips across his. "Come on in, but weren't we supposed to meet at my parents' house?" She stepped aside.

"Something came up."

"Oh, yeah?" She touched his body with hers and brushed against him. "Like what?"

He stared into her eyes, but he was afraid of what his next words would place there.

"I have to go to Houston." The look that flared in her eyes was too much like the one he'd seen eleven years ago.

She stepped away, and he realized that he had forgotten how lonely he could feel.

"Only for about a month."

He explained about Eric's call and the reason he had to go. As he talked, he kept looking for understanding to replace the distrust in her eyes. He was still waiting when he finished talking.

"Okay." She folded her arms across her chest. She reached around him and opened the door. "Thanks for letting me know."

"Sheila, don't."

"Don't what? I said it's okay."

"It's not okay, but I have to go."

"I understand. Good-bye."

"Don't say it like that. I'm coming back."

"I'm sure you plan to." She blinked, but Jeff still saw the moisture in her eyes.

"I'll be back. I promise you."

"I've heard that before." She stepped back even farther. "You shouldn't have left Houston, Jeff. How can you operate a business long distance?" She shook her head. "You never really left it."

"Sheila, don't do this." He reached for her, but she stepped out of reach.

"I won't." She stared at the floor. "You'd better go. It's getting cold with the door open."

"I-I'll call you."

"Why? Let's just accept that, no matter how much we want it, we aren't meant to be together."

"Sheila—"

"Good-bye, Jeff." She shut the door, but he stood on the porch for a while before he admitted that she wouldn't change her mind.

He went home and packed, but he couldn't pack what he needed more than anything else.

He took the paper off the jewelry box and looked at where he had placed his hope for the future. He slipped it back into his pocket. Maybe, if he had it with him, he could pretend.

He rode to the airport trying to figure out how to do that.

Twenty-two

"You need to go back to Philly," Eric told him. They were stopping early because it was Christmas Eve. "We're on track here. The plant is in full operation. Next week we can start spitting out the new parts. Paula is stabilized. She's coming home today. She has to stay in bed, but she'll be in bed at home. We hired a nurse to help with her and little Eric. I have things covered. Go back to Philadelphia where you belong."

"I'm not sure there's any reason for me to go back. I can manage the Homes project from here."

"You know there's a reason."

"I don't think she wants to see me again. This is the second time I did this to her. This time was worse. We had gotten closer than ever."

"If she loves you, she'll be waiting for you."

"I'm not sure she loves me that much."

"Only one way to find out."

Jeff shrugged and went back to his office. There must be something he could do to keep from going to the furnished townhouse he called home. He went over papers that were complete, checked work that didn't need it, and cleaned out his desk drawers. Then he checked the papers again. Finally he quit.

He let himself into the apartment and slipped off his jacket. To be truthful, he had lived at the plant since he got back, not here. He came here only late at night so he could pretend that he expected to be able to sleep.

He picked up the small blue box that stayed on the table in the hall. He rubbed the top as if it were a magic lantern and a genie were about to appear and grant him three wishes. He shook his head. One wish was all he needed.

He placed the box back on the table, noting that he had rubbed the top smooth. Still no genie.

He turned on the television for company and caught the newscaster signing off.

"We here at the station wish you all a merry Christmas." Tomorrow was Christmas Day.

Jeff turned off the television and sat in the dark. This was not the way he had expected to spend Christmas.

What was she doing? Had she left her parents' house with a promise to be there early the next day to help with the meal?

Had she really moved on with her life this time? Was she missing him as much as he missed her? Would she give him yet another chance if he went back?

He got ready for bed, but he knew he wouldn't sleep. His thoughts were too loud.

Close to daybreak he had decided: he had to try again. Then his body took charge and let sleep take over.

The doorbell shattered Jeff's dreams. He frowned. Dreams were the only way he could be close to Sheila.

"Eric had better have a good excuse or I might be minus a partner."

He forced himself out of bed. If Eric didn't have Eric Junior with him, Jeff would bless him out. He flung open the door.

"Merry Christmas, Jeff." Sheila twisted the straps of her purse in her hands.

Jeff stared, afraid that he was still dreaming. This wasn't real. He wanted it too much for it to be real. He wanted to touch her, to make sure, but he was afraid.

"Are you too mad at me to let me come in?"

"What? Oh, no." He stared at her. Then he remembered to step aside.

"I had a hard time locating you." She smiled. "I woke Eric up late last night, but he gave me your address anyway." She blinked. "I'm sorry."

"You're sorry? For what?"

"For not being understanding, for being so selfish, for putting you through what I did. I-I hope you can forgive me." She wiped her eyes, and Jeff felt his heart flip.

"Don't. Please don't cry." He touched her arm, but that wasn't enough. "You don't know how much I've missed you, how much I was afraid that I'd never hold you like this again." He held her close.

"I know. I've felt the same way, only it was my fault that we were apart." She placed her hands around his back and held him close.

His mouth found hers and swallowed her sigh. Her hands found the familiar spot at his waist. The kiss went on.

Finally he forced himself to ease away from her, but he didn't let her go.

"I don't have to stay here much longer. We have things pretty much in place. We—"

"Shh." She placed her finger to his lips. "Take as long as you have to. If you finish in time to go back to Philly with me, good. If not, I'll be waiting for you when you get back."

He stared into her eyes and saw the love there, stronger than ever. Almost as strong as his.

"I can't let you leave without me."

"If you have to, you can, and I'm all right with that." She brushed her hand down the side of his face. "Even if you want to move back here, that's all right, too." She swallowed hard. "After you left, I realized that where I live doesn't matter, as long as I can live with you for as long as you want me." She pulled his head down and captured his lips with hers. Her love for him filled her kiss. His love met hers. They stood wrapped in each other's arms, showing how strong their love was. Finally Jeff felt strong enough to ease his mouth from hers. He kissed her forehead, then took her hand in his.

"I have something for you."

He took the box from the table and opened it. He smiled. He didn't need a genie after all. "Marry me?" He controlled the shaking in his hands as he held the ring out to her and waited.

"Oh, Jeff."

"Is that a yes?"

"Yes." She was laughing and crying as she held out her left hand. She was shaking as much as he was.

Jeff slipped the ring onto her finger and folded her into his arms. "You made it home for Christmas."

"Yes." She touched his jaw. "Any place with you is home." She kissed him gently. "I believe in miracles more than ever."

"So do I." He looked at her, and his love for her swelled his heart.

He eased her against him slowly and gently kissed her. There was no need to hurry. They had all the time in the world to enjoy their miracle.

Dear Readers:

HOME FOR CHRISTMAS follows my first two novels, SNOWBOUND WITH LOVE and DREAM WEDDING, into publication.

HOME FOR CHRISTMAS takes place in Philadelphia, and those of you familiar with the Mt. Airy section of the city may recognize some of the streets and places.

Jeff Hamilton, the hero, begins a program to provide homes for the homeless. While the story is fiction, his program is modeled after a real program, Homes for Christmas, which was started by a professional football player.

I welcome feedback from readers. I do book signings all over the country. You might find me appearing at a bookstore near you. If you know of one where I might have a successful signing, let me know and I'll consider it.

Yours truly,

Alice Wootson
P.O. Box 18832
Philadelphia, PA 19119
E-mail address: agwwriter@email.com

ABOUT THE AUTHOR

Alice Wootson is a retired teacher who entered writing, her second profession, upon retiring from teaching in the Philadelphia school system in 1993. She follows her sister, Marilyn Tyner, into the field of writing romance novels. Her first novel, SNOWBOUND WITH LOVE, was highly rated. Her second novel, DREAM WEDDING, was released in April 2001.

Alice is also a prolific poet and a member of the Mad Poets Society. She has been the featured poet at many venues in the Philadelphia area. Last year she became a member of the Philadelphia Writers Conference, which holds a writers' workshop each June.

Alice has been married for forty-one years. She is the mother of three sons and had two grandsons and a granddaughter.

More Sizzling Romance From

Marcia King-Gamble

Do You Have the Entire
SHIRLEY HAILSTOCK
Collection?

___Legacy

0-7860-0415-0 $4.99US/$6.50CAN

___Mirror Image

1-58314-178-2 $5.99US/$7.50CAN

___More Than Gold

1-58314-120-0 $5.99US/$7.50CAN

___Whispers of Love

0-7860-0055-4 $4.99US/$6.50CAN